The Third Temple
By
Christopher Cartwright

Prologue

Namibian Desert, 1655.

It was just before midnight when Harper Smith climbed to the final rise of the highest sand dune. The air smelled richly of salt, giving him hope the coast was near. By his calculations they should have reached it before nightfall. If he'd made a mistake with his navigation there was no way they would survive long enough to see it corrected. He was badly winded. The muscles of his calves and thighs were hot with pain. He breathed heavily and peered out into the distance to where the Atlantic Ocean should have been. Instead, beneath the silent moonlight he saw nothing but the majestic rolling sand dunes of the Namibian desert.

He swore loudly, cursing his greed. It had already claimed the lives of twelve members of his original party. He felt no guilt at being responsible for their deaths. They knew the risks before they became involved in his treacherous and evil business. The rewards would never have been so high if their task had been less dangerous. Besides, his punishment would come in the morning, when the scorching new sun would send him to his grave – that was, if his pursuers didn't reach him first.

Smith remained at the crest until midnight so that he could take a reading of the South Celestial Pole using his kamal. The device consisted of a small parallelogram made of intricately carved ivory, roughly one inch by two inches wide. It had a single string inserted through its center, with a series of knots evenly spaced along its length. It was a simple device, but it measured latitude accurately. He'd traded for it three years ago with a small Arab man in Istanbul, who said that his people had used the device for celestial navigation since the ninth century.

The air was bitterly cold, but he didn't feel it as he searched the sky above for the Crux – the cross-shaped constellation that would later become known as the Southern Cross. He didn't feel much at all above the pain. Smith and his remaining party had been traveling west for seven days. Now, fatigue, piled upon the end stages of dehydration, had pushed him long past any sense of pain and left him physically as well as mentally numb. It was time to know the truth, even though it would do little good for him now.

Smith bit the end of the string with his crooked teeth and held the other end of the kamal up toward the horizon. He slowly moved the ivory card along the string until it was positioned so the lower edge became even with the horizon, and the upper edge occluded the Crux. He then calculated the angle by counting the number of knots from his teeth to the card. Each knot was precisely the same distance along the string, and each one represented approximately 1.5 degrees of latitude. He wasn't interested in any of the regular knots. Instead, there was one mark noted with a single old bronze coin. Smith adjusted the card until his hand reached the metal and then stopped.

His brother shared an identical kamal. Many weeks earlier, before he'd entered the wretched desert in search of the damned temple and its God-forsaken relic, he and his brother both added an additional knot on the string of each of their kamals by tying it around an old bronze coin so that it would be impossible to mistake. That way, when Smith and his party set out into the desert, all he needed to do was head west and maintain the same point along the kamal. The point identified the precise latitude along the African west coast, where his brother would be waiting for him aboard the *Emerald Star*.

He stared at the result and swore a violent oath. He took the sighting again and achieved the same result. It had been three days since he'd been able to take a reading. On the first, he thought he could hear the echo of his pursuer's war cry. Sound, he later realized, traveled miles across the open sand dunes of the Namibian desert. He couldn't rule out the possibility that he'd imagined it, either. Not that it mattered, the fact was it had sent a shiver of fear through his soul, which made him unwilling to delay their movement, even for a minute. On the second night, cloud cover had prohibited a sighting of the Crux, which meant that tonight was the first night he could get an accurate reading. He just hoped it wasn't twenty-four hours too late.

The coin had moved downward, which meant he and his party had somehow drifted north of their intended latitude. He mentally recalled the shape of the African coastline. It steered westward as they traveled north. If he'd maintained the correct latitude he would be staring at the Atlantic Ocean by now and the *Emerald Star*. Instead, he was staring at more sand dunes. It confirmed what he already knew – they were a long way off course. Despite the cold, sweat dripped and stung his eyes. He took out the compass from his right breast pocket and carefully took a bearing to the south-east. There was no way to know how much longer it would take.

It didn't matter. Without more water, they would all be dead long before they reached it. He'd gotten it wrong, but how he didn't know. Not that it mattered anymore. Fact was that he wasn't anywhere near where he was supposed to be. He glanced at the remaining men from his party. He should have told them, but he couldn't face it. Only two of the original fifteen men were left, and they had chosen to follow him because their greed had given them the image of a future where they were extremely rich.

The remaining two members of his party approached slowly. As though each step caused an immense pain, and they had to make the conscious decision to either overcome it and keep going or lie down and die. Jack Baker, who, at the age of twenty was by far the youngest of the group, and Thomas Hammersmith, who was nearly forty, and as greedy and selfish a man as he'd ever met.

Jack Baker stopped next to him. His wide dark brown eyes stared imploringly up at him for any good news. "How much longer do you make it, Smith?"

"Not long now, boys," Smith lied. His eyes fixed on theirs. His face, hardened by a lifetime of exploration, softened as he spoke. "Another twelve hours, at most and we'll be on board the *Emerald Star* – and very rich men."

Hammersmith swore. "Twelve hours! I may as well lie down here and die."

Smith shrugged, and said nothing. It didn't make any difference to him. They could follow him if they wanted, or they could give up and die. It was their choice. There was only one way to survive and that was to grit their teeth and keep walking. If they didn't have it in them to do so, they didn't deserve to make it.

Smith had no intention of letting Death win so easily. He clenched his teeth, glanced at his compass, and started to walk again. This time, he turned from a predominantly western direction and headed due south. He had to be quick. If the other members of his party lost momentum and stopped for more than a few minutes, they could never be cajoled into moving again. It's a rare thing to see a man so fatigued that he should rather lie down and rest, than keep walking and live. Smith took the first painful step. He felt his legs burn.

They walked on through the night without stopping again. Smith knew their movement was slow, but they had to keep going. If they didn't their pursuers would almost certainly catch up with them. He shuddered at the thought of what they would do to him and his men.

No, it was far better to push them hard and die of thirst than to get captured.

In the morning the sun crept steadily higher until it reached directly overhead. Once there, it appeared to linger and remain for eternity. The temperature soared a few degrees above a hundred Fahrenheit. He stopped, unable to continue without a rest, just before three o'clock.

Smith cursed another vicious oath and dropped his carry pack in the sand. He opened it and looked at his pitiful remaining inventory. He removed each item and placed it next to the bag in the sand, carefully making a mental note of the weight and value of each one. There was a single leather flask, almost entirely bereft of water, one sharp knife, his precious journal, and his Lazarino Cominazzo wheel-lock rifle. He glanced up at the sun. It burned with such heat that it would undoubtedly kill them all before it set.

Jack Baker asked, "Which way?"

Smith turned to meet the young man. His face remained impassive. "Same direction. Go on, straight ahead. I'll catch up."

Jack nodded and kept walking. Smith glanced behind. Hammersmith was still following, but slowly. If he had to guess, he figured the man wasn't going to make it. Smith didn't let the thought linger on his conscience. He no longer felt responsible for the safety of every member of his team. They'd all resigned that right when they joined this evil task. It was now up to each of them to dig deep and retrieve whatever strength they had left to survive.

Smith returned his gaze to the carry pack. The animal hide appeared worn. He'd never had to carry it before. It, along with his camel had traveled many miles over the past decade. After he and his party left the pyramid with the stolen relic, they had ridden their camels as hard as they dared. In the end, they had pushed their noble beasts to their deaths.

The creatures had proven their worth and given his party a significant gap ahead of their pursuers who were on foot. When the last camel went lame, they had to make the agonizing decision of what to keep. Their sleeping bags were the first to go, followed by additional bags of shot and powder and cooking equipment. Each of them had carried a large leather flask containing water, but only Smith was strong enough to labor through the grueling sand while carrying the camel's pack. The contents of which were now negligible.

He quickly consumed the last of the water and then threw away the flask. The Lazarino Cominazzo wheel-lock rifle had cost him a fortune and he hated to part with it, but he could quickly see the weapon was no good to him if he died. Besides, it would do little to dissuade the army of savages if they caught up with him. He dropped it into the sand and next to it he discarded the final bag of rifle shot, but not his remaining bag of powder – that he would still need, if he ever reached the Atlantic.

He looked at the journal. A lifetime worth of work and exploration was documented inside. The thought of discarding it was impossible to accept. Besides, without it, the artifact would be useless. He would never locate the buyer again, and even if he could, the man would refuse to pay the exorbitant price he'd agreed on. And why should he? Its gold value alone would be all it was worth, without the journal.

No. The journal must stay. He would rather die than lose it after all these years. In fact, he'd rather bury it. Better no man should find the truth, if he couldn't reach the place in time. Smith placed the journal inside the bag. It made him feel better to see it inside. A final reminder there was still hope. Albeit a very slim chance, but still, he hadn't failed entirely. His eyes darted toward his knife. It was a gift from his father who'd been an explorer before him. An old weapon with an even older Damascus steel blade kept rigorously sharpened to maintain a perfect edge. It had been with him a long time and seen most of the known world. But there was nothing it could do to save him now.

He left it in the sand, with a slight pang of loss, and then tied the top of the carry pack together to create a seal. In one movement, Smith lifted the heavy bag, and slipped his arms through the straps. The weight of it nearly knocked him to the ground. It was a burden none of the other men could possibly hope to bear. He looked at the kamal and dropped it unceremoniously in the sand. There was no point carrying it. If he didn't reach the coast by the end of the day, he never would.

There was one other item, concealed at the bottom. Of all the items, it was the heaviest. He knew he should have thrown the ancient relic away. The weight of the gold alone would kill him. That is, if its curse hadn't already set in motion his death. He shook his head. It was impossible to discard such an item.

He pictured the hideous golden skull, with its sweet flavored scent, burning at the center of the pyramid. It was more valuable than anything he'd ever seen. More valuable than anything he'd ever heard of, or even imagined. The grotesque device harnessed a certain power he would never have believed existed if he hadn't seen it with his own eyes. It was because of the relic he'd taken such risks and was now suffering more than at any other time in his life. Smith had been an explorer all his life, but this was the pinnacle of his achievements. And only he knew the extent of what he'd done.

He recalled what the purple-eyed devil who'd given him the map to the damned temple had told him. *They won't hurt you. They will replenish your supplies and welcome you. It will be easy to steal from such trusting people.* Smith had asked why the man was willing to pay such a high price for something that he could easily steal himself. *Because they will recognize me on sight and kill me.*

Thomas Hammersmith interrupted his thoughts. "When will we reach the *Emerald Star?*"

Smith said, "By nightfall."

Hammersmith stared at the rolling sand dunes ahead. "Are you sure. All I see is desert."

"I bet my life on it."

Hammersmith's mouth opened to object. They had already bet their lives on it. "I can't go on."

Smith said, "Not my problem."

"No. My legs are weak, my throat is dry, and my tongue is swollen. I can't go on any further."

"Okay," Smith said without looking back at the helpless man. It wasn't his fault. Everyone had a breaking point. Hammersmith would be dead within a few hours, if he was lucky. If his body managed to hold on any longer than that, they would reach him. Smith shuddered at the thought. He couldn't imagine what they would do to him – after what they had stolen.

Hammersmith screamed out. "Smith! You can't just leave me here, you bastard!"

Smith ignored the cry.

Hammersmith begged, "What about my ration of water?"

Smith ignored him again.

"I had two more rations of water left!"

Smith continued. He alone had the physical and mental strength to carry the remaining party's water. Every other person in the group would collapse under the weight of a single drop of water, and those who didn't, would succumb to the desperate need for rehydration. Their thirst would have overpowered the strongest among them, and they would have drunk it all in one, pitiful, gulp.

Smith didn't look back at Thomas Hammersmith. There was nothing he could say. The man was as good as dead, he just didn't realize is yet. It would be pointless to waste any more water on him. That's if there was any water left.

None of the lies mattered. He'd either got the navigation right this time and would see the dark blue of the Atlantic Ocean by dusk – or they would all perish. He breathed hard and pushed himself to keep going. There might just be a chance he would survive.

That's if my brother's still waiting.

*

Thomas Hammersmith was a lean, sinewy man with deep-set eyes the same dark brown as his hair. They spoke of a life filled with hardship and plenty of suffering. His face was hard, with a heavily defined jaw-line, hollow cheeks, and jutting chin. It would never have been considered very handsome. But it could have once been a pleasant face, too, warm and open.

He drifted in and out of consciousness throughout the day. During his intermittent periods of wakefulness he called out for Smith. Begging him for just one more drop of water before he died. He called to the other members of the party. Not just to Jack Baker. He called out to those who'd already perished, too. In his delirious state, he struggled to recall who was alive and who was dead. At one point he thought he saw his wife, who had died three years earlier, during childbirth.

She looked at him with pity. "Would you like a drink?"

"Please," he begged.

She smiled at him, silently. In her hand she held a flask out in front of her, but just out of his reach. He tried to grab it, but his arm wasn't long enough. He crawled through the burning sand, his face dragging through it. His mouth opened and he tried to reach it again, but her hands were still out of his grasp.

"Miriam, please, I need you to come closer!" he begged. "I don't have the strength to move."

She stared at him, her hardened face full of sympathy. "I'm sorry, Thomas, I can only help you so much. You'll need to take the final step yourself."

Thomas stared at his wife. *How could she be so harsh to him at a time like this?* Her hair was light brown, and her plump face was coated with the reddish blush of a woman who'd struggled through the cold hardship of the Northern Ireland winters all her life. No one would have ever considered her pretty, but she had loved him, and he had loved her. He had strengthened her resolve, and she had softened his anger. Together they had made a surprisingly good partnership – until God had taken her and his unborn child from him.

"Open your mouth and drink," she coaxed him.

Hammersmith tried to drink from the flask, but found it tasted like poison. He spat it out and stared at his dead wife. "Why would you give this to me?"

She shrieked with laughter. "Because they're coming for you – and you don't want to be alive when they get here."

Hammersmith opened his eyes in terror. He opened his mouth to scream. Instead he coughed. His mouth was full of hot sand, which burned the back of his throat, and he wondered how much he'd consumed. He'd heard stories of shipwrecked sailors becoming so desperate they drank seawater, only the salty water would inevitably speed up their deaths – *would sand have the same effect?*

He heard the war-cry from his pursuers. It was faint and melodic, as though they were repeating the same series of words over and over again. They were still far away, but it wouldn't take long for them to close the gap. He considered consuming more sand if it would bring about his more immediate demise.

The war-cry forced his mind to return to the temple he'd tried so hard to forget. Back to the kind people who worshiped there, and to those who his party had betrayed so much. The temple was a pyramid and it almost appeared as though it had been constructed by removing all the sand around it instead of building it up by piling layer upon layer of stone on top of one another. Hammersmith recalled the first time he saw it. The place looked like the largest stone quarry he'd ever seen. Like a giant had scooped out a massive hole in the earth's sandy crust. But instead of removing everything, the giant had left a pyramid of sandstone at its center.

Hammersmith had seen drawings of some of the pyramids found throughout the dry African continent, but he'd never imagined just how large they could be. He had no way of knowing that this was the largest pyramid ever built, or that great armies from around the world would gladly go to war to steal what it mined.

Inside was the most valuable thing anyone had ever seen. The local worshipers had been quick to show them. It was a skull made of gold, fashioned so that its teeth appeared to be stuck in some sort of grotesque grin, as though it knew just how much each of them had wanted to steal it. Like the damned thing was encouraging them to take it. Out of its mouth the strange religious relic burned with a darkened smoke. Each of them was allowed, even encouraged, to breathe the potent black smoke.

It sent them into a dream-like state. Everything somehow appeared clear to all of them simultaneously, as though every last one of them shared the same common goal – they needed to steal the relic and take it away, to where it wanted to go.

Hammersmith recalled the kind people who had found them nearly starving to death, dehydrated, and unprepared for the sheer intensity of the heat of the Namibian desert. The dark skinned men and women were kinder and more generous than any other people he'd ever encountered. They took them in and healed them with good food, water and shelter. These were the good people who they'd come to betray because of man's most cruel master – greed. And it was that greed which had convinced them to steal their most sacred possession.

Despite the generosity of native people, Hammersmith and the rest of the men who followed Smith were steadfast in their original goal. To steal a golden relic, so valuable, they had at first doubted its existence. They had come to the desert in search of it, with eighteen men and numerous weapons to take it by force. Only, instead of finding it, they had become run down and lost in the desert.

The golden skull had been laid out at the center of their beautiful temple on a pedestal. The inside of the skull was hollowed, and one of the native men, a religious man by the looks of it, reverently poured a blackened powder inside. He lit it and a darkened smoke, with a sweet scent, enveloped the temple. It had made him relax, like strong liquor. Only, unlike alcohol, which mellowed him to the point of drowsiness, whatever was inside the skull, made him feel good. It made him feel strong, powerful, and like the world was in perfect order.

It had a similar effect on the rest of the men in the party. All eighteen of them. They labored for the local people, moving large amounts of sand in giant human chains. They could work all day without rest and then wake up feeling energized and fully recovered by the morning. Hammersmith shook his head. It was the contents of that skull that had made them all so reckless. Something inside the darkened powder drove them with desire.

On the eighth day, their party had re-provisioned the camels and Smith, the best navigator among them, had determined it would be less than three days ride to reach the Atlantic. So, as humans do – they betrayed the very people who'd saved them. At one a.m. they stole the sacred artifact that meant so much to the people who had saved their lives. They carefully made their way out of the temple and climbed the giant sand dunes to escape the pyramid.

While being healed to good health, they had watched the hundreds, if not thousands of men, women and even children work every day to stem the tide of sand, which forever fought to drown their temple from existence. They were happy people and said they were privileged to have such a purpose, for their God had been very kind to them.

Hammersmith climbed the steep crest of sand until they were out of the temple's sandpit. He watched Smith take a quick compass bearing and they set off at a hurried pace, riding their camels through most of the night. If they were lucky, they would have a five hour head start on their pursuers. Their carry bags were full of water and supplies, so they could maintain a good pace. There was little reason to ration anything. They'd reach the west coast of Africa days before running out of supplies.

They might have made it, too, if their beasts hadn't become lame.

*

The sound was excruciatingly loud and appeared to approach from every direction. Through the sandy haze he tried to concentrate on the dune where the angry hoard approached. It looked like a black wave in a storm, rising up high only to soon crash down again, and take him with it to the next life. Like a mirage it moved slowly, and then it was upon him. Hammersmith knew Death had finally caught up. A broad smile crossed his cracked and bleeding lips. He'd made a final prayer to his God, and now had been granted his deliverance from this world.

At least a thousand men, women and children cried out. They wailed like possessed fiends – demons of the dark underworld. Their cries tormenting him as they charged past. He felt their tough feet and legs brush up against his body as they ran by. With each touch he felt the sting of Death upon his skin, but somehow that blessed relief never came.

Was this his final torment?

Would they simply let him die of thirst?

He was no longer frightened of Death. No fire in hell could punish him any more than his perpetual thirst. The army disappeared and he was left almost entirely on his own once more. He watched as one man stopped. The fiend sat down next to him, lifting the back of his head. The face, which had showed so much kindness only days earlier, now glowered at him with its whitened teeth and pure vehemence.

The monster held him down with his left hand and gripped a large knife in his right. He ran the knife over Hammersmith's face, as though he was choosing a memento before killing him – an ear, a nose, his scalp, or his dried tongue perhaps? He moved slowly, as though he was enjoying this final act. Hammersmith was too weak to resist, and let the man move his head freely. He no longer had the strength to care if he was to lose any part of his face. After all, what use did he have for any of his body parts? But what should the monster decide to take?

An ear. It turned out to be an ear. *His left one.* Hammersmith noticed with a numb and morbid curiosity, as the monster showed it to him. He felt no pain. No discomfort. Not even the loss of a body part he had once found so useful. He was about to die. It no longer mattered. Instead, he felt relief. There was no doubt now, the pain of his past few days was about to end permanently. He watched as the fiend lifted his right arm in preparation for the final stroke. The sharp blade, made of fragmented obsidian looked like it would perform its task with enviable ease. The fiend's arm came down with tremendous speed. Hammersmith didn't flinch. His eyes remained glued on the weapon that would take his life – but the blade never reached its target.

Instead, the wretched man's face exploded in a gush of broken bone fragments, skin, tissues and blood. Hammersmith heard the rapport of the rifle a split second later. He looked up and saw its owner approach. His skin wasn't dark like the rest of the local people. Instead it was deathly pale, like that of a ghost. The man's eyes were wide, and glowed purple as though he was able to see into his soul. Hammersmith had never seen anyone with purple eyes.

The ghost handed him a flask of water. "Here, drink this."

He slowly reached out and took it. The liquid sloshed inside. He stared at it for a moment. The water looked clear and there was no toxic smell coming from inside. He took a small, furtive taste. It was cool, sweet, and divine. A moment later he gulped the water down until he felt euphoric.

"Careful," the stranger advised him. "Your body's been profoundly dehydrated. You'll make yourself sick if you drink too much, too fast, now."

Hammersmith took another gulp of water. What did he care if he made himself sick now? He had water!

The ghost handed him another flask of water and a compass. "Keep the bearing due south. There's a Portuguese settlement no more than a day's walk from here. You should make it easily. Good luck."

Hammersmith stopped drinking and looked up. "Who are you?"

"I'm the man trying to retrieve what you stole from my temple." The man's words were spoken calmly, without any trace of vehemence or reprimand. Somehow, that made them sound even more frightening.

"I'm sorry," Hammersmith mumbled.

The ghost started to move again. He was following the army, who were following the last two remaining members of their original party.

"Why did you let me live?" Hammersmith shouted.

The man stopped. His voice was steady, clear, and held a certain undertone of the danger to come. "Because I want you to go back to my brother and give him a message – tell him he'll never get his greedy hands on it. I'd rather destroy it before I let him succeed."

"I've never met you, or your brother!"

"No?" The ghost didn't look surprised, and he definitely didn't look like he cared. "He knows you. And someone from your party knows him. Why else did you think you were sent to the temple?"

"We didn't know about the temple. We were sent to explore the land to the east of the desert!"

The ghost ignored his lies. "Just give him the message."

"But how will I find him?"

"Don't worry. He'll find you."

Hammersmith said, "But it might take years to find a ship back to civilization, and even longer still for your brother to find me!"

"That's okay. This is a family dispute. It's been going for centuries now. It can wait."

Hammersmith glanced at the man, his pale blue eyes weak and pitiful. "Am I dead, and are you a God?"

"Some might see me as that. Others might call me that. My brother would have you believe that." The ghost stared at him, his intensely purple eyes piercing at his soul. "The world is approaching the horns of a dilemma – my name is Death and I am here to set it on the right path."

*

Smith stared out from the crest of the sand dune, and the dark blue water of the Atlantic stared straight back at him. Baker followed him over and screamed in excitement. There were a series of sand dunes ahead progressively decreasing in height until the final one became swallowed by the Atlantic.

He opened his telescope and looked out toward the Atlantic. He scanned the area starting from where the sand dune entered the water, all the way out past the breakers. The water looked like a terrible mixture of white, frothy and turbid waves. Behind them, no more than three or four miles from where he currently stood, the *Emerald Star* rested at anchor.

They would reach it within the hour.

He felt his heart race in anticipation. His brother had waited for him. He'd played the most dangerous of gambles, and it was about to pay off. Smith grinned. He'd stolen what he'd set out to steal. He was going to be rich. The gold alone was worth a fortune, but the man with the purple eyes had offered at least ten times its weight in gold. Now that he'd seen what the relic could do, he didn't doubt for an instant such a tremendous price was achievable. He even had wondered whether he wanted to sell it for that price. It didn't matter. He had plenty of time to make a decision. Smith's delirious sense of happiness, disappeared as quickly as it had arrived – with the crack of a rifle shot.

At first he thought it was coming from the *Emerald Star*. A signal from his brother, perhaps. But a second later there could be no doubt about its origins. The sound had come from behind him. His head snapped around to where they'd come. It didn't make sense. The local people didn't have anything as sophisticated as a rifle. And he'd told Hammersmith to leave his weapon behind days ago. He focused the telescope. His eyes were wide and his mouth open. He stared into the distance, where he'd left Thomas Hammersmith five hours earlier.

He made a silent prayer that the poor man had lied about dropping his weapon and had now taken his own life. It would be a far better way than to let those angered barbarians reach him while he was alive. He stared at his pursuers, as they ran down the sand dune, like a flooded river, breaking free of its bank and running wild.

Smith breathed in deeply. It was impossible that anything could coax a human body to run at full speed through a desert. Even from his distance, Smith imagined their powerful muscles straining to propel their muscular frames across the thick sand. They were moving much faster than he or Jack could possibly run through the sand.

My god, but they move beautifully.

Jack asked, "What do you see?"

Smith said, "Nothing good. That's for sure. Come on. The water's not far now. It would seem preposterous that we're to be butchered so close to our safety."

Jack took the telescope and quickly assessed the men in pursuit. "They're moving with speed, aren't they?"

"That they are, but they're still five or six miles away – much too far for them reach us in time. We'll be safe, trust me my lad."

Smith continued to set the pace. It was slightly faster than a walk, but a long way off a run. He no longer stopped for rests. He wasn't quite terrified yet. All he had to do was keep moving, and he'd reach the *Emerald Star* with time to spare.

It wasn't long before he heard the strange battle-cry of his pursuers. It started out softly, barely audible, yet constant. At first he thought it might be the sound of the dangerous surf crashing on the sandy beach ahead. It was too relentless to be caused by humans. But twenty minutes later the sound resonated louder, and by forty minutes, Smith could feel the prickly fingers of Death, teasing at his back.

Jack asked, "What is that sound?"

Smith ignored him, unable to accept the only possible answer.

"They're close aren't they?" Jack persisted, without attempting to hide his fear.

Smith nodded. He couldn't believe that humans could make such a persistent and horrifying sound, but there was no denying its origins now. It was the sound of the fiends who chased them approaching fast. It caused fear to rise in his throat like bile. "Run!"

Adrenaline commanded his muscles to move without hesitation. He ran all the way to the beach. Dusk turned to nightfall by the time he reached it. With nightfall, the sound of the battle cry had finally ceased. Somehow, the eerie silence felt far more terrifying.

They reached the final sand dune. It stood approximately sixty feet into the air, and descended all the way into the cold, unfeeling waters of the Atlantic Ocean. He was badly winded. The muscles of his calves and thighs were hot with pain. His heart thumped so hard he could barely hear the waves crashing on the shore, above it. Smith glanced behind him. His pursuers were still another hour away, even at their fantastic speed. He grinned, it was close, but they were going to make it.

Jack turned to face him. His eyes were wide and his breathing hard. "Where's the *Emerald Star*?"

"Don't worry," Smith grinned. "She'll be out there, somewhere."

"Your brother's left us!"

"No! My brother might be a greedy, selfish bastard, but he will be there."

"How can you be sure?"

Smith removed the golden skull and leather shot bag from his satchel. "Because he wants this as much as we do."

"But how are we going to contact him?"

"With this," Smith said, as he poured a small amount of the contents of his shot bag onto the ground in three separate piles. The blackened powder mixed with the sand. He then struck the first one with his fire-striker. Ferrocerium struck steel's heated shards and ignited the gunpowder. In an instant, the first pile ignited, followed by the second, and third, in a rapid staccato like gunshots.

He stared at the sea. The *Emerald Star* was now blanketed by the night sky. *Where are you, brother?* Nearly two hundred feet out, he saw the golden light begin to flash.

*

Smith watched the skiff approach. The sailors rowed hard against the rough seas. Not one of them was chatting. They were all focused on the cadence and fighting not to be overturned by the waves breaking along the shore. Smith looked up as the skiff caught its final wave and slid onto the beach. The men pulled her up a few feet until they were confident the swell wasn't going to reclaim the boat before they were ready.

Smith looked at Oswald, his brother, and captain of the *Emerald Star*. Smith grinned as he offered his hand. "Christ, are we glad to see you, brother!"

"You're welcome." Oswald's eyes darted to Jack and back to Smith. "You took your time. What happened to the rest of your men?"

Smith looked toward the peak of the second sand dune behind them. Small white dots appeared to be moving across its crest. The whites of the eyes of his pursuers were unseen, but they were there, and they were very close.

He turned to his brother. "It's a long story and we're not on our own, so I'll tell you on the way."

Oswald glanced toward the peak of the sand dune and nodded. "All right gentlemen, it looks like Smith and Jack didn't make any friends with the locals, so let's get back on board the *Emerald Star*."

The sailors didn't need to be told twice. They worked quickly. Smith and Jack climbed onboard the wooden skiff as the rest of the men pushed it back into the water. Smith gripped the leather satchel, which contained the ancient relic, holding it close to his chest. There was no way he was going to lose it in the dangerous surf, so close to the *Emerald Star*. Following Oswald's command, the sailors waited until the wave broke onto the shore, and then rowed hard to meet the following wave.

Now afloat and into the violent waters, Smith realized he wasn't safe yet. The next few minutes might be the most dangerous of his entire trip. His mouth was set hard and his heart raced so much he could hear blood pounding in his ears. Where he gripped the satchel his knuckles turned white. The waves came in endless sets. Each one capable of flipping the skiff and drowning them all.

No one, he realized with mixed feelings, could swim in such violent water. It meant if they reached the *Emerald Star* they were safe from the savages who pursued them. If they didn't reach the ship, they would never survive in the water. No man, no matter how strong a swimmer, could stay alive in such a torrent.

"Hold on, men!" Oswald yelled, as they reached the second breaker.

The skiff's bow lifted high into the air. For a moment Smith was certain they were going to flip. The two sailors who rowed closest to the bow saw it too. They jumped forward, moving the weight further toward the bow. Smith watched in horror as the seawater from the breaking wave – white and frothy – rushed through the back half of the skiff. Helpless to avoid the unfolding series of events, he hung on the edge of the boat. Water ripped past him, sending sea spray over his face. The saltwater stung at his eyes and filled his mouth with the bitter taste as two sailors, and Jack Baker were washed overboard.

The bow crashed down hard.

Ahead, a third breaker approached quickly. Smith glanced behind him. The two sailors were barely afloat – the whitewash so full of air that it provided barely any buoyancy at all – and he couldn't even see young Jack. He wondered how his brother was possibly going to rescue the three men before the next wave drowned them all. The rest of the sailors paused on their oars for a split moment.

"Keep going men," Oswald screamed. "Or every one of us will be lost!"

The men rowed in silence and none of them had to be told to leave their friends behind. It wasn't an option of helping their friends. It was save themselves or drown. They struck the third wave at speed and the momentum carried the bow over the top of its crest. For a moment, the skiff appeared to remain stranded in the middle of the wave as the flow of water tried to drag them toward the beach.

"Heave you bastards!" Oswald shouted.

Smith held his breath. The skiff remained motionless for another split second and then began moving forward. He slowly exhaled as the efforts of the men rowing started to be rewarded with movement. They cleared the fourth and fifth waves without any trouble. After that, the deeper water settled and they picked up speed.

Two minutes later the skiff came alongside the *Emerald Star's* portside and Smith climbed up the cargo nets. He kissed the deck. He had cheated death.

Oswald waited until the skiff was pulled up onto the deck and then turned to him. "You okay, little brother?"

"Fine. I'm sorry about your men."

"Don't be. They knew the risks. Death is part of the life of a pirate. You lost more men than me today, by the looks of it."

Smith nodded. He'd felt the same about the men he'd lost earlier. They'd all chosen this life. "All the same. I'm sorry."

Oswald shook his arm. "It's good to see you. I was starting to think you weren't coming back. You could have picked a better time though."

"Why, what's wrong with the timing?" Smith asked. "I cut it fine, but I made it."

"We were about to set sail. There's a storm coming, and if you'd waited another hour or two, we'd have had no choice but to leave you here. Either that or the *Emerald Star* would have been smashed to pieces along this frightful coast!"

Smith smiled. "Another hour and you'd have been picking up our dismembered pieces. In case you haven't noticed, we're not alone."

Oswald looked at him, appraising him in a new light. "My goodness, you did it, didn't you? You actually stole their damned relic?"

"Yes. And what's more, I know why it's so valuable to them."

*

The *Emerald Star* was a Spanish Galleon sporting four masts, and armed with a total of sixteen canons – seven to the port and starboard sides, and one each in the forecastle and aftercastle. Smith's brother had captured the Spanish galleon while it was heaved to, making repairs, off the coast of Gibraltar ten years earlier. Since then, Oswald had her refurbished so she would be unrecognizable to her original owners. Her sail canvas was increased to make her fast, and her load kept light so she could be used as a pirate ship.

His brother had been successful in his endeavors. He was an extremely lucky man, and it had made him rich. Smith smiled as he saw Oswald admire the ancient relic. Neither of them had ever made such an incredible haul. It was the first time he'd gotten away with such deceit. His brother appeared calm. After all, his brother was a pirate.

Oswald studied the evil looking skull. "I can't believe you went through with it!"

Smith said, "There will be plenty of time to admire it later. Now let's bring up the anchor and get away from this God forsaken place!"

"Soon."

"No. Now, it can't wait. We have an angry army after us!"

"Don't worry. It won't take long. We've struck the sandbar and are trapped for the time being. The tide is coming in and she'll float free, soon. Within the hour, for sure."

"We don't have an hour."

"What are you worried about? We have a crew of 120 men armed with muskets. I think we can take a few natives. Besides, you saw how rough the surf was coming out here – it's impossible to think they'll be able to swim through it. And, even if a few might get lucky, they'll never have the strength to then board us."

Smith stared out at the darkened shore. "There might be a thousand out there. They're driven mad like wild beasts."

"My god, you really stole it, didn't you?"

Smith pulled the golden skull and handed it to him. Its wicked smile stared at him, as if to say, *I told you I could get away with all of this, didn't I?*

Oswald undid its leather satchel and admired the ancient relic. A wry grin on his face. "I can't believe you got away with it!"

"We haven't yet!" He glanced up at the darkened sky, from where he'd come. In the night Smith couldn't make out the shape or movement of his pursuers. But he knew they were out there, driven by rage. He shook his head, it was going to be one hell of a storm.

The sudden gust of wind bellowed from the shore, sending painful specks of sand shooting towards them. It passed as quickly as it had struck – only a teaser of what was soon to come. Oswald looked pleased.

Smith asked, "What are you so happy about?"

"This wind is going to be perfect. It's going to blow us off the shore, instead of into it. As soon as the tide lifts, we'll be blown out to sea."

He breathed in a sigh of relief. It was going to be okay. He'd committed a terrible crime and stolen from the very people who'd saved his life, not more than ten days ago. But he was going to get away with it, and he was going to be a very wealthy man. Smith's heart started to race again – because along the shore the fearsome and hypnotic battle cry started again over the roar of the angry sea.

*

The portside of the *Emerald Star* was quickly lined with men aiming muskets toward the beach. Smith noticed the battle hardened pirates seemed unfazed by the angry war-cry resonating from the shore. It was amazing to see so many of the native warriors preparing to attack. Despite their massive numbers, they were outmatched. Oswald's men had superior weapons and the advantage of being up high on the deck of the ship, whereas the warriors would need to swim through the impossibly rough surf, then climb the hull to reach them.

Smith forced himself to relax. There was nothing the attackers could do. The screeching cry from the shore increased pitch until it became deafening. He pressed his hands over his ears. The sound was unimaginably loud, and like nothing he'd ever imagined – and then it stopped completely. Carrying simple weapons of wood and fractured obsidian the army advanced into the deadly sea.

"Hold your fire!" Oswald ordered. He walked along the deck, making certain that each of his men felt his presence and maintained discipline. "They've a long way to swim before they can harm us. There's nothing they can do. So keep calm. We might still have to pick off the few stragglers who survive the swim, but they'll be easy targets."

Smith followed his brother. "You're certain your men can keep hold of the *Emerald Star*?"

Oswald grinned. "You can't tell me you're afraid?"

"Afraid? Of course I'm afraid."

"Why? There's nothing they can do?"

"Look at them. They're driven crazy by the need to return this damned relic." Smith cursed. "How much longer until we're off the sandbar?"

"Not long. Not long now."

Smith watched in horror as his pursuers were driven into the deep water by their religious fervor. Few were capable of swimming. Terrified and relieved, Smith felt his gut wrench at the horrible sight of men, women and children drowning to reach them. Not all of them could swim and those who could were unlikely to make it past the breaking waves.

It was a pitiful sight, and made Smith feel sick to the stomach. He watched a young man, no more than twenty, walk into the water until his head dipped below the surface and then never return. Followed by an adult warrior, nearly six feet tall, who simply ran into the surf, and was swept away by the first wave that reached him.

Not a single shot was fired, and still they came. Warriors advanced into the sea by stepping onto their drowned brethren with the sort of fanaticism that made them believe that with enough deaths they could build a bridge with their dead into the sea. Smith wanted to vomit as he watched the first hundred or more people become buried beneath the waves.

Oswald glanced at him. "Why don't they stop?"

Smith shook his head. "They're as powerless to stop as we are to move off this damned sand bar. They're driven by a higher power, to return their precious relic. Its loss eats at them and tortures them so much that the pain of death pales by comparison."

"And now it's going to drown them."

Smith nodded, solemnly. He may be a selfish bastard, but he wasn't completely devoid of human feelings. They were good people, and had treated him and his party kindly. He'd stolen something of immense value from them, but that didn't mean he wanted to watch them all die.

Smith spotted one man who had dropped his weapon and concentrated on swimming had made it past the breakers. The man appeared to have gotten lucky and swam hard during a slight pause in the set of waves. He was now swimming easily toward them.

"Oswald!" Smith shouted as he pointed at the man.

"I see him." Oswald shook his head in disbelief. "There had to be one, I suppose."

The warrior swam quickly until he reached the side of the *Emerald Star*. Smith watched as the poor wretch stared up at the massive freeboard – the distance between the water and the deck – and suddenly realized there was nothing to climb. The warrior then quickly swam toward the front of the ship, where the bowsprit netting was tethered from the bowsprit to the hull just above the waterline.

Oswald drew his pistol and waited as the savage climbed onto the bowsprit. The instant the man's foot touched the deck Oswald squeezed the trigger and the shot ball fired. It struck the boarder directly in the middle of his forehead. The ball lodged inside the man's skull and never left again. The warrior's eyes stared vacantly up at him and he fell backwards into the water, where he floated lifelessly.

Oswald turned to Smith. "Well. I stand corrected. One of them managed to reach my deck."

Smith said, "More are on their way!"

"My God, so there are. They are persistent, I'll give them that. But don't worry. My men will take care of them." Oswald grinned and then his eyes narrowed with curiosity. "But what in the world are they making?"

*

The human chain involved more than two hundred men and stretched from the shore to well past the breaking waves. The tallest and the strongest men gripped each other's arms to form an intricate structure like ants forming a bridge. The line was roughly eight men wide and each man had a second person on their shoulders. Individually, the waves would have broken them, but together they appeared to be holding their position.

No other civilization in the world had achieved the same amount of human unity. They were working together as a single, defining object, without any consideration for the individual men, women and children who formed the bridge. Smith's eyes darted to the deeper end of the bridge, where some of the men were sacrificing their lives to form a platform beneath the waves.

Oswald opened his mouth to speak. Paused and then said, "They're killing themselves to build the foundations of the human bridge in the deep waters!"

Smith nodded without saying anything.

"I've never seen anything like it. I thought my men were disciplined in battle, but this is a whole new level. Have you ever seen anything like it?"

"No," Smith lied. How could he tell his brother he'd seen something exactly like this back at the pyramid where the entire civilization worked as one machine? And what's worse, he knew exactly how they were achieving it.

Smith watched, mesmerized by the sight. It was a phenomenal achievement of engineering and bravery. *But would it work?* A moment later he witnessed the answer. Crawling on their knees, four at a time, the warriors who were still on the shore made their way along the top of the human bridge. Once they reached the end, past the breaking waves and into the deeper waters, they were able to swim toward the *Emerald Star*.

"My God," Smith said, "they're going to reach us!"

Oswald turned to his men. "Save your shots. Wait until they're right below us and then shoot on my command. Make every musket ball count!"

There was a loud roar of, "Aye, aye, Captain!"

Smith watched as the first set of men swam toward the ship. He looked at his brother, "I'll need a weapon."

"Go down below. Marcus will find you one from the armory. Not that I think you'll need it. We'll be off this sandbar any minute now."

Smith nodded, wishing he shared his brother's confidence. He placed his leather satchel over his shoulders again. There was no way he would let the ancient relic out of his sight while on board a ship full of pirates. His brother's men or not, they couldn't be trusted with such a fortune in gold. He moved quickly toward the open hatchway to the aft.

He wished he felt more confident about his brother's sentiment. The men and women who were attacking them might be little more than savages, but they were focused with religious fervor and would fight ruthlessly to the end. He definitely felt much less confident now than he had twenty minutes earlier, when he assumed they held the infinite advantage of musket shots against their attacker's much larger force. He would feel a lot better once they were off the sandbar and sailing out to sea.

He climbed down the steps and into the ship's hold. He hadn't made it any further before Marcus, the ship's armorer met him. The man was short, with broad shoulders. Multiple scars lined his bearded face like medals from previous conquests.

Marcus grinned and handed him a musket, with a bag of powder and shot. "I heard the Captain. You'll be needing this, then?"

Smith nodded and took the weapon. "Thanks."

"Make every shot count." Marcus had the hardened face of a man who'd seen enough battles to realize that they were never won until they were over.

He simply nodded at the man. "I will." He then returned to the deck, where the first wave of forty or so warriors approached the *Emerald Star*.

The men on deck were already aiming their muskets at the first wave of attackers. The ship rested on the sandbar, while the men silently prepared for battle. The weapons had been primed and loaded and there was no more for the men to check. Their muskets would either fire or not. Some kissed lucky charms, while others closed their eyes and made promises to their Gods. Smith could hear their heavy breathing, and feel their uncertainty and eagerness to fire.

"Wait for it men… wait until they're just below us!" Oswald commanded.

A moment later, the first attacker's hand touched the chain that supported the bowsprit. Oswald pointed his pistol and squeezed the trigger. The warrior fell back into the water. "That's close enough – fire!"

A series of shots fired. The deck became blurred by powder smoke and the scent of burned sulfur and saltpeter wafted through the battlefield. The men worked in three groups of shooters. Group B loaded their weapons while group A fired, and group C prepared to take the next shot. That way the pirates of the *Emerald Star* were constantly capable of firing at their attackers.

Only group A and B fired before the first wave of attackers were killed. Smith studied the sea which quickly turned pink as blood intermingled with the saltwater in a multitude of deathly swirls. Silence filled the air, and for a moment he thought every single one of the attackers had been killed. Then he heard the ghastly scream.

Smith's eyes shot toward the sound in the water. It came from just aft of the *Emerald Star*, where one man desperately tried to keep his head above the water. He'd been shot in both shoulders and was now struggling to stay afloat. His head would dip below the water and Smith assumed it would be all over, but then somehow he'd find the strength to kick his legs and reach the surface again. Drowning was the worst imaginable death to any sailor, and it made him feel sick just to watch. Yet no one was willing to put the poor wretch out of his misery.

Smith quickly examined his own weapon. It was an old flintlock musket. His Lazarino Cominazzo wheel-lock rifle would have been much more accurate. He gritted his teeth. From this distance it didn't matter, it would be hard to miss with anything. He pulled the hammer back to the half-cock position and carefully set the flint. He poured the black powder charge into the measuring flask until it reached the firing mark, and then poured that into the muzzle. He carefully tapped the sides of musket barrel to settle the powder.

Smith opened the bag of shot and removed a lead ball. He slid it into the muzzle and gently used the ramrod to seat the bullet securely on the powder charge. Resting the musket horizontally, he opened the frizzen – the L shaped piece of hinged steel used to enclose a small priming charge – and filled the shallow flash pan with powder. Confident the weapon was ready to fire, he closed the cover tightly. His jaw was set hard as he took aim.

Oswald yelled, "Don't waste your shot!"

Smith carefully leveled the musket at the only survivor and squeezed the trigger. The ball struck the man in the back of his head. His arms stopped thrashing in the water, and water settled once more. It was the only gift he could give to the poor man.

"You shouldn't have done that!" Oswald said.

He looked up, ready to argue, but stopped – because the second wave of forty warriors attacked.

*

Smith watched as the second wave of attackers fell as quickly as the first, and the third followed immediately after. The third focused its attack on the bow of the *Emerald Star*. It was the only place where they had any chance of climbing onto the vessel. It should have made it easy to defend. Instead, it made it exceptionally hard, because there were only so many spaces for the men to load and fire their muskets. While their attackers were spread out around the ship, it was easy to pick out individual targets and take them out. Now, the same attacker was being hit by multiple shots while the person behind, was able to continue the advance.

When the fourth wave of attackers reached the bow they did so with the same unity as the human bridge. They locked arms and gripped the bowsprit and chain, to form a semi-rigid platform. The attackers quickly scrambled over their backs and up on to the deck of the *Emerald Star*.

Muskets fired and the deck was filled once more with the familiar cloud of smoke of burnt gunpowder. The men rotated through the process of priming, loading, and firing so that they could keep a constant barrage of shots at the boarders. Smith noticed, for the time, the method worked – but how long could the muskets keep firing? His eyes glanced at the army of warriors, impatiently waiting on the shore to join the fight. He knew the answer – *not very long*.

Their only hope was that the tide would rise sufficiently so they could flee before being overcome by the superior numbers. He turned to check with his brother and stopped. A small party of attackers had managed to form a small human chain, and climbed up the portside to the no longer guarded aft section of the *Emerald Star*.

"Boarders aft!" he said.

Smith aimed his musket and fired at the first attacker to step foot on the deck. He then dropped the weapon, and replaced it with a pike. The sudden success of the boarder's attack, sent a surge of adrenaline to his system, and his fear turned to bloodlust. He charged at the men trying to scale the railing. He stabbed at their fingers as they gripped the gunwale, before they had a chance to overcome the railing.

Behind him, he heard his brother shout, "You five! Help Smith. The rest of you, stay at your posts – if the boarders breach the bow, we're done for!"

"Aye, aye, captain!"

The five reinforcements joined Smith and quickly killed the remaining boarders. Smith felt his heart pounding in his ears. He paused on the edge of the ship, struggling to catch his breath. He glanced as the growing number of attackers surrounding the ship was swelling again. It was hard to tell the living from the dead. He stared at them, stunned. With their own superior weaponry, how could they possibly lose? But it was clear their dominance was beginning to wane and struggle to keep up with the endless number of assailants, willing to sacrifice their lives to win. Soon, he knew, the muskets would start to fail. They would misfire, the powder would fail, and their shot balls would run out. Then what would happen?

Smith knew the answer with the simple certainty of a man who knows that he cannot fly like a bird, or breathe water like a fish – their attackers would overcome them, and the crew of the *Emerald Star* would be slaughtered.

Unless they changed their tactics, now.

Smith stared at a row of dead men floating in the water below. Despite the gruesome sight, he suddenly grinned. The solution had presented itself to him. He couldn't believe his brother hadn't thought of it already. He turned to tell his brother. But a hand stretched through the railing and clasped his leg.

He looked down and saw a fiend from the dead suddenly rise out of the sea. Smith stabbed his pike at the man, but the attacker gripped the head of the weapon and used it to pull himself up. Smith let go, but he was too late. The fast moving boarder had already cleared the railing. The man appeared young, no more than fifteen or sixteen. He wore nothing but a small animal-hide loincloth. His muscles were lithe, and he moved about with the agility of a circus performer. He used a small dagger of fragmented obsidian and sliced one of the men in the process of priming his musket.

Someone else fired a shot, but the lead ball went wide. Another pirate threw his dagger, but it missed. The attacker slipped past three men who were reloading their muskets and ran forward. Oswald stood toward the bow of the ship, where most of the crew still fought off the main boarding assault. He noticed the unfolding disaster and ran toward the assailant, with his cutlass drawn, ready to slice the small man. The boarder glanced at the large man and turned. He was now trapped between Smith and his brother. Smith reached for his musket and quickly began the tedious task of priming it to fire.

The attacker stared at him. The assailant's eyes darted back toward Oswald, who stared back with the vehemence of a seasoned pirate with blood on his drawn cutlass. It was enough for the attacker to make a decision. The attacker turned to run away, directly toward him. Smith quickly filled the muzzle with gunpowder. He didn't measure the amount, and then shoved a round shot ball into the barrel. He dropped his ramrod, and opened the frizzen to fill it with an unmeasured priming charge. The attacker jabbed at him with his small dagger. Smith parried the attack with the barrel of his musket, and stepped back. He closed the frizzen and squeezed the trigger. The shot ball fired and struck the man's belly…

The soft lead flattened on impact. Unlike a modern spitzer-type bullet, which enters and exits tissue quickly, the deformed ball doesn't travel through tissue very efficiently. Instead, it transfers most of its kinetic energy to the tissues, organs and bones of the victim causing unimaginable damage. The boy gripped his abdomen with his right hand. Abject horror in his eyes, as blood started to gush out. It was a mortal shot, but the man still moved.

The boarder howled with rage. Driven by some unearthly force, he pushed passed Smith and clambered up the ratlines to the main-mast. He reached the maintop and continued to climb up to the topgallant. Once there he started to cut the rigging. Smith cursed and swiftly started the process of reloading his musket.

"Forget about him," Oswald said, as he glanced up into the rigging. "He won't live long, and if I don't do something to change their attack, we won't have a ship left to protect."

Smith nodded. "I'll take care of him."

It took less than twenty-five seconds to finish priming and loading the musket. Smith then climbed the ratlines to the maintop. He stopped and tried to aim at the dying man. The shot was obstructed by the main mast and second stage of ratlines. If he had his rifle he could have made it, but not with the musket. The dying man above appeared to be making the most of his last few minutes of life by cutting as many rigging lines as possible. *Why doesn't he just lie down and die?* Smith breathed hard and started to climb again. Immediately, the man above started to move toward the very end of the crosstree, toward the portside.

Standing on the small platform at the main-topgallant, Smith looked at the end of the crosstree where the man he was chasing had finally stopped running. He studied the native's face, realizing he was little older than a boy. His eyes were focused. There was fear inside, but it wasn't of losing his own life. It was something else. Something somehow far more frightening. Whatever it was, Smith intended to put him out of his misery without hesitation. He took aim. They were close and it was an easy shot, but he didn't want to get caught out if he missed.

The boy looked crestfallen. Like many of the men from the pyramid, he'd learned to speak basic English. "Do you have any idea what you have done?"

"I'm sorry," Smith muttered, silently.

The boy shook his head. "Not as much as you will be once you discover what the demon with the purple eyes will do with it."

Smith stopped himself from squeezing the trigger. "What do you know about the man with the purple eyes?"

The boy stared back at him. His eyes were sardonic. Smith recognized that look. It was the same one the damned skull had given him. It was like a curse. A challenge. It said, *do you dare open Pandora's Box?*

"What will he do with it?" Smith persisted.

The boy cut the end of the mainsail sheet, and jumped. He swung like a pendulum, and landed on the fore-topgallant platform, toward the bow of the ship. Smith immediately took aim and fired. But he was too late – the boy had already chosen to dive, head first with his knife held outward. He landed on the deck with a sickening thud, which broke his neck in an instant, and killed one of the pirates.

*

The defiant act served the attacker's cause more than the death of one musket-wielding pirate. One glance at the crew, and Smith knew exactly why the boy had done it. The act had simultaneously invigorated his brethren, and demoralized the crew of the *Emerald Star*. It showed them that their attackers would stop at nothing to win.

Smith clambered down the ratlines. He needed to do something. Otherwise the outcome of the battle was indisputable. Oswald's face, which was earlier cheerful and confident, was now set hard. His jaw was rigid and his eyes wide. They were winning, but for how long? He knew as well as every one of them that the muskets would fail well before the enemy had depleted its supply of men and women willing to die to save the relic.

He looked up at Oswald. "How much longer until we're off this God-forsaken sandbar?"

"I don't know," Oswald said. "It may be a few more minutes. Definitely no more than an hour or two."

"An hour or two!"

Oswald shrugged. "The ocean can be capricious. Working out how much time it wants to take to raise the *Emerald Star* to float is not a precise science."

Smith said, "The muskets won't fire indefinitely."

Oswald pointed his pistol at another boarder, and fired. The ball struck the man in his neck. He gripped it, and fell backward into the sea. "I know. I'm still trying to work out what to do about it."

"What about the fore-cannon?"

"We're too close," Oswald grunted. "There's no way we could maneuver it to hit the boarders."

Smith shook his head. "I wasn't thinking about the boarders."

"No?"

"No. I was thinking about destroying that human bridge."

Oswald glanced out toward the strange construction of men used to overcome the breaking waves, as he thought about it for a moment. He turned to one of the shorter men, and said, "Matthews, take the rest of the forward gunner team down below. I want you to start battering that human bridge!"

"Aye, aye, Captain!"

Five minutes later, Smith watched as the fore-cannon was loaded with a standard iron cannonball known as round shot. Matthews struck the light and the cannon fired into the human bridge. The heavy ball of steel missed by several feet.

A spotter ran down into the forward hold. "It's short."

Matthew cursed. "By how much, man? Be precise!"

"Seven feet."

Matthew nodded and quickly resealed the cannon's touch hole with a leather thumb sheath to eliminate air from entering. "All right, men. You heard him. A small adjustment and we're going to destroy that bridge. Let's do it again."

"Aye, aye, Mr. Matthews."

Smith watched as two men hastily sponged the barrel to prevent any leftover embers from prematurely sparking the next round of gunpowder. The third man wormed the cannon – a process of running a piece of coiled iron called a worm through the barrel to remove any remnants from the previous firing – and the barrel was then sponged again.

Matthews examined the barrel carefully. He nodded, satisfied the barrel was clean of any embers. "Okay. She's ready. Let's do this right, this time."

The powder monkey said, "Aye, Mr. Matthews," and passed the heavy powder charge to the powder handler at the front of the gun.

Matthew's gave the order, "Load."

"Aye, Mr. Matthews," the powder handler acknowledged, as he placed the charge in front of the bore of the gun, and the rammer slid it in until it bottomed out at the back of the barrel.

Matthews removed the leather thumb sheath from the touch hole and used the prick to test the charge was seated properly by pushing the powder prick into the touch hole and into the charge. Satisfied with the result, he yelled, "Home."

The powder monkey passed the second canon ball to the powder handler, who placed the ball in front of the barrel bore with his hand below the barrel. He glanced at the gunner.

Matthew yelled, "Load!"

The rammer said, "Aye, Mr. Matthews," and rammed the ball with a wad of rags down the barrel until it was seated against the charge.

Matthews carefully sighted the gun. He adjusted the telemetry and height so the iron ball would fall past its previous location. Confident of the new position, he primed the gun by pouring black powder into the touch hole. "Ready."

The gun crew covered their ears and stepped clear of the gun. Smith took an additional step backward, and blocked his ears. He watched as Mr. Matthews lit the fuse. The wooden rod with a piece of lit saltpeter glowed orange.

"Fire!" Matthews yelled, as he touched the saltpeter to the powder in the touch hole.

This time the cannonball sliced straight through its human recipients, severing one head and multiple limbs in the process. The human bridge swayed for a moment, and then the surviving members closed the gap and a new wave of attackers started to crawl along its top.

Oswald came down the gangway, into the forward gunner's hold. "Great shot, Matthews! Let's hit them again!"

Smith glanced at his brother. He was grinning and covered in blood as he gripped the handle of his cutlass with enthusiasm. Smith gritted his teeth as he watched the horrific sight. He'd never had the stomach for the battles, but it was obvious this was what his brother lived for. Still, if someone was going to die, he'd rather it be them instead of him.

"Smith," Oswald looked at him. "You'd better follow me on to the deck. Some of the muskets are starting to foul. We need every hand we can get to stop them from over-running us."

"Of course," Smith said.

He raced up on to the deck with his loaded musket and joined the fight. Smith looked around. His eyes darting between the bow and stern, where the greatest number of attackers congregated, and pushed forward. Around him, his brother's men were beginning to show signs of fatigue. Muskets were being loaded with the careless disregard of soldiers overwhelmed by their attackers. As a consequence, the muskets were starting to foul and fail. They were still winning, but not for much longer.

An attacker somehow reached the gunwale to the port side of the ship. Smith aimed his musket at the man's head, and squeezed the trigger. The attacker fell back into the water, but more people continued to climb the railing. He grabbed a cutlass from the rack and sliced through their wrists, forcing them to fall back into the water.

He heard the third cannon fire. Its steel ball made a sharp whine as it sped through the air. Smith took a deep breath and held it. If the shot didn't destroy the bridge, they would struggle to keep command of the *Emerald Star* for a fourth one. His eyes followed the shot. It was directly on target. This time, the human bridge parted moments before ball struck. It dipped into the ocean, without injuring a single warrior, and sent a small plume of seawater into the air. Immediately afterwards the human bridged closed the gap and held firm – while another wave of warriors quickly climbed over the top and past the breakers.

*

Smith swallowed hard, and reloaded his musket.

Behind him, Oswald stormed down below into the gunners hold. "Same target. This time, load the grapeshot!"

Grapeshot consisted of small iron balls about three quarters of an inch in diameter, which were then packed into bags. The bags disintegrated when the powder ignited, releasing a cluster of balls in a wide shot pattern. This load was very deadly against crewmen at extremely close range, and often used to repel boarders. It was rarely used to hit a target fifty feet away.

Smith heard the loud boom of the fourth canon shot. His eyes traced the grapeshot's trajectory as it whined through the air. This time the lethal concoction of deadly projectiles struck the middle of the human bridge.

At a guess, it killed at least thirty of the warriors in the process. It would take much longer to re-establish the human bridge this time, but Smith wasn't so certain they'd won, and neither was his brother. The disconnected, outer section of the human bridge floundered in the water. No longer able to stabilize itself amongst the men whose feet were planted firmly in the shallow waters, the outer men started to float.

Oswald met his eyes. "One more shot and the bridge will be washed away in the breaking seas, and this all will be over!"

Smith nodded as he shot a man who started to climb the stern. "I hope that shot comes soon, because we're not going to last much longer."

"Don't doubt my men." Oswald grinned as he hacked at another boarder. "They'll hold as long as we need them to."

Behind him, a second boarder climbed. Smith looked at his shot pouch. It was empty. He was out of musket balls. He dropped the musket and picked up the cutlass instead. He hacked at the attacker, slicing him across his chest.

He turned and yelled, "Marcus. We need more musket shots."

Smith didn't hear the response. Instead he heard a loud explosion coming from the bow! Smoke erupted from the forecastle where the cannon were housed. He looked at his brother. "What the hell was that?"

Oswald shrugged. "The fore-cannon just exploded. Some fool must not have sponged the embers well enough!"

"Can we get the other cannon?"

"No. Not fast enough to make it do us any good."

Smith glanced back at the shore. The human bridge was starting to form again. "Now what?"

Oswald growled. "Now we fight for our lives!"

"It would take a miracle to hold them off much longer."

Oswald looked up at the sky behind. A massive storm was moving in toward them, whipping sand from the Namibian desert at them like tiny shrapnel. The once-unified human bridge appeared to disintegrate under the barrage.

"See, Smith – the Gods haven't forsaken us!" Oswald was grinning with delight. "That wind storm is going to blow us right out to sea!"

*

The easterly wind screamed along the Namibian desert, picking up sand along with it, and sending it out to sea. The human bridge failed to form, and the warriors were scattered throughout the surf, which had been whipped into a turbid boiling pot of angry sea. Smith watched their arms flailing beneath the light of the crescent moon, as they struggled to keep their heads above the seawater. The few who were close to *Emerald Star* were now being blown further out to sea, despite their best efforts to reach the ship.

Smith carefully found another bag of shot balls, reloaded his musket and smiled. He'd beaten the odds, and survived. He searched the ship for any signs of boarders. The last thing he wanted now was to risk being killed by complacency.

His brother grinned. "I told you we'd be all right!"

"You did!" Smith embraced his brother. His eyes darted to the shore, where a dark, amorphous shadow stared back at him. "I'll feel a lot better when we're off this damned sandbar."

"Any minute now. I can already feel her lifting in the swell."

"We got lucky."

"Yes. We did. But God knows I've made enough luck for myself over the years. It was time she paid me back some."

Smith nodded. He wasn't sure how much he deserved to be lucky, but he was none-the-less thankful for it. He climbed down below to avoid the tiny sand particles, which were cutting at him. Once there, he carefully opened the leather satchel he'd been carrying, and admired the cause of all this death. Of his entire party, only he had survived. The hideous relic stared back at him with hollowed eyes.

They teased at his conscience – *was it all worth it?*

Smith covered the relic with its protective cloth and placed it back inside the leather satchel, as though he could hide its accusatory eyes. A gust of wind howled as it screamed toward the *Emerald Star*. He felt the ship slowly list to her starboard side under the sudden pressure. He waited for it to right itself, but instead she remained slightly on her side.

The wind shrieked as it continued to thrash the portside of the ship. Smith slipped his arms through the straps of the satchel and stood up. Bracing on the side of the hull, he closed his eyes and made a silent prayer.

Please, let me survive, and I promise the man with the purple eyes won't ever have you.

The ancient relic wasn't in the mood for listening to his prayers. Instead, Oswald opened the deck hatch and said, "All hands on deck!"

Smith climbed up top. "What's wrong? We have an easterly wind. Why aren't we being blown out to sea?"

"It's the sand!" Oswald yelled. He voice barely audible above the cry of the wind. His skin was speckled with his own blood where the sand had sliced at him. "This wind is dumping the dunes of the Namibian desert onto our deck."

Smith felt his heart drum faster. *No, it can't be. The curse can't be true!* "What can we do?"

"We need every man to do his part to lighten the ship's load. There are some shovels and buckets in the bilge. Those who aren't getting rid of this damned sand, need to go below and make a human chain to remove the cannonballs and anything else that can be thrown overboard!"

"Aye, aye, Captain!"

Smith shoveled the sand from the deck. It lined the deck thinly, but the combined weight was enough to keep the *Emerald Star* well stuck where she lay. He struggled to breathe through the dense barrage of sand pellets. He covered his mouth with part of a small piece of cloth and kept working.

Sweat dripped from his arms as he shoveled quickly. His head pounded hard and the muscles of his arms and chest burned from the strain. He continued for as long as his body would allow, and then stopped. His feet had already become buried in the new sand. Sections of the deck which hadn't been attacked with shovels were now knee deep in grit and the weight of it all began crushing the ship deep into the sandbar below.

Despondent with the certainty his battle was hopeless, Smith glanced at the deadly weather formation that would kill them all. It looked dark, ominous and evil to its core. Smith had spent nearly thirty years venturing into unexplored regions of the world. He'd seen every type of weather pattern known to man, but he'd never seen this. It was a once-in-a-generation meteorological event. The ferocious winds were leveling the monstrous sand dunes of the Namibian desert and dumping them out to sea.

His eyes turned to the warriors who lined the coast. They were going to win. He was going to die, but he doubted any of them would live long enough to revel in the knowledge. The storm was indiscriminate. It would kill all of them. Smith blinked, trying to see through the sand. When he opened them again, he saw an even more ghastly sight – the fiends had started to walk on water.

It was proof they were unearthly creatures. For a moment, he questioned whether or not he was still alive, and if he was now being punished in hell. He'd already accepted his fate, as impossible as it had seemed only a few hours earlier, he was going to die. But this was different. This was something evil, from the darkest unknown. Because no one walks on water.

A gust of wind knocked him onto his back. Nearby, one of the crew fell overboard, and Oswald screamed for the remaining men to keep working. Smith glanced at the fiends of his nightmare. There was something eerie and unnatural about the way they moved across the surface of the water. Like some sort of ethereal wraith, they glided above the water, and slowly stalked him.

Smith heard a man cry out for help from the sea. It was the man who'd fallen overboard. Smith clambered to the starboard railing. The crewman was standing in ankle deep water. *My God! The ocean's being swallowed by the sand!* He reached down and helped pull the man back onto the deck.

Oswald had seen it, too. "Forget shoveling the sand, men. Prepare to repel boarders!"

*

Smith stared in horror as the warriors from the sand temple slowly approached. Their original numbers had been decimated, but they were still much greater than Oswald's men, and they looked terrifying as they approached the *Emerald Star*. Smith followed the rest of the crew and fired his musket at the onslaught of warriors. His replenished supply of shot would outlast the weapon's ability to continue to fire.

The first set of shots was fired and the smell of burnt sulfur and saltpeter filled the deck once more. Sand tore at their fragile skin, while the storm buried the meager light from the crescent moon. Their attackers advanced in an eerie silence, and the howling wind mocked them. Visibility was quickly reduced to nothing. The muskets rapidly failed under the sandy conditions. Flints broke, powder was spilled, and barrels became jammed with sand.

"Cutlasses and pikes out!" Oswald yelled. "This is it lads. Do or die!"

Smith rammed the butt of the musket into a boarder. The man fell backward and Smith dropped the weapon. He picked up a cutlass and swung it at the next man he saw. In the darkness, only the cries of the crew of the *Emerald Star* could be heard above the cold wind. He had no way of telling how many of the pirates were still alive.

It no longer mattered. They had been overrun by boarders, whose numbers and savagery would inevitably slaughter every last man. He heard his brother growl like a wounded beast. It could have been his bloodlust, or he could have been killed. Smith had no way of knowing. What he did know was there was only one place left where they might survive.

"Into the hold!" Smith yelled. "Retreat into the ship."

He ran forward along the deck, through the darkness. One man stabbed at him with his dagger. Reflexively, Smith sliced back with his cutlass. The attacker's gut opened up and Smith kept running. He climbed into the open hatch.

Once inside, he grabbed a pike off the rack, and pointed it upwards. If one of the boarders were to try to advance inside, he would pierce the man with the blade. He waited a few seconds for the other members of the crew. One of the attackers tried to drop down into the hold. Smith lifted the pike so it stood upwards, and the man was killed as his own weight drove the weapon through him when he landed on top of it.

Smith grabbed another pike off the rack, and waited ten seconds for more survivors, but none of the crew came. He knew he should wait longer. But how long could he keep fighting off the rest of the attackers? Sweat filled the palms of his trembling hands, and made the pike slippery. He climbed the ladder, and looked out into the darkness. Three of the attackers ran toward him. Smith closed the hatch and locked it shut. He wondered if their daggers of fragmented obsidian would be capable of penetrating the hardwood hatch. Smith dismissed the thought. There was nothing he could do about it. He quickly slid down the ladder, and lit a lantern.

"Is there anyone else down here?" he asked.

Only silence returned.

Above, the cries of men being slaughtered had finally dwindled to nothing. Smith carried the lantern and continued to search the bowels of the *Emerald Star*. He was on his own. He recalled the words the man with the purple eyes had said to him about the ancient relic – *He who possesses it shall rule in solitude. For that is the price of unimaginable power.*

He quickly opened the leather satchel, and unwrapped the protective cloth that surrounded the golden skull. He stared at the wretched artifact. Its hollowed eyes were tormenting him – *Aren't you glad you stole me?*

He wanted to throw it overboard. Get rid of the cursed thing, but the outward opening hatch was now filled with sand and unable to be opened from the inside, even if he wanted to. His eyes darted to the porthole. Maybe there was still time to open it and escape. But even if he could, where would he go? The answer came to him immediately – to his death. Anything would be better than being buried alive.

Smith kept staring out the porthole in horror. It was pitch dark outside, and the light of the lantern flickered and reflected back at him on its glass. The porthole was too small to escape through. It was barely large enough to squeeze his arm through if he tried, and nowhere near large enough to expel the golden skull.

Above, he heard the unnerving sound of fingers scratching at the deck. The people from the pyramid were trying to dig their way through the sand and the hardwood to reach him. Not him. They didn't really care about him. He glanced at the skull. Its sinister hollowed out eyes were mocking him. *You know why they're really here, don't you?* They had come for it, and the sweet smell of its burned, blackened powder. He would gladly give it to them, if he could.

His eyes focused on the porthole, as he watched the last remnants of the outside world being taken from him. Suddenly a man's face peered through it, staring back in at him. It was one of the warriors. The man was silent. His eyes wide, longing for one last glimpse of it. Smith was no longer frightened of the creature. To him, the poor devil outside, looked just as pained and tormented as himself.

The man pressed his eyes hard against the porthole, as though he was trying to squeeze his head through the much smaller, brass hole, in an attempt to get a better look at the golden skull. Smith grabbed the ancient relic and picked it up and brought it to the porthole window.

The warrior smiled as though its sight had somehow relieved his pain, and given him some sort of peace in his death. The two men were locked, their eyes staring into each other's souls as the sand continued to rise around them. Time came and went, but still the sand rose, until long after the warrior outside was buried alive, and his now lifeless eyes stared at him with accusation.

The storm lasted two whole days. When it finally stopped, Smith fought to open the hatch, but there was nothing he could do. The hatches opened outward, and now unimaginable amounts of sand weighed heavily above. He tried the other hatches, but each of them opened outward. He felt his way around the bowels of the ship, searching for an axe or anything to help free himself from his curse.

He struck a match and lit the lantern again. He studied the artifact under the poor light of the oil lamp. The skull stared back at him. Its white teeth grinned hideously at him as though it had known all along what the outcome of its theft would be. Smith spun the skull upside down and stared at it from below. Solid gold had been flattened to make space for a unique image, delicately etched inside. It depicted two mountain peaks, leading together with a small lake or possibly snow in the middle. He'd never seen the place, but there was no doubt in his mind of the image's purpose – it was a map.

As fear took over, he could no longer resist the urge to scream. He cried out to anyone who could help him. To his brother, to the other members of his party – all of whom were now dead – and finally, when fear and hysteria had taken over his rational mind, he cried out to God, and asked for forgiveness.

He then held the ancient relic close to his chest and laughed hysterically. Because his final act of redemption was to ensure the man with the purple eyes would never achieve his goal. That he would never get a hold of the artifact – because it had been entombed forever.

Khor Virap, Armenia – 2005

It was still dark outside the defensive walls of the monastery. Billie Swan stared over the stone parapet to the north, past the closed Turkey-Armenian border, where the snow-capped twin peaks of Mount Ararat glowed orange under the light of the crescent moon. The mountain stood at a near-quadripoint between Turkey, Armenia, Azerbaijan, and Iran.

Her eyes were almond shaped, and hazel colored, with tiny speckles of gold that glittered in the light. They were luminous and intense, befitting her intelligence, as she stared at the holy mountain. She had regular features that betrayed her Eurasian ancestry, and a sensual, full-lipped mouth. She breathed deeply, and watched her breath crystalize in the night. In two hours the first light of winter's solstice would shine through the twin peaks, turning them a golden red. And, if her grandfather's notes were to be believed, that first light would show her the precise location of the opening to the ancient temple.

Billie had been following her grandfather's notes since he died, years ago. Every lead she'd taken led to a tangent, and she had nearly given up hope of finding her grandfather. This time felt different. This was the closest she'd ever come to finding the temple. This lead had taken her to Mount Ararat, which was enshrined in mystery and biblical myths. The most predominant of course, being that the top of the mountain was where Noah had first stepped off his Ark.

In the seventh month the Ark rests on the mountains of Ararat, and in the tenth month the tops of the mountains are seen – Genesis 8:4

She smiled. The place was mysterious all right. And the Armenians were right to worship the sacred mountain, but it had nothing to do with Noah and his Ark – and everything to do with an ancient civilization who were genetically and mentally predisposed to greatness.

In the silence, she allowed her mind to drift, and she imagined what she might find inside. An ancient database of information by one of the greatest civilizations who ever lived? Or nothing more than a Neolithic cavern, and further evidence the Master Builders never existed? She thought about the last person to enter the ancient temple, before it was permanently sealed because the information stored inside was deemed too dangerous to humanity. The forbidden fruit. Gregory the Illuminator had seen that knowledge – he then spent the next fourteen years of his life imprisoned inside Khor Virap.

She lowered her gaze from Mount Ararat to the walled monastery. Her expressive eyes were pensive as they examined the grounds. The old stone fortifications provided a meek wall surrounding a modest stone church. Nothing about its appearance suggested such a rich and fanciful history. That the birth of modern Christianity once originated on the very same ground, seemed preposterous – but that didn't make it any less true.

The Armenian name for the monastery, Khor Virap, translated to Deep Dungeon. Until the start of the fourth century, that was all it was. A two hundred foot pit, dug into the hillock at the base of the Ararat plain.

It was said that when King Tiridates III ruled over Armenia, his assistant was Grigory Lusavorich, who preached the Christian religion. Tiridates, a follower of the pagan religion, became displeased with his assistant for having another religion, and ordered that Gregory's hands and legs be tied and that he be thrown into the Khor Virap to die in the dark dungeon located in Artashat.

The King waged wars and persecution against the Christian minorities. However, Gregory did not die during his fourteen years of imprisonment. His survival was attributed to a Christian widow from the local town who, under the influence of strange dream vision, regularly fed Gregory by dropping a loaf of freshly baked bread into the pit.

While Gregory was imprisoned in Khor Virap, King Tiridates III was said to have gone mad. Tiridates's sister, Khosrovidhukt, had a vision in the night, where an angel told her about the prisoner Gregory in the city of Artashat who could end the torments. Few people believed her visions, as most thought that Gregory had died within days of his being cast into the pit. But Khosrovidhukt had the same dream repeatedly, eventually threatened that if the dream's instructions were not followed, there would be dire consequences.

Gregory was brought out of Khor Virap in a miserable state. He was taken to the king, who had gone mad, tearing at his own skin. Gregory cured the king and brought him back to his senses. Gregory knew of all the atrocities committed, and saw the bodies of the martyrs who were later cremated. The king, accompanied by his court, approached Gregory, seeking forgiveness for all the sins they committed. King Tiridates III embraced Christianity as his religion following the miraculous cure effected by Gregory's divine intervention and proclaimed Christianity as the state religion of Armenia in 301 A.D.

Billie had spent hundreds of hours reading through the stories of Gregory the Illuminator. For the most part, she believed they were based on fact. All, except for the reason why he'd been imprisoned in the pit in the first place. That was the part she was most interested in. It was the early section of the myth that brought her here today.

In the year 286 A.D. Gregory made a pilgrimage to Mount Ararat in search of his God, where high up in the larger of the two volcanic peaks, he had seen a vision of God at work. When he reached the place, where he'd often seen a halo of light in the night, he was met by a cavern filled with information, so far advanced from his own, that he believed the owners to be Gods.

What those Gods had told him was so remarkable that he quickly returned to King Tiradates III to tell him the truth. When King Tiradates III heard Gregory's story, he found it so impossible to believe, and yet so damaging, that he ordered a second team to seal the ancient temple, so that no one else would ever find it. When Gregory confirmed to the King that his wishes had been carried out, King Tiradates ordered him taken to the Deep Dungeon and left to die in solitude. Tiradates III knew he needed to send him to a place where no one would ever hear him speak the truth. But just as importantly, he knew that he couldn't kill the man, either.

According to Billie's grandfather, the entrance shined golden red just once a year on the morning of winter solstice. Billie's eyes returned to the monastery's stone fortification. Jeremy Follet carefully climbed the wooden ladder, carrying a lit monk's candle.

"Good morning," he said.

"Morning," she replied. "You couldn't sleep, either?"

"No. I didn't trust my alarm with something like this." He smiled at her, as though he understood what she was thinking. "We're getting close to reaching it, aren't we?"

She smiled, and nodded. "Closer than I've ever been."

His eyes narrowed. "You're confident you have the right temple, this time?"

"Yes." She watched him smile. Deep creases formed in his face, giving him an older, but rugged handsomeness. He had intelligent dark brown eyes. They were kindly, and full of love and admiration. He was her father's best friend and her Godfather. He had a shallow cleft chin that some women found attractive. She imagined he would have been considered quite a handsome man in his youth. She looked up at him. "What is it?"

Jeremy said, "It's an amazing achievement to get this close. Your father would have been so proud."

"No. My father would have been furious with me for taking the risk."

"Your grandfather lost his life following that dream."

She turned her head so that he couldn't meet his eyes, "You know as well as I do that it's real, don't you?"

He nodded in silence.

"Grandpa found it, didn't he?"

Jeremy looked at her face, but she could tell he was envisioning a time long past. He nodded. "And it's what got him killed, too. Some secrets weren't ever supposed to be discovered."

"Maybe. But soon I intend to find out exactly what those secrets were."

Jeremy sat down on a small stone alcove. "I was afraid that's what you were going to say."

They both sat there in silence, until the sun penetrated the horizon. She measured the precise distance from the sun, to the horizon. The bright light reflected on a location, two thirds of the way up the ancient volcano dome of Ararat Greater.

She took out a small gadget that appeared to be nothing more than a hand held GPS with a telescopic lens. She focused it on the exact spot where the mountain turned red. It was fixed to a tripod, and she quickly ran her finger along the touch screen surface. She clicked the capture button once. Miles above Mount Ararat, eleven separate satellites triangulated the exact location where the light was set.

The expedition had been backed by big money. Professor Jeremy Follett had refused to disclose to her who his backer had been, but the money flowed well, and that was all she cared about. She'd never even thought why someone would spend so much money to provide the means to discover the location of the ancient civilization in the clouds.

Jeremy asked, "Do you know yet?"

She grinned. "I've got it, but it's going to be one hell of a climb to reach."

*

The Armenia-Turkey border was less than a mile away from Khor Virap. Billie Swan could clearly see the border's fence and lookout towers from the monastery. She was close to where she needed to go, but the border was closed to everyone. The only way to reach Mount Ararat was to go through Georgia and then fly back to Turkey.

She left Khor Virap immediately. From Armenia they drove to Georgia and then flew into Istanbul, where the rest of the climbing team were preparing the heavier archeological equipment for transport. An old Bell Jet Ranger helicopter was hired to take them to the base of Mount Ararat with a small team of local guides. Once there, they spent three days acclimatizing on the lower outskirts of Mount Ararat and one day climbing the small nearby peak of Mount Hasan to an altitude of 10,672 feet before making the final ascent.

They hiked north on the Anatolia trail toward the sacred mountain. Leaving behind the juniper trees and fields of grass, often used for breeding sheep, she began her ascent. The remains of a monastery and village constructed on the mountain could be seen high above, where an avalanche in 1840 had destroyed all but a handful of small buildings, which had since been rebuilt.

The party stopped for a short rest at a Kurdish stone hamlet positioned at a little over six thousand feet. Nearby, a small boy tended to four goats without making eye-contact with any of the party. Billie stared up at the mountain peaks ahead. A deep, thick fog was setting in, burying their peaks in obscurity. She'd been warned not to climb during the height of winter, but what she needed to find couldn't wait until summer and the safer climbing months. As the twin peaks of Mount Ararat disappeared, she turned her gaze to where they'd come from. She took in the sweeping views of the plains of Anatolia, which stretched all the way to the Black Sea. Her mind followed the landscape, drifting with it, all the way back to Istanbul and her recent discovery there.

When her late father died, she had received a digital key and number to a locked box for a Bank of Turkey located in Istanbul. It had been left there by her grandfather with a single note – *If I don't come back, it is imperative that you take this key and finish my research.* The note had been for her father, and not for her. It was only when she was going over some of her father's things with her mother that she found the key. Her mother had warned her that it was likely to be something her grandfather had been involved in and it was best to leave some things alone. Billie had nodded with graceful understanding. She swiftly took the key and flew to Istanbul – to find answers.

Instead, she found more questions. The locked box contained hundreds of handwritten notes on an ancient race, who had been genetically and physically superior to other people of their time. She had spent nearly three months sifting through them before she found what she was after.

This was the first positive lead she'd found in nearly two years of searching for her grandfather. It was the first time she'd discovered confirmation of where he'd been looking for the temple before he died – if he was even dead? She recalled his note, which had made her heart race.

The golden gates of the Temple of Illumination, high up on Mount Ararat, will only be revealed to those who are present at Khor Virap during the sunrise of winter's solstice.

From there, everything had moved quickly. Her window of opportunity was about to close. It hadn't left her with a lot of time to prepare, and if she missed it she would have to wait another year to pick up the lost trail – a thought entirely abhorrent to her.

The next day, Jeremy Follett, one of her closest allies in the world of archeology and lifelong friend of her late father, arrived with funding for the expedition. Guides needed to be hired, equipment sourced, bribes made, and passes obtained to climb the mountain. She hired Ahmet. He had a surly disposition, and sense of superiority to women that made her instantly disdain the man, but he'd been guiding in the region for the better part of twenty-five years, and had an excellent reputation. More importantly, he could leave immediately. Five local men were taken on to help carry the heavy equipment. She had left Ahmet in Istanbul while she and Jeremy had traveled to Khor Virap to witness the sunrise of winter's solstice.

They left the Kurdish hamlet. The slope toward Mount Ararat steepened and Billie returned her attention to the task at hand. She maintained a constant speed, at first matching the rate of the local guides, and then surpassing it to set her own pace. She was tall and lissome. She moved with the assertive gait of an athlete. Even in shapeless mountaineering clothes, she had a willowy elegance about her as she climbed.

For the most part, the climb was nothing more than a steep incline of thick snow. The team was tethered together with a single rope for safety. Although it was not a technically difficult climb, any mistake or lack of attention, would cause her to commence a slide down the icy precipice which might not be stopped until it reached the ground thousands of feet below. She wore crampons, and carried an icepick. Her thighs burned as they slowly increased altitude.

At twelve thousand feet, she stopped. They'd reached the rough altitude of the temple, but would now need to traverse across the southern face until they reached it. The guides set up camp and the party rested there for the night.

Billie stared out as the scattered lights of Cappadocia glittered like starlight. The Black Sea appeared dark and foreboding with the occasional flickering light from a ship able to be visible. Her eyes stared out, trying to picture the underlying landscapes and cities, all the way back to the vague glow illuminating from beyond the darkened horizon, where the city of Istanbul rested.

She thought about the Temple of Illumination. She was getting close to it. Her heart raced in anticipation. It was an incredible achievement. Her grandfather had previously told her that he'd narrowed the location of the secret temple down to Turkey – most likely buried underground – otherwise it would have undoubtedly been discovered well before now. But that was akin to finding a needle in a haystack, inside a country known for its farming. Turkey was renowned for having upward of four thousand underground dwellings, cities, and temples. The soft volcanic rock of the Cappadocia led the Phrygians, an Indo-European people, in the 8th–7th centuries B.C. to build an extensive network of tunnels and cities. If it had been buried, she might never have found the hidden temple – that is, assuming tomorrow she'd find it.

Jeremy came and sat down next to her, and interrupted her thoughts. "Are you excited?"

"Nervous, more like."

"Nervous. Really? I've never known you to be afraid of anything since you were a three year old girl who'd discovered a talent for climbing that frightened your parents to death. So, what are you most afraid of, now?"

Billie's piercing brown eyes, stared out at the dark outline of the Black Sea. "What we find tomorrow."

"And what will that be?" Jeremy persisted.

"Answers."

"You don't want to know the truth?"

"Of course I do. I'm just not sure I'm going to like what I find."

Jeremy glanced at her. His eyes showed a certain amount of hope, as though he could finally persuade her to quit. "We don't have to go there, you know?"

She shook her head and smiled, as though the notion was absurd. "I've spent my whole life wondering about that temple. I don't know if my grandfather was insane or a genius. If he was right about the temple, it's going to change everything, for everyone. The whole world is going to need to hear the truth…"

Jeremy took her left hand in his and squeezed it gently. It was a gentle show of almost fatherly affection. "It's going to upset a lot of people. Some might not be very happy for you to hear the news."

Billie took a deep breath in. She watched it turn to mist as she exhaled. "Even so, the world has a right to know."

"Just be careful. Some might be willing to kill to protect such a secret."

She nodded in silence. She could think of many who would pay to protect such a secret. That was, if her grandfather had even been right, all along. They sat there, silently watching the lights of distant cities flicker, far below. Billie was glad Jeremy had decided to join her. He had been one of the few constants in her otherwise disjointed life.

Born into a family of archeologists, she had traveled extensively throughout her childhood. Rarely staying long enough to settle into a school, she had often tagged along with whatever expedition her father and grandfather were involved in. Often, her only education came from homeschooling. Home being the remote tent or camp their expeditions occupied. Her father and Jeremy worked together on their first Doctorate, and so he seemed more like an uncle to her. He had even spent numerous hours trying to teach her geometry at one stage. And now, he would see the truth with her – whatever it might be.

Jeremy stood up. "It's late. I'm going to get some rest. Tomorrow, we'll see what this was all really about."

"Goodnight." She stood up and embraced him, giving him a gentle kiss on his cheek.

Billie's glance turned from the distant lights, to those stemming from the camp of a second climbing team, two thousand feet below. It was unusual for there to be another team on the mountain this far into winter. She recalled the warning Jeremy had given her – *Some might be willing to kill to protect such a secret.* She dismissed the thought. It was impossible for anyone else to have learned about the secret of the hidden temple.

*

They set out early the next morning. Lengthening the rope tether between them, Billie's party set out east, along the steep face of the mountain. It was nearly eleven a.m. by the time she stopped and checked her GPS. The ground was thick with snow. She kept moving and stopped again. Billie kicked her crampons into the snow. It had been wind blasted so that it was hard as rock. She took another reading of her GPS.

She watched as three, four, then five overhead satellites geo-synchronized, providing her position within a matter of feet. Billie carefully drove a peg into the icy wall and attached her climbing tether to it. She sat down and waited for the rest of the team to catch up.

Jeremy asked, "What is it, my dear?"

She said, "I don't know. This is definitely the place, but I can't see any sign of the temple."

He glanced around. The entire area was full of snow that had covered the region for centuries. "There's nothing here. How much variance do you think there might be between where the light shined and where we are?"

"None. The ancient people knew extensively about astrology, and would have been able to predict precisely where the sun would have shined during the sunrise of winter's solstice."

"Then how close are we?"

"No, you're misunderstanding me, Jeremy. This is precisely where the sacred entrance must be."

"Really?"

"Yes. Why do you seem so surprised?"

"It just seems…"

"Unremarkable – for the entrance to a temple containing the most important knowledge of the human race?"

"Exactly."

"Even so, that's what it is."

Billie began chipping away at the icy wall, using the back of her icepick. The rest of the party caught up, and together they took it in turns to attack the side of the mountain. Two hours later, they had dug a tunnel into the snow, nearly twelve feet deep.

"You're certain you have the right place?" Jeremy asked.

"Yes."

"But there must be any number of variations in the sunrise since the ancient people set their gate."

Billie shook her head. "This is the right place…"

"Then why haven't we found any trace of it?"

"I don't know… we'll have to keep digging…" she didn't finish her sentence.

Instead Ahmet came out of the tunnel. "I think we just struck something – and it's made of metal."

*

It took nearly three hours to clear away enough of the snow to open the ancient door. Billie told Ahmet and the guides to wait outside and guard the entrance. If any other climbers were to approach, they were to tell them the tunnel had been used as a snow-cave to camp in overnight.

She examined the ancient door. It looked like it had been made out of solid iron. She tapped on it, and the metal resonated loudly – meaning that it was hollow behind the door. Her heart raced as she worked quickly with the acetylene blowtorch to melt the snow and ice surrounding it. She reached the edge of the door, where it met perfectly with rhyolite, the glassy volcanic stone. Billie ran her gloved hands along the edge, and stopped at a set of massive iron hinges. They were frozen solid. She focused the acetylene blowtorch gently over the top of them until the ice turned to liquid.

She put the blowtorch down and ran her hands along the edge of the door again. It started to move. She stopped what she was doing and gently applied pressure to the ancient door. Again, it moved freely. Centuries of ice had protected the iron from oxidizing and turning to rust. She stopped pushing, as though she needed to savor the moment.

Her eyes, dilated and piercing, focused on Jeremy. "It's free. I think I can open it."

"This is it," Jeremy said. "Moment of truth. Are you sure you want to know what lies behind this door?"

Billie switched on her flashlight. "No, but I need to."

"Good luck." He shined his light at the door.

She pushed hard and the iron door moved inward. It slid easier than she expected. There was no creak as it opened. A strong scent of decay teased at her nostrils. It was distasteful but not overtly offensive. More like opening the lid to an antique box left sealed for centuries. It was the absence of life, yet a cold and solemn sense of what there once must have been. The only thing close to it she could remember was the first time she entered a sealed section of the King's Chamber inside the Great Pyramid of Khufu near Giza. Billie shined her flashlight in horizontal swathes, revealing the entrance to a large obsidian vault.

She'd never seen anything like it. The ebony colored, glassy volcanic stone had been carefully chipped away with rudimentary tools to form a large, vaulted room. The smooth walls reflected the light so powerfully that for an instant she thought someone was alive inside, shining their own flashlight out at her. She took a breath and paused.

"Are you all right?" Jeremy asked.

"I'm fine." She took her first step inside. "I just got startled by the sight. It's not quite what I was expecting."

Billie heard the echo of her voice as she walked toward the center of the room. She shined the flashlight around until she could gather a clear image of each end of the room and then stopped. She turned to face Jeremy and swallowed hard. Billie couldn't believe what she was seeing. She felt her stomach cramp, and wore her heart in her throat as she spoke. "It's empty. The Temple of Illumination's been stripped bare!"

*

The place was completely deserted. Billie cursed loudly, like a teenager who'd only just discovered the length and breadth of the more colorful elements of the English language. After all these years of searching, and to get so close, only to discover it had been raided before she could reach her legacy, made it all more painful than had she never found the hidden temple at all.

"Someone's moved it!" she said. "I thought it was too easy to open the iron doors after all these years. Someone must have more recently discovered we were on the right track and broken inside to hide the evidence."

"The evidence?" he asked. "I wasn't aware we were investigating a crime?"

"I'm talking about the truth. You said yourself that there were many among us who would go to dire lengths to make certain it was never discovered."

"Or it was never here to begin?" Jeremy suggested.

She breathed out a sigh. "No. It was here."

"Must have been raided years ago. There was nearly twenty feet of hardened snow above the gateway."

She nodded. "It could have been stolen at any stage in the past seventeen centuries since Gregory the Illuminator first sealed it. It was all for nothing!"

"Some secrets are best left hidden," Jeremy said. His voice was soft and sympathetic.

She took a couple steps forward and stopped. "Wait. I see something."

Jeremy placed his hand firmly on her shoulder. His voice suddenly hard as his cold, steely gaze. "Are you sure you want to see it?"

She shrugged his hand off her shoulder without saying a word, and moved to the back of the vaulted cavern. There was a small ledge near the end of the room. Carved out of the same piece of pitch black obsidian, the two ledges formed a visual illusion of the continuation of the floor.

The closer she got to it she realized with certainty, that it formed a small canyon. There was part of a small handprint on the edge. It appeared dull, making it stand out compared to the gloss of the obsidian floor. At a glance, she guessed the owner had placed his or her hand into some sort of liquid. It was so dull and impossible to accurately determine without equipment.

She peered over the edge. It was pitch dark. There was something that felt sinister about the scarred opening in the earth. Like some sort of evil abyss. She felt cold despite her thick mountaineering jacket. The dry almost musky smell seemed richer, too. She shined her flashlight into the chasm. At one end the light never reached the bottom. The crevasse simply swallowed the light indefinitely. She shined the flashlight in the other direction. This time the light reached the bottom. The crack had formed all the way through to the left of her and it appeared to have been unwilling to rip clear through the one to her right – the result was a second ledge, where the depth of the chasm was no more than twenty or thirty feet. She was close enough that she could clearly see the bottom as she shined the light across it.

At the far end, where the chasm ceased, sitting with his back against the wall was the remains of a long since deceased mountain climber. The cold weather and high altitude had protected him from bacteria, and most of his bloating had been contained within his clothing. He almost looked lifelike from that distance. Billie had to climb down to see the man. She had to be sure. She owed that much to him after all – didn't she?

She felt Jeremy's hand on her shoulder again. "I'm sorry," he said.

"It's all right," she said. "I always knew in my heart what we'd find."

She had a fair idea what she would find, but she needed confirmation. She moved to the right where the edge of the chasm stopped mysteriously at the base of the obsidian wall. It was as though the tectonic shift that had caused the scarred crack to form was unable to splinter the impervious obsidian room. It was as though some kind of higher power had forbidden it to do so.

Billie studied the opening. The chasm was narrow enough that she could have comfortably stepped over it, yet wide enough for her to easily fit through. She carefully placed one hand on either side of the opening and slipped her legs inside until they found a foot-hold to support her. She focused the majority of her attention on each hand and leg individually as she progressed. Confident the dark stone wouldn't crumble under her weight, she started to climb down.

She glanced at Jeremy with a hardened resolve. Her brown eyes piercing and challenging. "Are you coming with me?"

"Me?" He shook his head. "I'm afraid if I climbed down there I would never make it back up again."

She nodded. It wasn't his place. He didn't have to see it. The truth wasn't his problem to solve. It was hers. Billie climbed down slowly. She made careful, purposeful movements. Testing each hand-hold and foot-hold as she climbed. A few minutes later she reached the first ledge.

Billie carefully tested the strength of the ledge with her weight while bracing the walls with her hands. Confident the ground wasn't going to fall away from under her, she flashed the light along the crevasse, until it reached the remains of the man. The body, well protected by the cold, was still intact. He could have been any other mountain climber, taking refuge on a ledge to catch his strength.

She stopped right next to the body. Three small holes were visible in his jacket. She didn't need to look closer to realize they were bullet holes. She shined the flashlight on his face. His swollen eyes protruded hideously from his face, like some sort of incarnation of an evil clown that would have fit well in a Stephen King novel. Despite the decayed remains, she recognized the face of the man staring back at her instantly.

What were you involved in grandpa?

A heavy golden chain hung from his neck. His frozen hand still clutched at the bottom of it, where a pendant or something had been grasped when he died. Billie carefully opened his hand to reveal an ivory crucifix inside. The upper section of the cross was carved intricately in the shape of a horseman, holding a bow and wearing a crown. The lower section was smooth and unimpressive. She'd seen the chain before, but the pendant that hung from it had always remained hidden beneath his shirt. She'd never known her grandpa to be religious. She started to search him for what she was really after, without giving the crucifix another thought – after all, the strength of one's faith often raises quickly when facing death.

She checked each of his pockets in his jacket, followed by his trousers. There was still nothing. She swore. *How could he have lost it?* She unzipped the climbing jacket and continued to rifle through it until she found his pocket-sized journal. Her grandfather always kept intricate notes during any expedition he was on. She kissed the journal. If he was killed for getting this close to the truth, he would have made a note of it.

Billie shined her flashlight on the last entry. *We're getting close. Soon, the Four Horsemen will ride together and the Third Temple shall rise.* She glanced at her grandfather's crucifix again. It had a horseman made of ivory, carrying a sword and wearing a crown – the White Horseman – AKA the Conqueror.

She bent down and slowly removed the ivory crucifix and horseman. *Sorry grandpa.* She once saw a painting called, *Death on a Pale Horse* at the Pennsylvania Academy of Fine Arts. She recalled it had some sort of biblical ties. Something about The Lamb of God opening the first four of the Seven Seals, which summoned forth four beings that rode out on white, red, black, and pale horses – Conquest, War, Famine, and Death.

But there was no mention of the Third Temple...

A moment later, she forgot about the Four Horsemen, because the ground beneath her started to vibrate, and the obsidian room above echoed the roar of thunder. *Had there been another movement of the tectonic fault?* She stared at the ground below. It was perfectly still. She tried to call out to Jeremy, but other sounds drowned out her voice – they were the sounds of gunshots.

*

The gunshots finally ceased, and were replaced with more sound of thunder. The shots might have caused an avalanche. She hung the crucifix around her neck. She placed her grandfather's journal into her inside jacket pocket and zipped it shut. Whatever happened to her from here, she needed to know the truth. She studied the wall again, and prepared to climb out, before there was no longer an obsidian vault to climb to.

"We've got company!" Jeremy shouted at her.

"I'm on my way up." She took one last look at her grandfather, tucked the crucifix into her climbing jacket and started to climb out.

She reached the top of the crevasse and inside the obsidian vault. Her pulse was racing and she was breathing so hard that the muscles in her chest burned. She took a couple deep breaths in, and exhaled slowly. She could feel the lactic acid pounding the muscles of her arms and legs.

Jeremy glanced at her. "Are you all right?"

"Fine. What have we got?"

"I don't know yet. It must be the second climbing team we saw following us last night. Ahmet must have shot at them. Maybe it caused an avalanche. Ahmet's well armed, and we have the high ground. They won't reach us. Even so, we should get out while we still can."

"Of course," she said, thankful that Jeremy had the foresight to arm their climbing team. At the time, she thought he was being overly dramatic, but now it was clear she was lucky to have his good counsel to rely on. "Just let me catch my breath."

"What did you find?" he asked.

"My grandfather."

"I'm so sorry, my dear child." He swallowed hard and held his breath for a moment. "As you know, there was a sudden storm. I pleaded with your grandfather to turn around. He refused. He was certain we were getting close. I came back down the mountain, and your grandfather continued. It turns out he reached it, but he mustn't have had the strength to climb back down again."

Billie jaw was set hard. "It's all right, Jeremy. I knew long ago he wasn't coming back. At least now I have some sort of closure. Say, what do you know about the Four Horsemen of the Apocalypse?"

His eyes narrowed. "What did you say?"

"Do you know anything about the Four Horsemen of the apocalypse?"

"A little. Not much. The Christian apocalyptic vision is that the Four Horsemen are to set a divine apocalypse upon the world as harbingers of the Last Judgment. The world will be purged of its great wickedness and purity of the new world shall rise. Why do you ask?"

"I found grandpa's journal. His last note was that the Four Horsemen of the apocalypse would soon rise." She stood up to leave.

"Did he mention anything else?"

"Yeah. He wrote about the rise of something I'd never heard of."

"And what's that, dear?" He spoke casually, more like the Godparent he'd been, but his eyes were studying her, scrutinizing her somehow as she spoke.

She met his eyes and said, "The Third Temple."

His breathing paused for a split-second. She saw instant recognition in his eyes. The muscles of his jaw tightened, and then he smiled. "The Third Temple?" he confirmed.

"Yes, have you heard of it?"

He broke their eye contact and shook his head. "No. It certainly sounds quite mysterious though, doesn't it?"

Billie heard heavy breathing coming from the entrance of the obsidian room. Suddenly reminded of the more pressing need to escape, she stood up to leave. Broken snow from the tunnel above the opening fell in through the iron doors. A moment later Ahmet arrived. He was wild with adrenaline. His face was covered in sweat and his pupils were massive like an ice-addict at the peak of psychosis. The man roared as he approached. Blood stained his jacket where a shot had clipped his right shoulder.

Her eyes darted to Jeremy. He looked suddenly terrified, but there was something else there, too. *Was he surprised to see Ahmet still alive?* She needed to know what happened, and quick. Her mind raced. Was there still time to hide somewhere inside the crevasse? Or did they still have the ability to break through their attackers and make it down the mountain? She opened her mouth to speak, but Jeremy beat her to it.

"For God's sake, man!" Jeremy yelled. "What happened?"

Ahmet tried to speak, but the words came out garbled. He spat dark red blood. Evidently, the one of the shots had penetrated more than his shoulder. He had internal bleeding, and would probably die this far away from medical help.

Jeremy softened his voice, but maintained his authority as he spoke. "Sit down. Tell me who attacked you?"

Ahmet spat more blood and then began to speak. "We were ambushed. The climbing team who were following yesterday must have split in two in the night. Some of them left in the darkness of the early hours of the morning and climbed ahead. They waited until we reached the inside of the temple, and then attacked from above and below us.

"Who else is alive outside?" Billie asked.

"No one."

"What happened to the other men?" Jeremy asked. "There were six of you, and you were well armed!"

"They had more men, and they came with machineguns."

"You're equipped with Israeli Uzis!" Jeremy spat the words out. "So what the hell happened?"

Ahmet stared at Jeremy, but his eyes were distant. He was vacantly reliving the moments just past. "They outnumbered us. One by one, they took out each of our men. When I was the last one alive, I decided to play the last card I had left to play – I opened both of my grenades and destroyed the entrance."

"You caused an avalanche, didn't you?" Jeremy asked. "Did any of the attackers survive?"

"I don't know. But I doubt it. Half the mountainside came down in the avalanche. I only survived by sliding back down into the entrance."

The edge of Jeremy's lip curled upwards. It was more of a smirk than a smile. There was something sinister about his reaction. His eyes betrayed bewilderment at the turn of events, and then he started to laugh. Without any hesitation, he withdrew a handgun and fired twice. The shots hit Ahmet in the chest, and the man fell to ground, as blood quickly filled his lungs.

Jeremy glanced at the dying man. "Ahmet I do believe you just did me a tremendous favor. It appears I no longer have to contend with Conquest for a place in the Third Temple."

Billie's eyes darted to the Uzi lying on the ground next to Ahmet, and then back to Jeremy. It would be impossible for her to reach it before Jeremy got a shot off. Her eyes fixed on Jeremy and she spoke with the confidence of a woman who knew she was about to die. "You killed my grandfather, didn't you?"

"Guilty, I'm afraid," Jeremy said. "I'm so, so very sorry, Billie. Really, I am. I was worried when you saw your grandfather's corpse that the bullet holes would give it away. But even that I could have easily justified by telling you it was further proof of the lengths some would go to keep the truth hidden. I was happy, truly I was, that you could finally achieve closure. I always did love you, and never wanted it to end like this. But you had to bring up the news about the Third Temple, didn't you?"

She studied his eyes. He looked frightened, like he didn't want to kill her, but he no longer had the choice in the matter. After all, he was her Godfather for God's sake! "What is it? What is so damned important about the Third Temple?"

He leveled the barrel of his handgun at her. "If it was up to me, I'd let you live – and then hope to hell you never found it. But I'm afraid it's not up to me. It's up to the man I work for. The man paying for this expedition was quite explicit – if we found it, there were to be no survivors."

She held her palms outward, in supplication. "Wait! Please. Found what?"

"You still don't know, do you?" Jeremy grinned as he aimed directly at her head.

"Know what?" she asked. "Who paid for the expedition?"

"His name is Death – and he's been waiting a long time for the Third Temple to rise."

*

Billie heard the report of the weapon fire multiple times. She held her breath, expecting the pain to follow quickly. It took a moment to realize the shots weren't aimed at her. They were aimed at Jeremy, and they'd gone much too wide. She reacted fast, and it was a split second before she saw who had fired. But Jeremy responded faster. He turned to face Ahmet and fired a further two shots into the man's chest and one in his head, killing him instantly.

Ahmet's Uzi dropped to the floor. His failed attempt to save her life, had cost him his. She didn't wait for Jeremy to turn around and kill her. She launched herself at him. Her speed had caught Jeremy off guard. Instead of trying to reaffirm his footing, he made the mistake of concentrating on shooting her instead. Billie swung her left foot into the back of his knee and pushed him hard with every ounce of force her muscular and lithe frame could assemble. He pulled at the Glock's trigger. The shot went high, and he fell backward into the chasm.

She heard his scream as he fell into the same blackened abyss that had earlier swallowed the focus of her flashlight indefinitely. Jeremy pulled at the trigger as he continued to fall. The last thing she heard was the clicking sound of the Glock's firing pin striking the empty chamber. She never heard him hit the ground.

Billie shined her flashlight into the chasm. The dark and sinister looking opening toward the earth had swallowed his body whole. There was still something evil about the crevasse, like it had been drawn to the darkness inside her Godfather. She shook her head, cursing herself for not seeing the darkness before. She'd known Jeremy her entire life, and yet she'd never predicted his wicked nature. Her mind drifted to the past few weeks, trying to find a time when she should have picked up on his real nature.

She found none. Instead, the sound of thunder roaring from outside the tunnel interrupted her thoughts, and returned her to her more pressing concern – was there still time to escape from her pursuers? She picked up Ahmet's Uzi and climbed out through the ancient iron doors, and into the ice tunnel.

She scanned the new landscape. The avalanche had rendered the previously steep but traversable slope into a vertical cliff face. No longer covered in snow and ice, her crampons would provide little benefit in climbing the volcanic stone wall, and the rest of her ropes and climbing equipment had been lost in the avalanche. To her right a jagged ledge of volcanic rock ended in a vertical drop of nearly eleven thousand feet. Without climbing equipment, or a lot more experience, she had no way of descending or even traversing it. To her left the ledge was narrow and barely traversable. She looked up. There was no way she could climb, and down, was out of the question.

She carefully moved along the narrow volcanic rock-shelf. Her heart raced as she concentrated on moving quickly along the delicate route. She wasn't afraid of heights, but she wasn't all too keen on falling to her death either. She made certain of the strength and placement of each footing and handhold as she moved along. Her eyes continuously scanned the area for signs of her pursuers.

She made it probably three hundred feet around the face of the avalanche before she spotted her goal. It was an area another four hundred feet away, where the spur of Mount Ararat met a minor saddle, before descending steeply into the Nakhchivan exclave of Azerbaijan. Her eyes followed the spur toward the Armenian plains, where the Aras and Murat rivers ran through the closed Turkey-Armenian borders. She swallowed hard. Even if she made it, she would have trouble crossing the border.

Billie continued to move along the route, and then stopped. She dropped down as low as she could along the rock-shelf, reducing her visual silhouette as much as possible. Ahead of her, by no more than ten feet, the volcanic rock scattered into a hundred smaller fragments, as a heavy machine gun pummeled large caliber shots at her. The sound of machine-gun fire echoed throughout the mountain. For a moment, she was worried the damned thing would cause another avalanche.

The sound stopped, and she struggled to find its original source. She shuffled backward, trying to find any form of cover. Billie made it twenty feet and then stopped. The ledge rose about a foot and then dipped again. It wasn't much, but it was better than nothing. She stretched out, and dipped her head close to the ground, lowering herself as much as possible. Billie picked up the Uzi and stared through its scope, searching for the location of her attacker.

A few minutes went by and there were no more shots fired. Her eyes followed the narrow pathway, if it could be called that at all, until she reached the spur running down Mount Ararat. In an instant she spotted her attacker. He was positioned about two hundred feet away from her, and just up from the path. The man was lying down, looking straight at her. He had some sort of machine gun set up on a tripod. *Why did he stop shooting?* She wondered if he'd somehow lost her through his sight, or simply accepted that she was an impossible shot from that distance. It was unlikely. Her attacker had already managed to place a close grouping of bullets less than ten feet from her head, proving he could hit her from that distance. So why hadn't he? *Could he have intentionally missed her?* She considered why he hadn't killed her. Maybe he wanted her alive, but why? Then she recalled the words Jeremy had said to her – there could be no survivors once it was found.

The obsidian vault was empty. They found nothing. But maybe her attackers still didn't know that. Or maybe they needed her grandfather's journal. She shook her head. None of that mattered right now. What she needed was a way off the damned mountain. Then she could set about working out what this was all about.

She tried to shuffle slightly further forward. Maybe she should fire a burst at him. She might get lucky. It was unlikely, but what other choice did she have? Billie carefully lined up her attacker through the fine cross-hairs, and carefully prepared to make the shot. She'd been to a shooting range only a couple of times in her life, and tried all the tips her instructor had given her. She settled into a comfortable shooting position. Took in a deep breath and slowly exhaled. Her right trigger-finger gently squeezed on the trigger, but she didn't take the shot.

Falling snow tumbled onto her back. She quickly glanced upward. At least thirty people, covered in snow-camouflage worn by the military were abseiling toward her. That's why the sniper hadn't taken another shot. His purpose was to stop her from retreating. They needed her alive. She stood up and turned to run toward the entrance to the Temple of Illumination.

She heard the roar of the machine gun start to fire, but none of the bullets struck her. She raced all the way back to the entrance of the temple forgetting about any caution over the life-ending drop to her left. She reached the opening and backed into the tunnel. Billie checked the Uzi's magazine. It had less than ten rounds. Even if she made every shot count, her attackers still outnumbered her.

Her mind raced to find a solution. She considered the dark chasm that ripped its way through the middle of the obsidian vault. Could she hide inside? She recalled the bullet-holes where her grandfather had been killed taking the same sort of refuge. It certainly wasn't her first choice, but what other one did she have?

She slid back down the tunnel and stopped. Set against the back of the rock above the iron doors was a bomb. Its digital timer showed a few seconds under five minutes. She tried to move it. The back of the device had been drilled into the volcanic rock-face, and glued in position with a rock-hard climbing adhesive. Ahmet must have fixed it there while she was down the crevasse. Jeremy had said that some people would kill to make certain that some truths remained hidden.

Billie was confronted with the impossible decision of choosing between hiding and possibly becoming entombed after the explosion, or taking her chances on the outside of the mountain. It wasn't a choice. And it wasn't like she had long to consider her options.

She climbed back out of the tunnel and into the open again and turned right. She knew her options had run out and her only option was to gamble big. She ran along the narrow ledge. Below her, the heavy roar of rotary blades whined. They were close to fourteen thousand feet. Few helicopters were capable of reaching such heights. Whoever was after her, wasn't taking any chances – they had spent a fortune to capture her.

Behind her, the small group of soldiers was now on the narrow ledge and approaching fast. The clock was ticking on the timer, and the bomb would explode at any moment. She ran fast. No longer interested in looking back at her pursuers, her only chance was to get past the final edge by the time the explosion destroyed the entrance to the temple. If she got really lucky, she might just escape in the pandemonium.

The sound of the helicopter's turbojets screamed and the ground began to vibrate. She heard the sound of multiple automatic weapons firing. Billie kept running. A stray bullet was the least of her problems now. She glanced at her wristwatch. One minute and forty seconds to go. She was three hundred feet from the end of the ledge, and then she saw it – an entirely black helicopter.

It rose quickly and hovered less than twenty feet above her. She knew little about helicopters, but this one was clearly special. Even just to fly at this altitude placed it among some of the most advanced in the world. This one was entirely matt-black, and covered in strange, angular, radar absorbing materials, like those on stealth planes seen in movies. It was a deadly predatory machine, probably worth hundreds of millions of dollars. Nowhere were there any lights, colors, or identifying markings to be seen aboard the aircraft.

And it was after her.

Her eyes darted to the men behind her and back to the helicopter. Above her, more pursuers were descending diagonally. It made her run faster, as though she could outpace the helicopter. The strange predator continued to follow her, matching her speed closely.

She heard more weapons fire, but the bullets scattered nowhere near her. The helicopter suddenly banked heavily to the left and dipped suddenly, disappearing below the height of the ledge. She ran along the edge of the mountain, looking for any means of escape.

Billie suddenly reached the end of the ledge. She glanced at her watch. Forty seconds to go. She looked at the drop below her, and wondered if she could ever survive it if she just let herself go? There had been many stories over the years of climbers surviving hundred plus foot falls as a result of continuing to slide. Her pursuers were close – less than fifty feet behind her and she had nowhere else to go. She closed her eyes and glanced at the snowy slope hundreds of feet below. It would take a miracle to survive the fall, but it was the last option she had left.

On the count of three…

She braced herself to jump, and breathed in deeply.

Two…

She forced herself to breathe out.

One…

She stepped forward and stopped. The helicopter's rotors whined sharply as the predator turned and rose from beneath the ledge until it was facing directly at her, about three feet above her head. The windshield was covered in some sort of pitch dark tinting that made it impossible to see the pilot inside.

Billie watched the twin rockets ignite from its fuselage, sending powerful missiles screaming past her. She dived onto the ground and covered her head. The missiles hadn't even exploded before the helicopter's Gatling-style heavy machine gun started to rotate, sending hundreds of large caliber bullets skyrocketing past her.

She closed her eyes and heard the massive dual explosions as the missiles struck their targets. She heard the screams of the few attackers still alive. When she opened her eyes the helicopter was right above her. The downward pressure of its rotor blades sent a torrent of air down on her. A small opening appeared in its undercarriage and a man in a completely black flight suit stared out at her.

"Doctor Swan?" A man's voice asked, through a loud speaker.

"Yes?" she nodded.

"You better come with us."

She looked at the snowy slope hundreds of feet below and the dozen or more men who were pursuing her in the distance. It was probably a trap, but she'd run out of any other options. She nodded, and the man reached down with one hand.

Billie reached out and gripped his hand. It was firm and locked with hers in a grip that reassured her she would be safe. She saw the brief flash of tracer rounds as the helicopter banked to the north, swinging her violently, to avoid the shots from below.

An instant later the man pulled her inside, and the door below closed. Inside, the helicopter was lit up with hundreds of instrument displays. It looked more like the cockpit of something out of a Sci-Fi film than a helicopter. She doubted more than a couple countries in the world possessed such technologies. A moment later, the contents of her gut rose, as the helicopter dropped its altitude and left the side of the mountain.

"Are you all right, Doctor Swan?" the man asked.

"Having just saved my life, you can call me Billie." She smiled, revealing a set of perfectly even, white teeth. "And yes, I think I'll live." She eyed the man in front of her. He pulled up the dark visor of his helmet, revealing the most intensely blue eyes she had ever seen, reminding her of the ocean.

The man smiled back at her.

It was a warm and reassuring smile. For all Billie knew, her troubles were only just about to begin. She had no idea who owned the helicopter or why they had gone to the effort of saving her life. But this man's smile seemed to disarm those fears in an instant.

Behind them, a large explosion rocked the site where Ahmet, at Jeremy's request, had set a large timed, bomb. The helicopter, now several hundred feet out from the explosion site, gave a minor shudder, as the blast-wave slipped across its smooth airframe.

"What was that?" the man asked.

"A bomb was set to go off at the entrance to the Temple of Illumination."

"That would make sense, Dr. Swan." The man nodded as though he were merely discussing tomorrow's weather forecast. "By the way, my name's Sam Reilly, and I've been looking for you a long time."

Chapter One

Underground City of Derinkuyu, Turkey – Present Day

Sam Reilly sat down at a small table with three chairs, positioned outside an empty café that overlooked the gated entrance to the underground city. Tom Bower pulled up a seat opposite and sat down in silence. The sky above was a myriad of dark grays, ochre, and purple shades of predawn, speckled with a few remaining stars. To the north, nearly a hundred hot air balloons competed with the rising sun for space along the horizon over the Fairy Chimneys of Cappadocia.

A waiter with short dark hair and a thick mustache approached. "Good morning, gentlemen. You're up early to see the balloons?"

Sam nodded. "That and we want to beat the crowds at Derinkuyu."

"A good idea," the waiter replied. "But you know they don't open until nine, don't you?"

"That's okay. We're happy to wait until then," Sam lied. "Besides, it's a surprisingly warm morning."

The waiter smiled as he poured water into two empty glasses. "It's the warmest summer we've had on record. I've heard that large amounts of the snowy caps of Mount Ararat have started to thaw for the first time in more than two hundred years."

"Is that so?" Sam asked, genuinely interested. "We were thinking of doing some climbing over the next few weeks. It might be interesting to climb the sacred mountain."

"Good for you," the waiter said. "What can I get for you?"

Sam said, "Just a coffee, please. Black. No sugar."

"And for you, sir?" The waiter turned his gaze to Tom.

"I'll have the same, please."

"Of course, sir." The waiter smiled, cheerfully, and disappeared inside the shop.

Sam studied the café in a glance. It had been built into the soft volcanic rock face, along with the flock of gift-shops, restaurants and other tourist traps which had popped up to cater for the ubiquitous tourists who had flocked to the region to see the nearby underground city. None of the shops had existed before 1963, when a resident of the area found a mysterious room behind a wall in his home during a renovation that revealed access to the tunnel network and led to one of the largest underground cities ever discovered.

Next to him, Tom Bower sat with the same expression Sam had seen fixed to his friend's face for the past six weeks. It was set with the hardened stare of a man who knew that definitive action was needed, but had no means of determining what that action should be. Tom's dark brown eyes were fixed on the horizon, while his mind was a thousand miles away, searching silently for answers. At a guess, Sam assumed Tom was recalling the pyramid they'd discovered on Infinity Island six weeks ago.

The submerged island had risen after a large tectonic shift had disturbed the base of the Mediterranean Sea. Inside the pyramid they had discovered a Looking-Glass. It was the second one that Tom had witnessed, and the first Sam had seen. The device was built by an ancient race known as the Master Builders, who were unrecognized by the history books. They used the device as a means of visual communication between temples that spanned thousands of miles. It was made out of a translucent orb, capable of conducting sound and light hundreds of times faster than any other material found on earth – either natural or synthetic.

Like the first looking-glass, this one displayed the current views of a number of temples, as seen from above. If the device had been built today, Sam would have accepted it was merely powered by some sort of video calling system, such as Facetime or skype – but it had been constructed thousands of years ago, by the Master Builders. They were perhaps the most intelligent, far-reaching, and longest surviving group of people in existence. At times, Sam harbored the possibility that some of them remained, scattered throughout the globe – of course, it was only a theory, and there was no proof.

This time, the device showed a series of ancient dilapidated temples, and one modern temple currently under construction. Inside were hundreds of people – primitive in their appearance – and quite dark skinned. Their faces were painted blue. They were almost completely naked, with the exception of some kind of loincloth. Both women and men were bare breasted. And all of them were working vigorously to finish building the chamber. They all looked focused. Almost mesmerized by their desire to perform their task without any consideration for their own rest and wellbeing. They were working hard and constantly. No one was whipping them. There was no one guiding them. But like a group of ants, they were all simply taking part in completing their individual tasks so that the main project could be completed. And then there was one who didn't belong.

She was slightly shorter than the other women, and her complexion was much lighter and smoother. Her face shared the same intense focus as those around her. She was mesmerized by what she was doing, as though she was performing the work of the Gods. She looked like a slave, or someone who'd been drugged heavily with amnesic and hypnotic medications. While all of the men and women there looked muscular, her appearance was more lithe and athletic. She had a different sort of bone structure, altogether. She wore a pair of tan cargo shorts and a white tank top. Above her right shoulder was a small tattoo of a pyramid. She was definitely pretty. Sam gritted his teeth as he thought about the discovery. Her name was Dr. Billie Swan and two years ago, before she disappeared, Tom Bower had aspirations of one day marrying her.

It had been six weeks now since they'd discovered that Dr. Billie Swan was still alive, and was now working as a slave on the construction of the new temple. The pyramid, along with the looking-glass, had sunk back into the ocean and they had no means of tracing where the image had come from. With the only direct link to the new temple being destroyed, this was their first lead to anything that might suggest the Master Builders were building again.

The waiter returned and handed them their coffees. Sam thanked the man and took a sip. He smiled. The coffee was rich, and surprisingly good. It warmed him from the inside, and made him feel confident about the meeting with the stranger who'd contacted him forty-eight hours ago.

After the pyramid had sunk back into the Mediterranean Sea and with it any direct connection to where Billie had been taken, Sam had sent out a series of requests through a network of antiquity dealers, archeologists, and climatologists around the world. The request was simple – *Have you ever seen anything like this, and if so, where?* Attached was a photograph of the ancient script written by the Master Builders. To date, the ancient written language had only been discovered in a total of five locations. Of those, three were no longer in existence.

There was only one positive response, and it came two days ago.

Mr. Reilly. I believe I have seen something written in the same script. In the past three years since I discovered it, I have made more than a hundred enquiries about its origins. So far none has been able to identify who wrote it. I assumed it was an ancient civilization, because there was nothing similar anywhere, on any document. I've searched the archeology archives, internet and spoken with many archeologists. None has seen this type of script before. Last year, I had a section of the wood it was written on carbon dated. To make the mystery greater, the results returned with a dating of around 400 years old, which places it somewhere around the early part of the 16th century. It definitely doesn't match any form of written language anywhere within Turkey, and definitely none from such a recent century. If you're interested, please come to Derinkuyu. I would love to hear from someone who's seen it before and might be able to explain its origins.

Attached was a copy of the image the stranger had found. It was indeed written in the language of the Master Builders, and if his carbon dating was correct, it was by far the youngest known writing by them that he had ever seen. The question remained, could it be possible a descendent of the Master Builders had survived, and was currently in the process of constructing a new temple?

Sam considered the possibility as he sipped his warm coffee.

"Mr. Sam Reilly?" A man asked as he entered the café.

Sam nodded. The question came from a short man in his mid-forties. He had an olive complexion and gregarious smile.

The man offered his hand. "My name is Kahraman Sadik, and I'm so glad you came straight away."

"And this is an associate and good friend of mine, Tom Bower." Sam stood to greet the stranger, taking his hand. "Can I get you a coffee or tea?"

"Pleased to meet you both," Sadik said, his eyes furtively darting between the two of them. "I'm afraid we must leave right away. I'll tell you what I know along the way, and you can fill in what I long to hear, but we must leave now. We must descend underground before the sun's fully up."

"Descend?" Sam smiled, awkwardly. "Where?"

Sadik grinned. "Why into the depths of Derinkuyu of course, where no tourist has ever been."

Chapter Two

Sam stood up and placed a red ten lira banknote on the table to cover the bill. He studied Sadik trying to decide whether the guy was crazy and had just seen the image of the Master Builder's script on the internet or something, or whether he really had something to offer. Sadik's eyes were wide, and constantly glancing around furtively. He was out of breath, like he'd just run half a dozen blocks or something.

"You okay?" Sam asked, looking at Sadik.

"I'm fine, fine. We just need to be below ground before Derinkuyu is open to the public, shortly after sunrise."

"Okay. We'll follow you." Sam looked at Tom. He didn't need to say anything. It was obvious Tom shared his instant distrust of the stranger.

They left the café and followed a series of stone walkways and stairways along a shallow valley, where the once eternal stream that carved its way through the region appeared long departed. The path traversed upward and downward thirty or more feet as they moved in and around a variety of caverns that formed the local houses and shopfronts for the vicinity.

"I thought the entrance to Derinkuyu was back there?" Sam asked.

"It was," Sadik confirmed. He glanced over his shoulder, behind him – holding his gaze purposefully for a few moments, as though he was expecting something. He smiled briefly, and turned to Sam again. "I'm sorry. What did you say? Ah, that's right. The main tourist entrance? Yes. It was back there. There are many entrances to the ancient subterranean city. I'm taking you to one of the most northern ones. It's actually a ventilation shaft. Very few people know about it."

Tom's lip curled into the slightest of grins at the lie, but he remained silent.

Sam met Sadik's eye, and asked the question. "And still, we need to be inside before the sun comes up?"

"Yes," Sadik confirmed.

"Why?"

"Because you're not the only person to take interest in this discovery."

Sam said, "Someone is watching the entrances?"

Sadik nodded. "There are many people watching all of the entrances."

"You said you discovered this piece of wood with the unique writing on it almost three years ago. Have they been interested in this location since then?"

"No. Only for the past six weeks."

Sam asked, "Why?"

Sadik said, "Because you posted your damned query about the ancient script on the internet, and suddenly nearly everyone I showed the image to over the past three years is dead."

"And yet you trust me?"

"No. But what choice do I have. If you wanted to discover something the others hadn't, you wouldn't have been posting it so the world could see, would you? Two of my very good friends have died – I need to know why."

"And you think I might provide those answers?"

"I think you're the only one I've ever met who has an idea who wrote that strange script." Sadik took a pause to catch his breath. "And once you've seen where I found it, I'm hoping you'll be able to provide me with some of those answers."

"I'll do my best." Sam regathered his thoughts as he carefully followed Sadik. "In the last six weeks, has anyone else approached you to see the strange markings?"

"Yes," Sadik confirmed. "There were two other people interested in this information, just this week." Sadik nodded. "And they were both willing to pay big."

"What did you say?"

"I said I'd sent the piece of wood away to Europe to be studied by experts, but I'd love their input when it gets back."

Sam said, "Good man."

Speaking to Sadik, Tom asked, "Do you have any idea who's following your movements?"

"No." Sadik crouched down, close to a stone wall marking out the edge of a small open field.

"Then how do you know you're being followed?" Sam asked.

"I see them. There are people who don't belong here. They act as though they have a purpose, but they have no other purpose than to watch me. I've carefully checked all the entrances over the past few weeks. Every single one has been guarded, with the exception of this one."

"This one isn't guarded?" Sam asked.

"No." Sadik increased his pace, walking straight past the entrance and going further up the hill beyond. "Very few people know about its existence."

"So what are you afraid of?" Sam asked.

"The two men who are following us right now."

Sam glanced behind him. There were two men, casually walking along the path about thirty feet apart. Both looked like tourists. Sadik stopped and both men kept walking past them. Sam glanced at Sadik who shrugged and kept walking. Two hundred feet along the path, Sadik stopped again. The two men had stopped in a cave to buy something. Sadik waited and in a few minutes both men walked past them again.

Sam watched until the two men disappeared up ahead. "You still think they're following you?"

Sadik nodded, looking less confident. "They don't belong here."

"Of course they don't, they're tourists."

After another couple minutes Sadik started to walk back toward the entrance to the ventilation shaft. He made it less than a hundred feet before stopping again.

"What now?" Sam asked.

Sadik glanced up ahead to his left. "Look at the Aria Cave Hotel up ahead. Do you recognize the two gentlemen reading the paper?"

The stone chimney had been carved out to make a five story boutique hotel. At the bottom of the hotel there were two men reading the paper. Sam recognized them at a glance as the two who Sadik said were following them. They must have sped up and then looped back around a second path, so they could get in front of them again.

Sam breathed in calmly and said, "I believe you're right, we're being stalked..."

Chapter Three

Sam kept walking until he was no more than twenty feet from the two men who had been following them and stopped. He made no attempt to appear inconspicuous. They were the ones who wanted to keep a surreptitious eye on Sadik and possibly him, not the other way round. So Sam didn't see any reason why he should go out of his way to pretend not to be staring directly at them.

They were seated out the front of a subterranean hotel called Nexus. The lobby of the hotel was built into a large natural stone chimney which stood approximately thirty feet above ground. The accommodation and entertainment were all deep below the surface. Out the front a large glass revolving door stood unnaturally as a grand entrance, moving in a slow and continuous clockwise direction.

He stared directly at the two men. They were reading the Financial Review, but they definitely didn't look like any businessmen he'd ever met. They wore identical dark shades, with similar cargo shorts, beige V-neck tee shirts and thick climbing vests. There was a conspicuous bulge in both of their cargo pockets. It might have been caused by a weapon – maybe a handgun and spare magazines? Or they might be tourists carrying their wallets and cameras. Both looked genuinely interested in what they were reading. *Perhaps they knew Sadik had to backtrack eventually?*

Both men were of a roughly average height, with a slim and athletic build. They looked very similar, but not close enough to be brothers. Their rigid postures and definite movements suggested they had a military or paramilitary background. There was also the chance they were in some sort of policing role. If he was stateside, Sam couldn't have ruled out FBI or even CIA agents. In Turkey, they might work for Interpol – or they might work for whoever it was that didn't want him to find out what secret Derinkuyu held about the Master Builders.

"How long have those two been following you?" Sam asked.

Sadik thought about it for a moment. "I saw them yesterday afternoon, when I finished work, but didn't think anything of it at the time. Then again, they were there when I left my house. They've been with me since then. Do you have any ideas how we can lose them?"

"We could just go ask them directly to leave us alone?" Tom suggested. "I mean, their cover's no good to them if we know they're following us. We may as well confront them head on."

"I was hoping to avoid a direct confrontation," Sadik said. "Wouldn't it be easier just to lose them?"

Sam turned to face Tom and Sadik. "No. Tom's right. Let's go have a chat to them."

Tom smiled, as though confrontation was exactly what he needed right now. Sadik swore and started to walk away. Whatever Sam and Tom were going to say or do to the two men, Sadik wanted no part of it. Sam shrugged. He didn't care what Sadik wanted. He walked directly up to the table next to the two men and pulled out a chair for himself. He moved the chair so that he faced them directly. "My name's Sam Reilly. What's yours?"

Both men shuffled in their seats and pretended to focus more on their newspapers.

"Is there something you guys want to know?" Sam asked.

One of the men – the one closest to him – lowered his newspaper and asked, "I'm sorry, were you asking me a question?"

"Yeah. I want to know who you are and why you're following me?"

"I'm sorry… Mr. Reilly, was it?" Sam nodded and the man continued – speaking in a heavily Eastern European accented voice. "We weren't following you. We were following your friend, Mr. Sadik."

Sam shook his head. "I'm sorry. I'm really not very comfortable with being followed by a couple of badly dressed strangers."

"Didn't you hear me?" The man's tone was suddenly hard like ice. "I said we're not following you, we're following your friend. Now I suggest you leave if you know what's good for you."

Tom sat down at the chair next to Sam. He was a good seven inches taller than either of them, and eighty pounds heavier. He wore a thick grin as he spoke. "Gentlemen. If you will permit, I think I might be able to clear up this misunderstanding."

"Please be sure you do," the first guy said.

"You see, gentlemen…" Tom began. "My friend here is currently traveling with Mr. Sadik and therefore, if you're following Mr. Sadik, you're also following my friend. May I suggest you stop following my friend?"

The second guy stood up first. "All right wise guy. I think it's time we all have a talk, but not here."

"Sure," Tom said. He stood up, so that he had to look down on the man who was trying to intimidate him. "Let's start with why you're following Mr. Sadik."

"That's between him and my boss. Let's just say, he owes my boss something, and we're here to make sure he doesn't leave town." The first guy withdrew a handgun from his right cargo pocket, just enough to make it obvious he was carrying a weapon, before lowering it so it remained concealed. "So, given I'm the guy with the gun right now, I suggest you do as I say and come inside the hotel to answer some questions."

Sam watched as Tom's eyes swept the two men in a glance, trying to decide who he was going to have to take down first. He fixed his penetrating gaze on the second guy, who was slightly taller than the first, and hadn't yet revealed where he was carrying a weapon. The second guy stared hard back at him and Sam noticed with pleasure, the guy was holding his breath – it's hard, even for a man carrying a gun, not to be at least a little intimidated by someone of Tom's size.

Sam had no doubt he and Tom would come out on top in a fight. His first prediction that the two men had a military background appeared unfounded. No ex-soldier or professional would try and intimidate a person while their handgun was still in their pocket. If they were ever more than amateurs, it was long ago, and years of success had left them lazy and unskilled.

Sam stood up. "Tom. This isn't our country and we're the outsiders here. Let's not make a mess for anyone. We'll come and have a talk, but then we're out of here and neither of you will see us again, okay?"

The first guy met Sam's eye, and motioned to his partner to keep the situation hospitable. The second guy slowly breathed out and then spoke. "Of course. All we want to do is chat. No one needs to get hurt today."

"Where?" Sam asked.

"Inside the hotel," the first guy said.

Sam said, "All right, lead the way."

The tension seemed to disappear from the first guy as he walked toward the revolving door. He no longer walked with a rigid gait. The man clearly assumed he'd already won the dispute, and was feeling the relief at not having to fight Tom. He was so confident with his victory that he walked in front of Sam, leading the way – and why shouldn't he be? After all, he was the one with the gun. It was their first mistake – never turn your back to an enemy. Sam and then Tom followed next, with the second guy walking directly behind.

Sam figured he got the easy one out of the two men to take care of, while Tom got the only one with any sense of how to do his job. There were five separate partitions that made up the revolving door, which was designed to automatically start to move clockwise as you enter it. Sam entered the same partition as the first guy, while Tom took the next one with the second guy. This was their second mistake – never separate when there's going to be a fight.

Sam followed the revolving door around until they reached the hotel lobby. Just before the door reached the point where it opened up, Sam pressed the emergency stop button.

"What the hell did you do that for?" the first guy asked.

The guy reached for his handgun. It was still in his cargo pocket. Sam launched himself at the man, pressing him hard against the hard glass partition, so that he couldn't remove the weapon from his pocket. The confined space was the only thing that saved Sam's life. The guy's right-hand gripped his handgun inside his pocket, and Sam shoved all his weight against that arm so he couldn't withdraw the weapon.

The first guy glanced at him – as though he was trying to say, what are you going to do? I still have the gun, you're going to have to let go sooner or later – an instant later, Sam drove his right hand into the man's pocket. The man fumbled, trying to maintain control of the weapon. Sam squeezed his hand from the outside, forcing him to pull the trigger.

The semi-automatic weapon fired twice into the man's upper thigh. He wailed in pain, and Sam removed the weapon. The guy dropped to the floor, using both hands to stem the heavy bleeding to his leg. A moment later the revolving door started to move again.

Sam pointed the handgun at the guy. "Get out!"

The wounded man shuffled out of the revolving door into the lobby. Sam stepped into the lobby. Keeping the weapon pointed at the stranger, he glanced back at Tom. The next partition of the door came round. Inside an unconscious man laid on the floor, while a much larger man searched him and removed a small backpack.

Sam glanced at the bloodied heap on the ground. Reassured that the man was still breathing, he looked up at Tom. "Jesus. What the hell happened?"

Tom shrugged. "He made his first mistake."

"Yeah, what was that?"

"He picked a fight with me."

Tom dragged the second guy's unconscious body into the lobby. A concierge and security guard approached. Their eyes darted between Sam and Tom and the two badly injured people on the floor. No one spoke for a moment, as the hotel staff decided their next course of action.

Sam got in first. "I suggest you call an ambulance. This guy looks like he's going to need some serious help."

The concierge nodded, as though he was happy to be given a task. "We'll do that, right away, sir."

Sam pointed the handgun at the first guy, who was still struggling to stem the blood. He removed his leather belt and handed it to the man. "I suggest you wrap that around your leg if you don't want to bleed to death."

The man quickly took the belt and began trying to fit it to his upper thigh without saying a word. His eyes focused on his task, and he noticeably attempted to avoid making eye contact with Sam.

Sam said, "If you ever try to follow me again, I promise I won't stop with your legs."

"I won't! I swear!" the man promised.

Sam and Tom stepped back into the revolving door and outside. They walked casually back toward the main path they'd been using before Sadik had pointed out the two men following them. Poorly hidden behind three boulders, he spotted their guide.

"Come on Sadik, they've lost interest in following you, but they might have some friends who haven't – maybe we should check this place out before they do."

Ten minutes later they reached the hidden ventilation shaft. Sadik bent down and quickly unlocked the iron grate that blocked the entrance. It was a vertical airshaft, but large hand-holds had been carved into the volcanic rock, making it easy to climb. Sam and Tom followed him down into the ancient subterranean system. When they were all beneath the iron grate, Sadik locked it once more and said, "Welcome to Derinkuyu."

Chapter Four

The shaft continued about five stories down and then stopped. There was a total of six horizontal tunnels, leading in various directions. Sadik entered the fourth tunnel and headed toward the south. Sam switched on his flashlight. The beam illuminated the chalky walls of the tunnel. The tunnel itself felt like an overgrown rabbit warren. Made with rudimentary tools, the edges were rounded more than sharp. Sam and Tom followed Sadik a few hundred feet until the tunnel broke into three, with two horizontal tunnels and one narrow vertical shaft.

"Which way?" Sam asked.

"We'll take the long tunnel to the right. It's a little under a mile long. We've entered from a fair way out of the main city."

"Okay," Sam said, as he and Tom followed him.

"The name Derinkuyu translates to Deep Well," Sadik said, returning to his confident role as an informative tour guide. "It was carved out of the pliable volcanic ash rock the surrounds the entire region, called tuff. Inside, there is an extensive network of chambers for various daily activities, including temples, tombs, shops, living quarters, and even livestock pens. It has approximately 15,000 air shafts, and enough room to comfortably hold 20,000 people. Using geophysical resistivity and seismic tomography, it has been determined there are eleven levels, with some descending to a depth of 300 feet, with a total subterranean area of over four miles squared."

"It was a true underground city, wasn't it?" Sam said.

"Yes. With additional passages that connect it to other local underground networks, like the one we're in now." Sadik spoke reverently. "What's most unique however, is its ancient security system."

"A security system?" Sam asked.

"Yes. It's postulated the place was originally built as a hidden bunker to protect its people from any number of raids throughout the region. The city has many one thousand pound stone doors that could seal the city from the inside. They were on rollers that allowed them to be moved by a single person, but only from the inside. Additionally, each level could be sealed off from the next using the same system."

"Impressive technology for its age," Sam acknowledged. "How old is Derinkuyu?"

Sadik sighed, as though this was a common question with no real answer. "Aging the structure has proved very difficult because it was carved out of stone. Thus, there are no quarries to examine and carbon dating is irrelevant. Furthermore, there are no records documenting the construction, and the peoples who once lived here have long since vanished."

"But there must be theories?" Sam said.

"Of course, but without definitive proof, that's all they are – theories and guesses."

"So what are the theories and what do we know for sure?"

"Some of the caves were built by the Phrygians, an Indo-European people, in the 8th–7th centuries BC. When the Phrygian language died out in Roman times, replaced with its close relative, the Greek language, the inhabitants, now Christian, expanded their underground caverns adding the chapels and Greek inscriptions. Of course, there is no evidence that the Phrygians actually built the caves – only that they occupied the tunnels during the 8th and 7th centuries BC."

Sam asked, "What else is known for certain?"

"The earliest written mentions of Derinkuyu were found in the writings of Xenophon, dated somewhere between 431 – 355 BC. From Byzantine times of the 4th century through to 1923 Derinkuyu was known by its Cappadocian Greek inhabitants as Malakopea. It was greatly expanded in the middle Byzantine period to serve as a refuge from the constant raids of the Umayyad Arab and Abbasid armies, during the Arab–Byzantine wars that continued between 780-1180."

"Interesting." Sam flashed his light down an extremely deep ventilation shaft as they walked past. The hole swallowed the light well before it reached the shaft's bottom. "You said before there were some who suggested that Derinkuyu is even older than that?"

"Yes. Most of it is entirely speculation and deserves a place in the heart of conspiracy theorists rather than the works of archeologists and scholars."

"Go on," Sam said. "What are some of the theories?"

"Some suggest that the caves were constructed by the Persian King Yima around 400 BC." Sadik smiled, as though it was impossible. "Of course, Yima may have been a mythological figure rather than an actual king. It was said that he enjoyed a lifespan of more than 900 years – you may recall that this figure is common in many Biblical figures as well. The Zoroastrian text of *Vendidad* states that Yima built an underground city on the orders of the god Ahura Mazda, to protect his people from a catastrophic winter. Much like the account of Noah in the Bible, Yima was instructed to collect pairs of the best animals and people as well as the best seeds in order to reseed the Earth after the winter cataclysm."

Sam paused as the tunnel forked into two directions where a single ventilation shaft ran through the middle. "Which way?"

Sadik flicked his flashlight across the first rung of a more recent makeshift wooden ladder. "We're just going down."

Sam started to climb, followed by Tom. "What was the disaster Ahura Mazda said would come?"

"What?" Sadik asked.

"The winter cataclysm Ahura Mazda said would come – what was it?"

"Oh, he said it would come from the sky and cover the world in a dark cloud for a lifetime, before revealing a new world."

"It could have been in reference to a comet," Sam suggested. "Some of the ancient astronomers had extensive knowledge of the movement of the stars and comets above. A recent study just released has deciphered the Vulture Stone, which was found in the Göbekli Tepe in Turkey. It appears the ancient stone carvings show a comet swarm hitting Earth around 10,950 BC. This correlates with the mini ice age, known as the Younger Dryas, which lasted for around 1,000 years."

Sadik said, "Of course, Derinkuyu is nowhere near that old. So if they built it to protect themselves from a coming cataclysm from the sky, it never came."

Sam paused at the bottom of the ventilation shaft, thinking about it. "What if we're looking at this the wrong way?"

"How so?"

"What if we shouldn't be looking for the disaster that happened in the past?"

"If not a previous disaster, then what?"

"How about considering if the underground city was built to protect us from something that's still to come – something in the future?"

Chapter Five

Sam followed the next horizontal tunnel for about five minutes until they descended another two levels. The vertical shaft dropped maybe twenty-five feet and stopped. Two new horizontal tunnels broke off. Sadik took the northern tunnel without hesitation. Sam motioned to Tom to keep following, while he waited for a moment.

Sam waited until Tom's light dimmed and then switched his own flashlight off. He was instantly surrounded by darkness. A slight glow glittered to the north, ahead of him. Sam turned and faced the south, where a light radiated fiercely. He stopped, waiting for the light to come closer, but it remained where he'd first spotted it.

Had their pursuers found a way inside Derinkuyu?

He switched on his flashlight and quickly caught up with Tom and Sadik. "I think we have company."

"Really?" Sadik asked.

"There's a light behind us," Sam said.

Sadik exhaled deeply. "It's okay. That's coming from the tourist section of the Derinkuyu. They can't get in here without a key. I assure you, we're quite safe."

"How much of the underground city is accessible?" Tom asked.

"Only about ten percent of it," Sadik said as he kneeled down over an iron grate that protected another ventilation shaft. He rummaged through a large keychain until he found what he was after, and unlocked the padlock. "The rest is locked up for the safety of the tourists, or to avoid damage to some of the rooms of more archeological value. As you can appreciate, there are a number of wells and airshafts, which would swallow an adult whole."

Sam said, "Fortunately for us, you have a key."

"No. Fortunately for us, my discovery wasn't found in the tourist section of the ancient city."

Sam and Tom followed him through another series of tunnels, leading toward the south. They climbed down another two vertical shafts. It was a true rabbit warren, with no discernible purpose. After about fifteen minutes they reached a small opening, leading to a larger storeroom. It was oval-shaped and large stone seats were built into the ground.

Sam glanced at the stone structures. There were drain-holes at their base. "An old washroom?"

"Yes," Sadik confirmed.

Sam grinned as he studied Sadik's eyes. They were a dark brown color. His face appeared open and honest. A certain level of anticipation was evident, as though the man was waiting in expectation of being rewarded for his discovery.

Or had Sadik led Tom and him into a trap?

Sam glanced around the room. The entrance consisted of a gigantic rolling stone door that could seal the city from the inside. It seemed out of place to go to the effort to build such a defense system in order to protect a washroom and a dead end.

Maybe there was once more to this room, than now meets the eye?

In his cargo pocket, Sam felt for the handgun he'd stolen from their attackers. A Glock 31. The waterproof handgun had no safety, and could be fired in an instant, if Sadik had led him into a trap. He listened deeply for the sound of pursuers approaching, but none came.

Still waiting, Sam glanced at the walls for any evidence of the Master Builders being involved. He didn't believe for a minute that they had been involved in the construction of Derinkuyu. The walls were too simple. Carved out by using rudimentary tools, the edges were rounded, as opposed to sharp, purposeful lines.

His deep blue eyes focused on Sadik. "I don't see anything. Where did you find the wooden signpost?"

Sadik pointed to the end of the room, where a small well opened into complete darkness. "It was floating in there."

Sam focused his flashlight inside the well. The light reached an area ten or so feet below, and reflected back from the stilled water. "Where does that lead to?"

"Nowhere," Sadik said, looking blankly. "It's just a well."

Sam squinted, trying to see how deep the water went. "Sure. But where does it draw water from?"

"I don't know. An ancient subterranean river, I suppose. Why?"

"Does the water level ever fluctuate?"

Sadik thought about it for a moment. "Rarely. Once or twice in the past twenty-five years since I've been working here."

"Could it be possible that there were more levels below us?" Sam asked.

"And that the river below swelled and flooded it?" Sadik considered. "It's an unlikely possibility. No one's ever tried to find out as far as I know. It's clearly just a well. Like the rest of the city, it leads to a subterranean river that once supplied the city. A person can barely fit inside, so I don't think it was ever intended to be anything but a well. What were you thinking of doing, bringing SCUBA equipment to dive it?"

Sam smiled. "Actually, that's exactly what I was thinking."

Chapter Six

It was another twenty-four hours before Sam managed to get the dive equipment flown into Cappadocia. A further twenty hours passed before he and Tom carted it down into the Derinkuyu washroom. During that time, they opened the contents of their attacker's backpack. It held a flashlight attachment for the Glock, along with four additional magazines, each loaded with fifteen rounds. Sam and Tom split the magazines and Sam pocketed the Glock's flashlight.

At seven p.m. and two hours after the tourist section of Derinkuyu closed, Sam finally laid out the equipment needed to explore the well. Permanent lighting had been set up, so the small cavern was lit up like an office. Next to him, Tom began constructing a winching tower, the sort of aluminum frame used by rescuers to winch injured people out of canyons and off cliff tops. It quickly formed a tripod shaped structure with a series of pulleys on top.

Sam carefully checked his dive equipment. He'd brought two tanks. Unlike ordinary twin mounted dive tanks, these would fit singly, with one in front of his chest and the other behind. Each tank had its own regulator, and clipped on for easy removal. They were the common set he used when cave-diving in shallow water, where he needed to squeeze through tight spaces. He could take them off and feed them through a tight space in front of his own body, if he had to. His fins were compact and rigid. Instead of the typical rubber ankle strap, he used a spring heeled strap.

Sam carefully lowered the dive tanks into the water below and then tied off to the rope. Tom double checked his SCUBA equipment as Sam connected his carabiner from his harness to the end of a second rope, which ran through a pulley system. The plan was to remain attached to the rope throughout the entire dive. That way, if the subterranean river's current was stronger than expected he could make two hard pulls on the rope, and Tom would winch him back.

Sam met Tom's eyes. "Are you happy with it?"

Tom took up the rope's slack with a gentle downward pressure. "I'd be a lot happier if I was coming with you. We both know how much trouble you get yourself into when I'm not around."

"I wish you were coming, too." Sam's eyes darted toward Sadik. "But I still don't trust him not to leave us down there, if we both go together."

"I don't either," Tom said.

"Then I'm good to go."

Sam rested back into his harness until he felt the rope take his weight over the top of the well. It was narrow, but easily wide enough to take his solid frame without risk of becoming stuck inside. Not enough, though, that he could have carried the dive tanks on him while he descended. Not that it mattered to him he could easily attach them once he was out of the well.

Two thirds of the way down Sam switched on his flashlight. He carried a total of three with him on any cave dive, or wreck dive. One to use, and two for backups. He shined below, where it penetrated the crystal clear, stilled water.

His thin wetsuit felt painfully inadequate against the cold water as his legs touched the water. Tom stopped his descent, while Sam, found the two dive tanks and their regulators. He increased the air in his winged buoyancy control device, until he was neutrally buoyant. The benefit of the winged system was that as he breathed air in, it drew air out of the winged air seals, meaning that the overall displacement of water remained the same while breathing – allowing him to remain neutrally buoyant throughout the dive.

Sam fixed his mask so that it formed a perfect seal, placed a regulator in his mouth and placed a hand on his head to form an all okay signal for Tom. A moment later, he began his descent into a world of permanent darkness.

The round vertical shaft of the well continued for fifteen feet before opening to an enormous underground cistern. He swallowed a couple times until his ears equalized, and then glanced around his new environment. Sam guessed the original occupants of Derinkuyu were concerned about the subterranean river becoming dry, so had constructed a massive cistern to hold enough water to last a prolonged siege for months if not years. The only other option was that it wasn't attached to any underground river, and instead was simply a large holding cell. The second option was unlikely, given Sadik's reference to the occasional significant change in water levels. Either way, he'd find out soon enough.

Sam quickly and efficiently slipped into his dive tanks. He moved his flashlight around in slow clockwise swathes, sending out a powerful beam of light in a thirty degree arc. The flashlight never reached the end of the cavern. Every twenty or so feet, a vertical stone pillar reached from the ground to the ceiling, as though the original builders knew precisely how much the volcanic stone could take, before it needed to be propped up with structural support.

Sam corrected his buoyancy until he was completely neutral and then fixed his flashlight against the stony ceiling. He didn't move at all. The water was still, or if not, very close to it. He checked his depth gauge. He was in eighteen feet of water, and was carrying two full tanks of air. He would probably start to feel the adverse effects of hypothermia before he ran out of air. Even so, he hoped the cistern wasn't as big as it looked. He tugged on the rope firmly, once – sending a message to Tom to loosen the slack, so he could commence the exploration.

He kicked his fins and headed to the south. A couple minutes later he reached the opening of another well above him. It was narrow and impossible to climb without equipment. He continued to the south, finding a total of four wells before reaching the end of the room, approximately five hundred feet away. Sam made a note on his dive slate, and then returned to the starting point.

He followed the same process to the east and west, finding the shape of the cistern far narrower than he expected. Possibly two hundred feet wide at most. Sam found three more openings to wells, but none he could access without ropes from above.

Sam checked his dive time. He'd been submerged for nearly forty minutes. The water was cold, but he was maintaining his body temperature better than he'd expected. He decided to have a quick look to the north before returning to the bathhouse to warm up and prepare for another dive.

Roughly fifty feet out, he found the opening to a well. He ran the beam of his flashlight over it and stopped. This one had a vertical staircase dug into its edge. Sam unclipped each of his dive tanks, so they were trailing about seven feet behind, as he ascended the well. There was no light coming from above, giving him hope that he'd discovered a hidden chamber, once occupied by a Master Builder. He broke the surface of the well and removed the regulator from his mouth.

He climbed the vertical shaft nearly eighty feet before reaching an opening. An unlocked cover protected those above from falling into the opening. Sam briefly searched the area with his flashlight. He was at a crossroad in the underground city. Behind him, the tunnel had been intentionally blocked by the looks of it. Bricks had been laid with mortar to form a barrier to the south, which appeared oddly anachronistic with the tunnels carved by hand.

Sam disconnected his carabiner and attached it to the iron grate that covered the ventilation shaft where he'd just climbed up. He quickly searched the two tunnels to the east and west. They were short, and opened to large and empty storerooms. He walked a couple hundred feet down to the north, where the tunnel appeared to continue unhindered.

He turned around and returned to the ventilation shaft. From what he'd learned about Derinkuyu, some of the escape tunnels went for mile upon miles. As much as he wanted to know where it went, Sam decided to return to the water. This was the wrong place. No matter how much the river had flooded, it never would have reached eighty feet high, where it could wash anything away from the storerooms. Tom would be starting to worry about his dive time if he didn't return soon. It was most likely Sadik would know about it, anyway.

Sam quickly reattached his harness to the rope and carabiner. He descended the ventilation shaft, placed the regulator in his mouth and returned to the dark world below. He checked his watch. He'd been gone for nearly an hour and thirty minutes. Tom would be starting to get edgy. He should have returned, but instead he decided to swim north, just a little further. It was a bad decision, or an extremely good one, depending on the way you want to look at it.

He continued swimming for another two hundred feet and stopped. A set of stairs, chiseled into the soft volcanic tuft, rose straight out of the water about thirty feet away. Sadik had already told him that he didn't know where Derinkuyu drew its water supply, but if any of the known tunnels led to the water through a set of stairs, he would have known for certain. That meant, Sam had found a hidden grotto.

He began swimming toward the steps. He could see where the water broke the surface, but there was something else in that direction, too. He focused the powerful beam of his flashlight at it and stopped – because looking right back at him were the vacant eyes of another SCUBA diver.

Chapter Seven

It took a moment for Sam to recognize what he was looking at. He felt his pulse pound in the back of his head. He took several quick, shallow breaths. Anxiety and panic crept up upon him in an instant. His first instinct was to back away, and escape as quick as possible. But there was no reason to, because the wraith that was staring at him couldn't harm a soul – it was already dead.

Sam caught his breath and purposefully slowed his breathing. He quickly scanned the surrounding area with his flashlight in a three hundred and sixty degree arc. There was no one else, living, nearby. Sam studied the diver. He was wearing neoprene and twin dive tanks, leaving no air bubbles visible. The diver's eyes were still visible behind his mask, and stared vacantly at Sam – as though he was trying to warn him of some unknown horror.

Sam glanced at the man's dive tanks. It was impossible to think that even a moderately experienced diver would drown with twin tanks in such shallow water. He should have had hours to find an opening, and there had been a number of them, so what went wrong? Sam's eyes stopped at the edge of the multiple dive lines running off the twin tanks. Every one of the regulator lines had been sliced through. The poor wretch had his air source taken from him and left to drown.

The body didn't even look bloated. If he had to guess, the man had been killed in the past few days, at most. Sam briefly forgot about the stairs and quickly swam back to the well from which he'd been lowered.

He removed his dive tanks and surfaced. "Tom, you up there?"

"I'm here, you okay?" Tom's replied, in his cheerful voice.

"I'm fine, bring me up."

Sam reached the top of the well and detached his carabiner from the end of the rope. He removed the top half of his wetsuit and started to dry himself. He felt colder than he was. He glanced at Sadik, who appeared uncomfortable, but he said nothing.

Sadik asked, "Is everything okay?"

Sam turned his gaze to focus on the short man with icy steel eyes. "No. Nothing's all right. You lied to us, and now I want to know why."

Sadik said, "I don't know what you're talking about?"

Sam looked directly into Sadik's eyes. There was fear, but also a world of confusion. "You tell me, or I swear to you, I'll throw you down the well."

Sadik turned his gaze furtively at the well's entrance. He spoke in barely a whisper. "What did you see down there?"

"I found the remains of another person, searching for the rest of the writings you found."

Chapter Eight

Sam watched for Sadik's response.

"You found someone's remains?" Sadik asked.

"Yes and given you told me no one had ever been down the well, you can imagine my surprise."

"But… but… the body could have been there for centuries?" Sadik tried to spit the words out as though they were vile and unfair. "You can't judge me for this!"

Sam glanced at Tom who now appeared wide awake. He wasn't quite grinning, but something about his face gave the impression he was happy to watch someone else suffer for what had been done to Billie. Sam returned his focus to Sadik. "I'm afraid the person who died did so no later than the past day or two."

"The last day or two?" Sadik asked.

"Not an hour longer than that," Sam confirmed.

Sadik gritted his teeth. "He said no one was going to get hurt, so long as I cooperated with him."

"Who did?" Sam asked.

"I don't know his real name," Sadik said. "He was tall. He had a thick cleft chin and the most intimidating purple eyes I've ever seen. He said no one was to find the chamber, whatever the heck that is. Said it was supposed to remain hidden until the rise of the Third Temple."

"The Third Temple?" Sam asked. "What's the Third Temple?"

"I have no idea. You were supposed to come here and tell me all the answers about this strange piece of writing. Instead, all I'm getting is threats and more questions. You tell me what the Third Temple is?"

"All right, all right," Sam said. "What were you supposed to do?"

Sadik swallowed hard. "I was supposed to bring you here. Wait until you deciphered the ancient text inside the hidden chamber. Once I was convinced I had learned everything there was to know about the writings, he said he would return."

"When?"

"I told him it would take at least three days until you'd have your equipment to dive."

"Then what?" Sam persisted.

"He didn't say. All he said was that he'd be here to take care of it then, and I could go free. I'm sorry."

Sam wasn't sure that he believed him. He looked at Tom. "Go check out the surrounding tunnels. Make sure we're still on our own."

Tom nodded and left the room. His face more lively than Sam had seen it since their search for Billie had become dry.

"Don't you see?" Sadik said. "You need to get out of here now, while you still can."

"We came here to find answers, and I don't plan to be pushed around by a bully."

"You haven't met this bully. Your friend looked almost eager to meet the man, but he should be frightened."

"Tom?" Sam's upper lip curled into the faintest of smiles. "Have you seen the size of him? He's two hundred and sixty pounds of solid muscle. He really doesn't frighten very easily."

"He hasn't met this man."

Sam studied Sadik's face. There was a genuine fear, but there was also relief as though a giant weight had been lifted off him. A burden to betray someone he had no intention of harming. With the truth out, he was able to speak freely again.

"What name did this man give you?"

"He said his name was Famine."

Sam thought about it. "Any clue what the name might be in reference to?"

"Like I said, I have no idea and didn't ask. He didn't strike me as the sort of person who liked answering a lot of questions about his past."

"All right," Sam listened at the entrance to the washroom for the sound of anyone approaching. His eyes met Sadik's. He scrutinized him once more. "Have there been any major famines in recent or old history?"

"Are you kidding me?" Sadik asked. "There's been hundreds over the years. My country is rich in history, but poor in agriculture. Besides, our position in the region has seen us take in more than our fair share of refugees over the years."

"Okay, okay. Could he be referring to one of these famines?"

"It's possible, but I can't see how any discovery of an ancient historical artifact might allow him to make his point about an old or recent famine. Can you?"

"No. But it's the only lead I have so far."

Tom returned a few minutes later. He was breathing fast, like he'd just been running.

Sam asked, "Anything?"

Tom shook his head. "The tunnels are empty on this side of Derinkuyu all the way to the locked grates that block the tourists entering this side of the city to the south. I couldn't hear the sound of anyone inside the tourist section, either. So we should be safe, for the time being."

"Good," Sam said. "Because I need to get back down there."

Sadik stared at him. "Are you nuts?"

Tom answered for Sam. "Most of the time."

"Why would you want to go back down there?" Sadik persisted. "Don't you understand he's coming back, soon?"

"Does he have a key?" Sam asked.

"No. But he's expecting you to be here tomorrow."

Sam pulled his wetsuit back over his shoulders. "Then all the more reason we'll have to make sure we're done before then."

"You don't want to just forget about it, and leave now?" Sadik asked.

"No. Few people go to the trouble you've just described to kill a person in an underground water cistern. I want to know why? And besides, I still haven't found what I came here to get."

Sadik walked toward the door. "Well I don't want to stay any longer. I need to get out. Everything's changed if he's willing to kill someone."

Tom blocked his progress. "I'm afraid we really can't let you leave. Not now. Even if I trusted you, which I don't, I can't risk you notifying whoever this freak is outside that we know he's going to come for us."

Sam attached his carabiner to the end of the rope. "Relax. I won't be a minute longer than I need to be. What are you afraid of? Tom's here to look after everything and I assure you he has enough built up rage to take on even your demon."

Chapter Nine

Sam descended into the well again, slipped into his new dive tanks, and headed north. He switched his flashlight off and waited a couple minutes for any other sign of life. There were none. He was all alone, with the safety of the darkness. He flicked his light on, and continued swimming. It didn't take him long to swim the two hundred and fifty odd feet reach it.

About thirty feet away from the stairwell he spotted the dead diver, exactly where he'd left it. He switched his flashlight off and searched again for any other source of light. His eyes focused on the base of the stairs and the opening above them – searching for evidence someone was inside. The last thing he wanted was to be confronted by Sadik's demon as he climbed out of the water. Sam waited a little over a minute before switching his own light on and swimming toward the steps. The steps were formed out of white pumice, and ran all the way to the bottom of the water cistern. They were most likely used by the original builders of the underground structure, as a means of access when it was first being dug.

Sam breathed out gently as he slowly floated to where the steps met the surface. He took the regulator out of his mouth and flashed his light across the open space above. An entrance roughly four feet wide, by six feet high led to what appeared to be another stone chamber. He glanced around quickly, and listened for any sound coming from above. Hearing none, he removed his dive tanks and fins.

He removed the Glock 31 from a Velcro pocket on his right thigh. It was the same type of weapon the Navy Seals used. Equipped with a special firing pin, known as a spring cup, the weapon fired consistently post prolonged submersion in water. Normal spring cups are solid plastic, maritime spring cups have two channels cut into them to allow water to flow past them and empty out of the firing pin chamber, so that it can move fast enough to fire the handgun. The gun can fire submerged. The purpose of the maritime cups is that if the gun is submerged it can be retrieved and fired without having to perform maintenance. He drew it into a firing position with his right hand and switched on its Viridian tactical light and green targeting laser with his left.

Sam switched off his dive flashlight and carefully climbed the stairs. His feet felt cold on the porous steps. He moved his weapon around until he had a good vision of the entrance ahead. He cupped the light at the end of his weapon and searched one last time for any sign of an alternative source of light up ahead. Finding none, he slowly entered through the stone doorway.

Inside was a small stone chamber that appeared to lead nowhere. His eyes swept the room. It was possibly twenty feet in length by roughly ten wide. Its walls looked as though they had been made by digging away the volcanic stone using primitive tools. There was nothing about its construction that resembled the level of technological refinement and finesse achieved by the ancient Master Builders.

At the center of the room stood a large desk, made with the same porous stone found throughout the entire underground city. Sam glanced around the room. He ran his left hand around the walls searching for any hidden doorways. The entire room, right down to the stone desk, appeared to have come from the same piece of geology. Everything was solid, and Sam felt confident there were no secret openings.

He switched on the brighter dive flashlight and holstered his Glock to his right thigh. He covered the weapon with its Velcro strap and sat down at the desk. To his right were two small alcoves carved into the side of the desk. He reached inside and found two wooden placards.

Sam placed his flashlight on the desk like an ornamental reading lamp, and withdrew the two wooden placards. The writing on each of them was in the ancient script of the Master Builders. He carefully studied the words.

First Temple – Failed

Second Temple – Failed

Sam turned each of the wooden placards over. There was nothing written on the other side of them. He placed them back on the table. He ran his fingers across his forehead and through his thick, brown hair. Sam wasn't sure if he wanted to laugh or cry. Everything that had happened in the past few days… the murdered diver, the threats to Sadik, everything pointed to this hidden chamber – and it was a hidden chamber, designed from its first use to be kept a secret, away from the rest of the inhabitants of Derinkuyu – all of it, amounted to what? Sam glanced around the room – a strange empty chamber, a desk, and two wooden placards written in an ancient script, and referring to two temples, which had failed.

What the hell am I doing here?

Sam dropped his hands to the table and started to laugh – because he suddenly noticed the walls in front of him weren't blank. They had only appeared blank because of the bright LED light from his weapon. Under the less harsh glow of his dive light, the drawings along all of the walls suddenly glowed fluorescent green.

Chapter Ten

Sam stood up. His head was only about ten inches from the ceiling. His eyes swept the wall in front of him, as he moved quickly around the table to get a better view. The drawings were faded, as though the original artist had long since moved on, and his or her fragile landscapes had withered away in the same process. Even so, there was no mistaking the outline of the pictures.

They formed a primitive outline of the African continent, Mediterranean Sea through to the Black Sea. An asterisk was observed in the middle of the Black Sea. It was approximately fifty miles out from Istanbul, if the drawings were to a correct scale. Next to this, was the name, *Mary Rose*, 1653 – *First failed expedition*. Sam studied it for a few minutes, making sure he read each word correctly.

Expedition to what?

His eyes glanced around the rest of the painting. A small drawing of a ship was marked off the coast of Istanbul. The ship was followed by a series of dashes leading to an area about two thirds of the way down the west coast of Africa. An asterisk had been marked at the end of the line of dashes, and next to it were the words, *Emerald Star*, followed by the date 1655. Next to that, were the words, *Current Location: Unknown. Second failed expedition – all hope is lost.* With the exception of the ship's name, everything was written in the ancient script used by the Master Builders.

Sam took several photos of the image before moving on to the other walls. They were sparsely covered in the ancient script with no other images. They looked like notes, searching for the ship named the *Emerald Star*. It was last seen off the southwestern coast of Africa, where a large desert met the sea in 1556. Sam continued to decipher the writings. Apparently the ship possessed the key to the Third Temple – whatever the hell that was – but despite extensive searches, the ship was never located again. It was presumed sunk, and with its loss, all hope for humanity sunk to the seabed below.

The Third Temple?

It was the name that Sadik had mentioned, although neither of them knew what it was. He'd never heard the name before today. He recalled the *First Temple* of the Master Builders ever discovered. It was in Khyber Pass of Afghanistan. They'd never found a second temple. And had never heard of there being a third temple.

Sam stared at the words again – *Key to the Third Temple*. Was it in reference to a place, or an event? Could it be the third cataclysmic die off since humanity's existence? The rise of a third and massive event leading to widespread die off? He backed away from the wall, as though it might provide another perspective, and with it some more sense.

On the next wall was a simple map of the west coast of Africa. Most of the image was left unfilled, but inside what would now most likely be considered the Namibian Desert, a drawing of a large pyramid was observed. He'd never heard of any pyramid ever being found in the region. He made a mental note to have Elise do some computer searches for any reference to a pyramid within the region.

Sam completed taking photos of the other walls, and the ceiling. He took one last glance around the room, searching for signs of any clues he might have missed. Confident that whatever secrets the walls held were now captured on his digital camera, Sam returned to the steps. He donned his dive equipment, and made the short journey back to the well – to where answers might be waiting for him.

Chapter Eleven

Sam climbed out of the well. He quickly disconnected his carabiner from the end of the rope and started to remove his wetsuit. He glanced at Sadik, who appeared to be sweating harder than when Sam had left. He seemed to be battling that internal decision to run or wait it out – but for what, though?

Sam was wet, cold and hungry and all of these feelings were worsened by his heightened senses over Sadik's betrayal. It made him work quickly to remove their equipment. He decided he would throw the tanks and climbing gear into the well. Better to lose them than have Sadik's demon know they had finished their project.

Sadik approached, quickly. "Tell me, did you find anything?"

"Yeah. There's another room below this one."

"What was inside?"

"More writing like the one you found."

"What did it say?" Sadik persisted.

"Not much," Sam said. "Someone was searching for a ship a long time ago called the *Emerald Star*. Does that name ring a bell to you?"

Sadik shook his head. "No. Sorry."

"Me neither," Sam said. "What about the Third Temple?"

"We have a lot of temples in Cappadocia. Is there anything particular that identifies the one you're after?"

"No."

"Now what?" Sadik asked.

"Now, we must thank you muchly. Tom and I have to go. We're going to have to search for this ship, if it's still afloat somewhere, we'll find it."

"And if it's already sunk?" Sadik asked.

"Then we'll still find it, but it might just take a lot longer."

Tom started to disconnect the pieces that grouped together to make the winching tripod. "What do you want to do with the equipment, Sam?"

Sam looked at it. He'd used much of it over the past decade on various expeditions and he had a strange sentimental value to the dive gear, but he couldn't have anyone report they were finished with their search. "Ditch it."

"All of it?"

Sam nodded.

Tom took apart the last of the winching tripod and threw the pieces into the well, where they sunk to the bottom. Sam dropped the heavy dive tanks into the well. Despite being full of compressed air, they were negatively buoyant and dropped like stones.

"What did you find?" Tom asked.

"There were some old drawings, most likely done by one of the Master Builders. They looked like notes, searching for a ship named the Emerald Star. It was last seen off the southern coast of Africa, where a large desert met the sea in 1655. Apparently it held the key to the Third Temple – whatever the hell that was – but despite extensive searches, the ship was never located again. It was presumed sunk, somewhere."

"What do you want to do?" Tom asked.

"Let's get back to the Maria Helena and see if Elise can track this ship down for us. Also, see if she can find any reference to the Third Temple."

Sam crouched down to exit the washroom. He moved quickly, with Sadik following close behind and Tom casually following. They made it to the level above and nearly a hundred and fifty feet through the tunnel before they were stopped.

Three men approached at a walking pace. Two were armed with Winchester shotguns, with their barrels crudely sawn off. If either of the two men pulled their triggers, the effects of the short barrel would send a barrage of pellets down the tunnel with obliterating force.

A tall man at the center of the small group strolled with his hands in his pockets. "I'm afraid that's far enough, Mr. Reilly."

"Far enough for what exactly?" Sam asked. His tone was curious and nonplussed.

"They said you were a confident bastard." The stranger smiled. "Of course, they didn't mention you were stupid."

"He gets that a lot," Tom said.

The stranger ignored him. "I'm afraid neither of you is going to the surface."

"Who are you?" Sam asked.

"No one of significance," the man said.

His face appeared gaunt. It was narrow, with a patrician nose and high cheekbones. It was an ascetic face, like a monk or worshiper of self-sacrifice. He wore black robes. Hanging from his neck was a single pendant of a crucifix. At its center rode a horse of pure obsidian. Its rider carried a pair of weighing scales. It gave Sam Reilly the slightest of pauses. Violent criminals are dangerous, but the greatest of fear should be reserved with those religious zealots who believe they are acting for a higher cause. Criminals can be reasoned with on a human level. Greed, desire, need, lust – these are all things that a criminal can understand, but religious zealots are operating under a divine order that no mere mortal can begin to understand.

Sam stared at the man's face. "What are you after?"

The man spoke slowly, as though he was giving a sermon or making a prayer. "I'm looking for the Death Mask."

"What's that?" Sam asked.

"A sacred artifact. Something that will prove invaluable in the days to come."

"The days to come?" Sam asked. "What's coming?"

The man looked pitifully down upon Sam. "Haven't you read your Bible?"

"Not lately."

"The end of days is approaching. It's time to seek shelter – and the Death Mask is the only way to reach the Third Temple."

"Who are you?"

"My name's Famine, and my day of glory is coming soon."

Chapter Twelve

Sam glanced at the two men holding sawn off shotguns, and back to the man in black robes. Religious zealot or not, the man meant business. "What do you want?"

"I want you to tell me exactly what you discovered inside the hidden chamber."

"Why should I do that if you're going to kill me anyway?" Sam asked.

"Because if you don't I will torture you first and then kill you."

Tom said, "You must be the one called skinny?"

Sam said, "I think he said his name was famine."

"So that's it, then?" Sam asked. He glanced at Sadik. "You were always going to kill us, weren't you?"

Sadik said, "I'm sorry. They have my family."

Tom moved on instinct. His movements were quick and sharp. Tom held Sadik in front of him like a human shield, with his arm digging heavily into the man's throat and the Glock pressed hard into back of Sadik's head. "Yeah, I'm sorry, but I have a family, too."

Chapter Thirteen

Sam took in his situation in a silent glance. The two goons held the barrels of their shotguns low, as though they had all the time in the world to lift the barrels and shoot if they needed to. They looked bored, relaxed, like someone who'd spent their lives serving a master who always won by fighting with superior numbers. The ringleader was the worst. He was tall, and his face betrayed a hardened confidence of a man whose mere name evoked fear – Famine. Tom had Sadik, and he had nothing. They both had a pair of Glocks while the enemy had a pair of shotguns. They knew now that Tom was armed, but they didn't know Sam was.

Famine laughed and said, "There are three of us. We're armed, and you're not. Derinkuyu is crawling with my men, and every one of them is on their way here, as we speak. So, what do you think you're going to do?"

Tom tightened his grip on Sadik's neck. "I could snap his neck?"

Famine shrugged. "It would save me the trouble of having to go through the messy process of killing him and his family."

Tom's brown eyes were wide and focused with steely determination. His jaw was set hard, but at the same time he wore a genuine smile, baring a full complement of evenly spaced, white teeth. It made Tom appear insane. Almost eager for a fight where he held the unfair disadvantage. It was the happiest and most alive Sam had seen his friend in a number of weeks. The first time in a long time Tom had been given a real enemy to take out his anger and frustration. He'd almost forgotten how fearsome his friend could become when it was necessary. Tom's façade of being a gentle giant dissipated instantly when the need to fight arose, and all other options had been ruled out.

Sam said, "He doesn't look like he wants to surrender. I'll take the guy on the left, and you take the one on the right."

"Okay, that seems fair."

Sam reached into his right cargo pocket and withdrew his handgun. The Glock 31 was an extremely reliable weapon. He fired two shots before the first guy with the shotgun even lifted his weapon. The loud report of shots being fired from both Glocks echoed simultaneously.

His eyes darted toward the ringleader in the middle. Sam aimed directly at the man's chest. He was close enough he was certain he would hit it. Famine fidgeted with his right hand, as though he was contemplating reaching for the gun. It would take extraordinary reflexes for the stranger to get a shot off, let alone two before Sam or Tom killed him.

"I wouldn't," Sam said.

The tunnel echoed with the sound of footsteps running heavily in the distance. "My men are coming. You'll never get to keep me prisoner. You may as well hand yourselves over to me now."

"I don't think so."

Famine shrugged. "Suit yourself."

Famine feinted resignation, and then reached for his gun.

Sam puts two bullets into the man in an instant. Famine man fell backward, landing hard. Tom picked up one of the dead guy's sawn off shot guns. He fired a round down the tunnel, instantly stopping the progression of more attackers who were following the sound of gunfire.

Sam placed a firm hand on Tom's shoulder. "Come on let's go. You're not going to win the fight like this."

Tom pumped another shell into the gun in his hands, and then bent down to pick up the second shotgun. His eyes were now wild, like a possessed fiend released into the battlefield. "You got a better idea?"

Sam nodded. He pointed the Glock at Sadik's head. "You're coming with us."

"Where?" Sadik asked.

"Back to the washroom."

Tom fired another round down the tunnel. A second later he heard shots being returned. Tom moved quickly and followed Sam and Sadik back into the washroom.

"Now what the hell are you going to do?" Sadik asked.

Sam looked at the entrance to the small chamber. "Can you close that stone door?"

"Sure, but I don't see what you're going to do. What are you going to do, wait forever?"

Sam pointed the Glock back at Sadik's head. "Close it or I'll kill you myself."

Sadik nodded. He undid the steel locks, more recently installed to prevent the accidental movement of the gigantic rolling stone. He tried to shift the heavy stone, but it didn't move. Hundreds of years fixed in the one position had caused it to sink a miniscule amount into its stone cradle.

"Hurry up!" Sam shouted.

"I can't move it!"

Shots whipped past him inside the washroom. "Tom, give him a hand."

Tom fired a blast out the door from each of the shotguns and then ran toward the stone door. It was shaped like a giant wheel. He placed his shoulder on its edge, while Sadik pulled from the front of it.

It still didn't move.

An attacker stepped into the room. He fired a single shot from his shotgun, without aiming. The spray went wild. Sam stepped forward and placed two bullets in the man's head before he could reload. Another man started to climb down the ventilation shaft up ahead. Sam waited, watching the man climb down, until he was completely visible before firing at him.

He felt a stabbing pain right through his chest, as though he couldn't breathe. With whatever breath he had left, he swore – because it was the man in black robes. Sam fired another two shots right in the middle of the man's chest and still he kept walking towards him. He must have been wearing a Kevlar vest underneath his black robe.

The man laughed hysterically. "I told you, you can't kill me – I am forever… I am above death – I am Famine!"

Sam turned and retreated inside the chamber. "Tom! Close that fucking door!"

He joined Tom and Sadik, who were pushing the edge of the stone wheel with all their might. Sam's additional weight was just enough to start the movement. It rolled slightly.

"Don't let them close the door!" Famine said to one of his men.

Sam saw the man running. He'd taken the opportunity to move fast, while none of them were shooting outward. The door kept rolling.

The attacker dived.

He was too late. The door rolled across his chest and the weight of the stone sliced him in two from his upper chest downward. The man's eyes stared up at Sam in horror for an instant, before rolling into the back of his head.

Sadik quickly wedged a heavy stone next to the wheeled door, to make it impossible for someone on the outside to roll the stone back into its cradle again. Sam slowly walked over to the door, and tried to move the wheel. It didn't budge an inch. He breathed out deeply.

Sadik said, "Now we're trapped, what are you going to do about it?"

Sam smiled. "You can wait here if you want, but I think I've seen enough of Derinkuyu for the time being."

Chapter Fourteen

Sam leaned over the edge of the well and glanced at the stilled water looking back up at him. Behind him Tom still gripped the twin shotguns, as though he expected someone to break through the thousand pound stone door at any moment.

Sadik looked into the well and then back up at Sam. "I bet you wish you hadn't dropped your diving equipment already?"

Sam shrugged. "It doesn't matter. We're still getting out."

"How do you plan to do that?" Sadik's face was covered in sweat, as he studied the well as though he was only truly seeing it for the first time.

"There's a ventilation shaft about fifty feet north of here," Sam said. "It's not a particularly difficult swim."

"Do you know where it leads?"

"No," Sam admitted.

"You might be walking straight into them," Sadik pointed out.

Sam checked his compass, making a mental note of the direction where the ventilation shaft ran. "If we can't get through, we'll come back here and start again."

"If you can't get through there's always the front door," Tom said. He spoke with indifference as though he was just as happy to open the door and fight his way out, as he was to swim through to another exit. "There can't be more than twenty of them left?"

Sam glanced at Sadik and smiled. "See, we have lots of options."

Chapter Fifteen

Sam dropped like a pin into the well. He floated to the surface and looked up. The plan was that when they were all ready, he would dive down and start swimming toward the ventilation shaft to the north. Sadik would follow twenty or so seconds later to make sure he didn't land on Sam. Twenty seconds after that, Tom would follow last. So long as his navigation was correct, he would reach the ventilation shaft in under a minute. Sadik would then follow his light, and Tom would follow Sadik's light.

He looked up at Sadik and Tom. "You ready, Sadik?"

"Ready as I'm going to be," Sadik replied.

"Okay." Sam hyperventilated for about thirty seconds, before turning and diving head first down to the ancient water cistern below.

Without a facemask the water was an obtuse blur of refracting light. Sam squinted and tried to focus on the small arrow of his compass. He concentrated heavily, but his mind couldn't discern the shapes as an N for north, or S for south. He closed his eyes and opened them again. The image wasn't any better. It was a fifty, fifty gamble – with death awaiting all of them if he got it wrong.

Sam had checked the compass before descending into the water, so that he started out facing north, but it was impossible to know his current direction after spinning round to dive. Years of free-diving and SCUBA had given him an uncanny knack for navigation. His additional senses in his gut told him that he was facing north. It was good enough for him. He knew that he would become more disoriented each time he dived, and that his first instinct was usually the right one, even if he couldn't explain how he had reached such a conclusion.

He kicked hard, focusing on maintaining a straight line. He swallowed gently to equalize his ears, and relieve the slightly painful pressure. Sam started to feel heaviness in his chest as he fought the autonomic muscles of his diaphragm from contracting and forcing him to take in a deep breath. Time was running out quickly.

If he'd made the wrong choice, he knew there was no way he could reach the original well. More frightening still, was the knowledge he had no way of telling Sadik and Tom if he'd made a mistake. Unable to go backward, he continued to swim harder. He could hear his heart pounding in the back of his head. He normally had no trouble holding his breath for sixty seconds, but the situation, the cold, and the vigorous swimming were taxing his capacity. He knew that if he could make it, Tom easily could, also. They could only hope Sadik was fit enough and a good enough swimmer to keep up.

Thirty seconds later, he saw a darkened opening ahead. His only recognition of the image was that his flashlight no longer stopped at the ceiling, instead it was swallowed by a roundish vacuum. Sam kicked harder until his hands gripped the opening and pulled himself inside the ventilation shaft. He looked up and kicked harder until he reached the surface.

Gasping for air, Sam quickly turned his flashlight downward to highlight the opening for the others. There was just enough room for two people to squeeze into the ventilation shaft. He waited another forty seconds for his breathing to settle, and was about to dip down to make sure Sadik had followed his light, but instead Sadik broke the surface and gasped for air.

"You okay?" Sam asked.

Sadik nodded, unable to speak because he was breathing so hard.

Sam dipped his head into the water for a moment and saw Tom's light approaching. He started to climb the ladder to make room for Tom. Sam climbed to the about ten feet up and then waited for Tom to surface.

"You okay?" Sam asked.

"Never better," Tom said.

"Good. When you guys catch your breath, come on up."

He climbed to the top of the ventilation shaft and waited for Sadik and Tom to follow. By the time the other two men reached the top, Sam was waiting at the crossroads about thirty feet down the tunnel. Sadik was breathing hard after the swim and the climb, but he studied the room as though he was trying to place a mental image of his location.

"Do you know where we are?" Sam asked.

Sadik took a deep breath and settled. "Yeah, we're standing in the old Ottoman tunnels."

"The Ottoman tunnels?" Sam asked.

Sadik looked around at the two large store rooms to the east and west. "During the Ottoman invasion in the fifteenth century, these tunnels were built by the Cappadocian Greeks as a secret means of entering and exiting their underground refuge."

Sam shined his flashlight down the northern tunnel, where the light eventually trailed off to nothing. "How long is this tunnel?"

"Roughly three miles."

"And where does it come out?"

"Somewhere beneath the Fairy Chimneys." Sadik shook his head. "I'm not sure where exactly. It was closed years ago. It might not even be passable anymore."

Sam turned to the southern direction. "What about that way?"

"It comes out close to where we entered Derinkuyu."

To the south, the sound of voices speaking rapidly echoed toward them.

Sam turned to Sadik. In a whisper, he said, "Can they get into here?"

"No. Not unless they have a key," Sadik said.

A moment later, almost in response to the question, the tunnel echoed with the sound of a small explosion.

Tom withdrew his Glock, looking as though he regretted not making the effort to carry the shotguns. He looked at Sam. "It appears they found a key."

Sam said, "Run!"

Chapter Sixteen

Sadik was the fastest, with Sam and Tom following just behind. All three of them ran down the northern tunnel. It was the quickest three miles Sam had run in long time. His breathing was hard and his chest burned from the effort. They'd run the entire trip without stopping. On two occasions, Sam had considered resting for a moment, only to hear the sound of shotguns being fired at them from behind. The spread of shotgun pellets were still a long way off hitting them, but it was a good incentive to keep moving.

Sam turned the corner and the tunnel came to an end. The wall in front had been sealed with some sort of mortar long ago. He quickly studied the dead end, shining his flashlight in all directions, looking for any other ways out. There were none.

Sadik looked like he was about to collapse with exhaustion. His face was flushed and he was unable to speak because of the effort being used to keep breathing. Behind them, another shotgun fired. It was getting closer.

Tom took up a firing stance, aiming his Glock down the tunnel. "I guess we're back to square one. We're going to have to fight our way out."

"Forget it," Sam said, removing his dive knife and stabbing at the wall. "Give me a hand to break through this wall."

The soft, volcanic rock broke away and crumbled with each movement. It had been cemented up using a mixture of mortar made from volcanic rock and lime to make cement-like glue. Sam pried at the mortar that held a large stone in the wall. It was made using ground up pumice and lime, making it brittle and weak. The stone came free easily enough and Sam pulled it out. Tom threw his weight into the wall, and tried to pull out another stone using his bare hands. The wall started to move under his strength.

Behind them, another shot fired. A few pellets embedded themselves on the wall about ten feet away. Sam dropped his knife and started kicking the wall. Tom joined in, too, while Sadik fumbled away pulling at the remaining stones.

Another shot fired loudly.

It sounded like it was less than a hundred feet away. Sam turned and fired three rounds from his Glock down the tunnel, giving his attackers the tiniest of pauses. When they fired again, Tom ran toward the wall, putting all two hundred and sixty pounds of his weight into it. The entire wall shook and began to fragment. He hit it again, and more stone and mortar fell to the floor. Sam joined him on the third attempt, and both men fell through the wall.

It opened into the dining room of a cave hotel. The walls showed the classic stone formation found throughout Gerome. At least fifteen people were eating dinner, and stood up at their intrusion. A waiter still held a bottle of champagne in a bucket of ice.

"Sorry," Sam said, as he glanced at the waiter.

The room was suddenly filled with the reports of multiple shotguns being fired. Tom fired several shots back into the opening he'd just created. He yelled, "Everybody out!"

Pandemonium engulfed the quiet restaurant as people fled. Sam emptied the remaining rounds from his Glock into the opening. He looked at Sadik and Tom. "Let's go."

They ran up a series of stone steps, passing four levels before reaching the ground floor and entrance to the hotel. Two waiters blocked their exit. Tom pushed through the two waiters who tried to stop them, sending them flying onto their backs. He didn't apologize. Instead he kept running. They pushed through the large glass doors, and ran out into a world right out of the mind of Walt Disney when he conjured up Disneyland.

The Fairy Chimneys of Cappadocia appeared magical as they were lit up with thousands of fluorescent lights. The ancient stone towers looked perfectly suited for a fantasy ride in the Magical Kingdom. But this was no one's fantasy, and the ride they were on was starting to no longer be any fun.

Sam heard more shots being fired. The shotguns sounded like they had been replaced by handguns. He hoped his pursuers hadn't spotted them yet, and were just firing into the air to get his attention. A moment later several bullets whirred through the air next to his head – okay, they got it all right.

Tom fired back while Sam was still trying to work out where the shots were coming from. The report of multiple shots went quiet, and Sam spotted two men falling down a set of stone stairs about forty fifty feet away.

He turned to Tom and smiled. "Nice shooting."

Tom loaded another magazine. "Thanks."

Sam swept the landscape in a single glance. A series of stone stairs and walkways mingled around the brightly lit and colorful Fairy Chimneys through heights ranging from thirty to a hundred and twenty feet. Florescent lights lit up various aspects with deep blues, purples, greens and reds. A tall man with a barreled chest ran out of the Aria Cave Hotel, where they'd just left, holding a shotgun. He fired straight toward them. Sam and Tom ducked.

Sam heard the loud click of the pump-action ejecting the spent round and chambering a fresh one, over the sound of bystanders and tourists fleeing. It was instantly followed by the massive report of the weapon firing again and the soft volcanic rock above their heads was splintered into a thousand pieces.

Sam and Tom stood up simultaneously and sent two rounds each into the man's chest. His vacant eyes looked at his shotgun, unable to accept his fate, before rolling down the stairs – dead before he struck the pavement below.

"Sadik's run off without us!" Sam said.

Tom shrugged. "Can you blame him? We nearly got him killed. He's got a better chance of hiding without us."

"You're right, let's go."

They followed the pathway in a northerly direction. It meandered around several Fairy Chimneys, changing its height by more than fifty feet and crossing the valley multiple times, through a series of small tunnels and caves.

Each time they thought they'd gotten away from their pursuers, a new barrage of shots would fire at them from the south. They took it in turns to fire back, doing so only when one of them spotted a clear shot. They were both down to the last few rounds of their magazines. Sam had one more magazine left, and Tom was completely out. They would only risk a shot if they knew they could hit someone.

Sam and Tom were extremely fit. They were also driven with the primal will to survive. Adrenaline surged through their bodies giving them additional strength and endurance. The reports from gunshots were getting further away.

It took twenty minutes to reach the top of the hill, where the Goreme Yolu road met the end of the Gereme National Park – and more importantly, the last of their protective cover. Sam was breathing hard. It had been a long time he'd been forced to run so hard for so long. He studied the landscape. It became a mostly leveled plain, with minimal camouflage and even less protective cover. Across the road, and about three hundred feet away, some people were setting up a hot air balloon in a field.

A shot was fired somewhere behind them and its bullet went so wide they had no idea where it landed. The sound was all the encouragement Sam needed to keep moving. "Come on. Let's see what we can find over there!"

He made it several steps on to Goreme Yolu and a taxi pulled out in front of them. Its tires screeched as the driver came to halt just beside them. The yellow taxi, a Karsan V-1, smelled heavily of brake fluid and burnt tires, as though its driver had been driving it hard. The driver was honking the horn madly. At the end of the path behind them two men started to shoot. Sam ran around the taxi and ducked down below the driver's door.

The driver wound the window down. It was Sadik. "Get in!"

Sam and Tom didn't need to be told twice. Sam opened the front door and slipped inside. Tom climbed into the back seat simultaneously.

"Drive!" Sam yelled.

Sadik shoved his foot on the pedal and the taxi accelerated hard. Sam emptied his rounds into his attackers, until the Glocks's firing pin struck an empty chamber. Thirty seconds later, the taxi had disappeared out of their attacker's reach and the shots finally went quiet.

Sam sat up and looked at Sadik and smiled. "You came back for us!"

Sadik nodded. "Against my better judgement."

Sam loaded the last magazine into his Glock. "What happened to the taxi driver?"

"I told him to get out."

"Much appreciated," Tom said.

Sadik reached the T intersection of Kayseri and Nevsehir Yolu and stopped. "Where do you want to go?"

"Kayseri Airport," Sam said. "I have someone waiting to pick us up."

"Okay," Sadik said, and sped off to the north.

Sam asked, "What made you come back for us?"

"You saved my life. I save yours. Now we're even. Don't come back. I don't want to know what all this was about."

They reached Kayseri airport forty-five minutes later. Sam shook Sadik's hand. "Good luck with your family. I'll let you know how I go."

"No!" Sadik said. "Don't come back. Leave me alone. I don't want to know what this was about. I'm not interested. I just want to live my life."

Chapter Seventeen – Mount Ararat, Turkey

Gianpietro Mioli stood on the crest of Greater Ararat, the higher of the two volcanic peaks, and studied the snow-covered landscape that surrounded him in his search of a hidden secret. A place last seen in 1840 when the mountain last erupted, melting away the snow and revealing a series of ancient lava tubes below. Since that time, thick snow had permanently covered the upper third of the sacred mountain until this year.

As a result of the hottest summer on record, the ubiquitous snow which capped the region all year round had reached its lowest depth since the volcanic eruption of 1840. This year he'd postponed his studies at Italy's prestigious University of Bologna in order to search the sacred mountain. A mountain rich in mystery and Biblical history dating back to ancient searches for any remnant of Noah's Ark which some believe to have come to rest on the mountain.

Mioli didn't believe for an instant the Ark would be found – or any sort of historical treasure for that matter – what he was searching for was something altogether very different, and yet just as valuable. He wore a pair of dark snow goggles that hid his deep-set, gray eyes. He wore a thick mountaineering jacket, helmet and crampons, so that little could be seen of his appearance, except the broad crest of his smile. He felt his heart beat faster, and for a moment didn't even realize he was holding his breath, as he discovered his first lead in two weeks on the mountain.

Through a pair of binoculars, he studied the snowdrift wander aimlessly along the northern plateau. It turned sharply, as though it had suddenly been given a purpose and sped along the flat snow. Like a mythical beast with a mind of its own, it fought its way against the oncoming wind caused by the natural updraft, before losing momentum and slowing to a stop. A split second later, it spun around and began to move again as though suddenly energized by a secret enthusiasm. This time, it was turning in a large spiral formation. It gained speed as it approached the center, spiraling faster and faster, until it disappeared into an imaginary crevasse.

Mioli grinned and marked the precise location on his topographical map. This was exactly what he was looking for. As an avid mountain climber, he'd spent previous summers climbing throughout Europe. In two weeks, it would all be over, and he would have to take up his placement at the University of Bologna to resume his studies. In previous years he'd successfully climbed the Eiger, Mount Blanc, and the Matterhorn. This time, he'd come here in search of something very different – virginal spelunking.

It had become a craze with cavers around the world. The concept was to discover a brand new cavern, never before entered, and then map it out before the place had a chance of being overrun by other cavers and tourists. One of the tricks was to search for areas where wind shows an abnormal movement. For example a sudden down draft where the wind should be stagnant or flowing upward, might reveal an opening where the cold air below leads to a decreased pressure gradient.

Mioli carefully walked along the plateau, stopping about twenty feet short of the place where he'd seen the strange snowdrift formation disappear inside an invisible crevasse and downdraft. He fixed a climbing pin deep into the snow and attached the sixty foot climbing rope to the end of it. The other side of the rope was tethered to his harness, which he tightened until he was confident the rope would stop his fall if the ground opened into a massive crevasse. He wrapped the remaining bulk of the rope over his shoulder, and then slowly loosened the tether as he approached the point where the snowdrift had disappeared.

He was able to walk right across the section he was certain he'd seen the snowdrift disappear into. The entire place was full of hardened snow. He marked the center of the search grid and then started to examine the area with ever increasing counter-clockwise sweeps. After twenty minutes he'd thoroughly examined the entire section.

Mioli stopped and stared at his topographical map and the search grid. Had he got his navigation wrong somehow? It seemed impossible to him, but then again, the entire area was covered in thick white snow so it would be easy to confuse individual landmarks. He loosened his tether all the way and then made another series of searches throughout the initial grid using his ice pick to feel for any loose snow.

Ten minutes later, he searched confirmed one of two things. He hadn't seen snowdrift disappear down a crevasse or, he was looking in the completely wrong place. Mioli's mouth was dry. He'd been breathing hard in anticipation of his discovery, and it was only now the adrenaline had worn off that he realized he hadn't consumed any water for hours. He took off his backpack and withdrew a small thermos. He opened the lid and eagerly drank some of the lukewarm water inside.

He stared at the landscape again. What had he missed? He was certain he was at least close to the right place. A few minutes later, he stood up. There was a light wind in the area, and it was bringing with it an additional chill factor, now that he'd stopped moving and allowed his body to cool. He glanced at the sun, which was dipping over the horizon. It would be dark in a few hours. He contemplated making a note on his handheld GPS and returning tomorrow. The thought irked him like a gambler whose weekly numbers finally came up, only to discover he hadn't got around to submitting them this week.

Mioli untied the end of his rope from the tethered pin in the snow. There was no point using it if he was in the wrong place. Instead, he would need to start again. This time he reached into his bag and withdrew a forty foot piece of string with small pieces of yarn attached on each side every few feet. Like tell-tales on a sailing yacht, which indicated the tiny changes in air pressure to either side of a sail canvass, Mioli's device could pick up any downdraft or sudden updraft.

He carefully unraveled the tell-tale while moving backward until its yarn finally caught a light draft and began to flap lightly in the wind. He began to unravel the string from its reel, like a person trying to fly a kite. It pulled capriciously to the left and then the right, constantly moving slightly to the north. Mioli watched, gently loosening the string to give the tell-tale more freedom to move. After about three minutes the wind died off and the string and yarn settled gently on the snow.

Mioli breathed heavily and waited for a moment. He wound it in slightly and stopped. The tell-tale perked up, as though suddenly drawn upward by some mysterious power, and it shifted about a foot into the air and then due east. The reel felt firm in Mioli's hand. He held it tight, fighting the pull and then, like he was fishing, he quickly released more yarn to allow the tell-tale the freedom to follow its new desire.

He grinned. *Was it going to be a shared desire?* The string went taut, and Mioli instantly placed his second hand on the reel to keep from losing it altogether. The little pieces of yarn flapped vigorously and he started to follow the tell-tale. Whatever had caught its attention was powerful, despite there only being a light breeze on the plateau. His heart raced. *Could this be what he was searching for?* He'd heard a story from a climber three weeks ago, who said that a strange downdraft hit him like a hammer, nearly knocking him off his feet in the process, as he reached the summit.

The tension slackened for a moment and he released pressure on the string. *Had he lost it?* The tell-tale fell to the ground and he swore. Mioli slowly curled the string around the wheel as he moved to where the end of the tell-tale had fallen into the snow.

Mioli bent down, about to pick the end of it up, when it yanked to the side. He gripped the reel with both hands again. The mysterious downdraft seemed to be teasing him. Intermittently pulling hard and then releasing its prey. Now the string felt taut and he struggled to hold on. A moment later, despite Mioli trying to stop it, the tell-tale pulled away and unraveled the rest of the spool, and then disappeared into a small hole in the snow.

This was it – an opening to the hidden world he was looking for...

His breath felt light with anticipation as he bent down to examine the tiny opening. He was breathing hard and his heart raced from the effort of fighting with the tell-tale as much as with excitement. The opening was too small for him to climb through, but it wouldn't take much to widen it and he was certain it was only the tip of a large lava tube. Nothing smaller would have such a powerful downdraft.

Mioli sat down and started the process of winding up the spool. The string was still taut, as though something or someone was pulling it downward. It made him smile how hard it fought. Then it became too hard to keep hold of.

He dug both feet in and his crampons gripped the snow. For a moment he thought it was going to hold. He should have reacted faster. Maybe if he had, there was a chance he would have made it. Instead, he heard the crack of ice breaking beneath him. A moment later the string tugged hard, and the ground beneath him gave way.

His mind was still in the process of registering what had happened to the solid ground below him when his back struck the first piece of solid ice. It was heavily sloped downward and his general momentum kept going, which reduced the impact. He let go of the string and fumbled to grab the icepick, while at the same time trying to position himself so he was no longer sliding headfirst.

His right hand finally latched onto the hilt of the icepick. He swung it into the ice, but without any force, and the blade didn't even begin to take grip. Mioli swung again and this time the pick dug heavily into the ice. The same instant he felt elation that his icepick had taken hold, his momentum ripped it clear from his hand and kept sliding.

Only he'd stopped sliding – because there was no longer ground beneath him.

Chapter Eighteen

Mioli must have fallen twenty to thirty feet. Maybe more. He didn't know. At some point his rope must have caught hold on something because he felt it go taut over his shoulder and break part of his fall, before a moment later, being ripped away from whatever it had taken perch on above. He continued falling and struck the ground a split second later.

His back struck first.

Then his head and pelvis, and his entire body filled with a pain so intense he didn't know where his injuries were because everything hurt equally. Next to him he heard the deep resonant thud of rope falling to the hard icy floor, followed by a clanging sound as his icepick fell less than a foot from his head. The fall took the wind out of his chest and he was certain he'd broken his lower back, and possibly even his legs.

But he was alive.

Mioli realized he was unintentionally holding his breath. He forced himself to take a couple shallow breaths. They hurt his ribs like hell, but he was able to breathe at least. He made a small fist with each hand. The fingers worked, and like the rest of his body they were sending his brain millions of tiny impulses registering pain. He wiggled his toes next. The sensation made him want to cry. He could still move his arms and legs. That meant there might just be hope that he would still survive.

He fumbled in the total darkness for his helmet light and switched it on without moving from where he fell. He was inside a large tunnel. The walls were jet black and glassy. He grinned despite the pain – because he'd found his lava tube.

Mioli turned his head to the left. On the wall were a series of old cave-paintings. One of them depicted a man wearing nothing but a loin-cloth riding a woolly mammoth. Next to that painting was one of a similarly drawn primitive man fighting off a beast. It took Mioli a moment to realize the creature was a sabertooth tiger. He racked his brain trying to recall what his teacher had said about the two creatures in his ancient history class as a kid. They were both extinct – that much he knew for sure – but when had they died out?

His eyes darted to the top of the large tunnel where he'd fallen. It was made of ice and was at least thirty feet above him. He glanced back at the cave paintings. Only there was something different about them... There were no handprints. They were unlike any other Neolithic drawings he'd ever seen in previous ancient caverns he'd explored. He looked at a third drawing. It was of a young woman's face. She had intense eyes and strong facial features. She wore something golden around her neck, like a pendant, but the lower part of it had been worn off over time. There was no doubt she would have been splendid in whatever time period she'd lived.

The thought about time jogged his memory. He was twelve years old, sitting in an ancient history class in Scuola Giapponese di Roma. His teacher was telling him about mythical beasts. Only they weren't mythical, they were merely extinct. The sabertooth tiger and woolly mammoths became extinct around ten thousand years ago.

The thought jarred at his concussed mind – *the images were at least ten thousand years old!* He turned his head to the right. He took a deep breath in and held it. No longer concerned with the pain he slowly sat without taking his eyes off the image painted on the wall. He felt okay. He still had pain. That's for sure, but somehow he could get past it. Somehow, he had to, didn't he? He slowly breathed out. It was going to be okay. He would be all right. He would work out a way to climb out. He knew it with certainty. Everything was going to be all right from here. It had to be. He needed to survive so that he could tell someone what he'd seen.

He'd have to. The world had a right to know, no matter what the consequences. There in front of him – on the jet black wall of obsidian, in a cavern not seen by humans since the age when the wooly mammoths and sabertooth tigers roamed the earth, was a rendering of a human being. A perfect depiction of Jesus Christ nailed to the crucifix.

Chapter Nineteen

The Gulfstream G650 flew smoothly in a westerly direction at a comfortable 48,000 feet and well above the raging storm below. It flew toward Malta where the *Maria Helena* was having minor repairs and maintenance completed while her crew was taking vacation leave. Sam sat at his desk flicking through the digital photographs taken from the hidden chamber inside Derinkuyu. Opposite him, Tom searched the internet for any evidence of a pyramid ever being found anywhere near the Namibian desert.

Sam looked up from his screen. "You having any luck locating that pyramid?"

Tom closed his laptop. "If it did exist, any record of it has long since been destroyed. There's nothing on the internet."

"What about the *Emerald Star*?"

"There's been a few hits, but nothing that matches that time period."

"So we're at a dead end?"

"Yeah," Tom said.

Sam picked up the phone at the end of the table and dialed a number from memory. The phone rang four times before being picked up by its owner.

"You're getting slower, Elise," Sam said. "I remember a time when you used to pick up before it reached its second ring."

"Is that so?" she asked. "And I remember a time when you didn't interrupt me when I was on vacation."

Sam smiled. In the past three years since he'd hired her for her inhuman ability to solve complex puzzles and hack any computer on the planet, he hadn't recalled Elise ever taking a proper vacation. "That's right, you said you were going away while the *Maria Helena* had her maintenance. Where are you?"

"Laying on a sunny beach in a town whose name most people can't pronounce, and where few people will ever go looking to find me."

"Not anymore," Sam said. "I need you to get back to civilization and use that incredible mind of yours to locate something for me."

"What?"

"Two things, actually."

"Go on," she said.

"A pyramid in Namibia and a ship last seen in 1655 bearing the name, *Emerald Star*."

"Sure." Her voice betrayed her usual surprise by what Sam wanted from her, as though for all her knowledge and skills, he basically wanted her to use Google for him. "You want a pyramid that didn't exist and a pirate ship?"

"Yeah, something like that." Sam flicked over to the third photo of the pyramid on his computer. It was real, he was certain of it. "How long will it take you to get off the beach and find me some answers?"

"Oh, I'm not planning on leaving the beach today. I'm on vacation, remember?" Her voice was teasing.

"Elise, this is important. It's about Billie."

"Relax, I'm already looking it up for you."

"You take your laptop to the beach?" Sam asked.

"What can I say? I'm still a nerd even if I'm on vacation. And with the free satellite connection the company so generously provides, why shouldn't I?"

Sam smiled as he listened to the sharp staccato of fingers tapping on a keyboard. He waited on the line for her to tell him how long it would take to find something.

He didn't have to wait long, before she spoke. "Okay, I'm running two searches through a series of databases, ranging from African and Portuguese newspapers through to maritime and archeology reports. It might take a few minutes, but it's looking like there's nothing about a pyramid ever being found there."

"What about the ship, the *Emerald Star*?" Sam asked.

"Okay, there were eight separate ships built between 1600 and 1700 bearing that name. Can you give me anything else to make it more specific?"

"No. What have you got?"

"Three were built after 1655 and two were sunk before 1655," she said.

"And the other three?" Sam persisted.

"There's a Spanish merchant vessel, which sank on the way to South America in 1656, a Portuguese Frigate that sank at Trafalgar, and a Portuguese barquentine that was stolen by pirates in 1646 – after which, it caused a world of havoc for merchant vessels traveling through the Gibraltar Strait. Apparently it was one of the most successful pirate ships during that era."

"What happened to it?"

"No one knows. In 1654 it fired two shots at a Portuguese Frigate, before evidently realizing it couldn't win, and turned to run. It was never seen again."

"That's our ship," Sam said. "Where was it last seen?"

"Causing trouble along the north-west coast of Africa."

"That's it?" Sam said. "You can't get any closer port or anything? What about where she was sailing to?"

"Sorry, Sam – that's all I've got."

Sam felt the Gulfstream ease off its thrust, as it commenced descent into Malta still thirty miles away. "What about the pyramid?"

There was a pause on the line – maybe just enough to take a couple breaths. "All right, I think I've got something for you."

"What?" Sam asked, feeling hopeful.

"I don't know if you're going to like it. There was never any proof, but the story will definitely grab your attention."

"Go on!"

"A man named Peter Smyth, three years ago went searching for a pyramid his great ancestor once wrote about. He claimed he'd found a journal stored by his late father and written by a guy named Thomas Hammersmith. In the journal Hammersmith described a journey into an African desert that reached all the way to the Atlantic. The purpose of which was to steal a rare golden artifact from an ancient pyramid. He goes on to say the strange relic was a curse that led to the deaths of the rest of their crew."

"How did he survive?"

"Hammersmith wrote that he was saved by the generosity of an Angel with dark purple eyes who came cloaked in white robes, claiming to be Death, and told him to spread the word – Death was going to save the world."

Sam said, "I can't imagine why you thought I'd be concerned about the authenticity of this guy's story. What did the archeologist say about it?"

"Of course, he never found a pyramid, and the conservatorium of archeology generally placed the story as fiction with no credible basis to go off."

"But you think he might have been on to something?" Sam asked.

"Well, there's an interesting note at the end of the article. Apparently Hammersmith was part of a crew who had come there specifically to steal a priceless artifact. After doing so, they were chased like wild animals by the rightful owners who numbered in the hundreds, all the way back to their ship. Care to guess the name of his ship?" she asked, with a hint of a tease.

Sam grinned. "The *Emerald Star*!"

"Quite a coincidence for a completely made up story, isn't it?"

"What happened to the ship?"

"He doesn't know. But what he does know is that a sand storm raged that night, worse than he'd ever seen, and in the process, the entire landscape had changed forever – and he often wondered if the ship still lay buried in the sand."

Sam took a deep breath in and held it for a moment. "Elise. Tell me you have Peter Smyth's contact details!"

"No. He went on another journey early last year in search of the pyramid and hasn't been seen since."

"Can you find him?"

"Only if he's left a digital footprint, somewhere. If he walked into the desert and never came back I won't find anything. He's definitely not on social media or anywhere else on the internet as far as I can tell. There's a note somewhere here about him being considered a paranoid conspiracy theorist. Apparently he became concerned that the same people who went after his great descendant were now after him because of what he knew."

"What about facial recognition?"

"What about it?" Elise asked, and he could imagine her grinning at his naiveté.

Sam persisted. "I thought you said there's software out there that can locate any person on the planet based on their face."

"Sure. But the person would need to have the image of their face recorded somewhere for me to locate it. For example, if he went into a bank or a public library I could find it on their database."

"So can you do it?"

"Not if he's as paranoid as he appears to be. A man like that would know to disappear into the woods, away from any digital preying eyes."

"What about satellite images?"

She laughed. "I appreciate the vote of confidence, but now you're talking about the realms of science fiction or poorly described techno thrillers. I'll keep searching to see if I can find him on any photo taken in the past year. But it's going to be a miracle if I find something."

"Okay. See what you can do. I've seen you perform miracles before."

"Okay. Anything else?"

"Yeah. I need you to tell me the name of the closest airport to the Namibian desert."

A moment later, he hung up the phone.

Tom asked, "What did she say?"

"We're off to Windhoek Hosea Kutako International Airport."

"Why?"

"To find a lost pirate ship and a pyramid that doesn't exist."

Chapter Twenty – Namibia

Sam stepped out of the Gulfstream G650 and onto the tarmac at Windhoek Hosea Kutako International Airport. He took a deep breath and was surprised by the sudden change in temperature. Having crossed over from the northern summer to the southern winter, the temperature dropped to 34 degrees Fahrenheit. He gritted his teeth at the perversity of recent severe weather changes. If people didn't know by now that the health of the world was a global issue, they were never going to get it. While Turkey suffered its hottest summer on record, Namibia was struggling through its coldest winter. He was greeted by two men – one an official Customs Officer and the other an aircraft dealer.

"Good morning," Sam said, handing his and Tom's passport to the official.

"Welcome to Namibia." The Customs Officer stamped both passports without looking at them and handed the books back. He smiled obsequiously, as though he were used to dealing with wealthy businessmen who landed at the airport in private jets. "If there is anything I can do for you while you're here just let me know and I will arrange it for you. I have left my private cell number and will most certainly be able to find any service that you are after."

"Thank you, Romashall," Sam said, glancing at the man's name tag. He turned to the second man. "You must be Bjorn?"

"Pleased to meet you, Mr. Reilly," Bjorn offered his hand.

Sam took it and then motioned toward Tom. "This is a good friend of mine, Tom Bower."

"Pleased to meet you," Bjorn said.

Sam glanced around the tarmac where several small private aircraft were stored outside. "What did you find us?"

"I've got a Cessna 172 Turbo Skyhawk!" Bjorn whistled through crooked teeth and a single gold tooth, as though he'd done them a monumental favor. "There's less than three hundred hours on the clock, too. It was only recently purchased to use as a charter to ferry the various geologists and other professionals employed for oil exploration currently."

"There's a lot of that going on?" Sam asked.

"Oh yes, very much. Business has never been so good for me. They say that Namibia is the El Dorado of oil reserves. Lot of money coming into the country."

While Sam expected many Namibians still eagerly anticipate an oil discovery, he figured others were more circumspect. Oil discoveries, particularly in developing countries, have not always yielded positive results for the people. In many instances, the majority actually end up losing out, while the minority became exorbitantly wealthy. Moreover, competition for control of resources has been known to lead to bloody and pervasive conflicts in many developing nations.

"And I bet it's the people of Namibia who are the recipients of this new wealth?" Sam said without restraining his cynicism.

Bjorn ignored the comment. "People need my planes to fly the short distances to where there are no permanent airfields. The Cessna is fully booked after the end of the month, but you can have it until then if you like?"

The end of the month was still two weeks away. Sam hoped he'd have some answers by then. "It should do."

"Great. I'll take you over there now and run you through a few things. Do you have any other luggage?"

"No. We travel pretty light. We'll buy anything we need while we're here," Sam said.

"Good. Is there anything else I can help you with?"

Sam said, "You spend a lot of time flying around the Skeleton Coast and Namib Desert?"

Bjorn nodded. "That's how I've spent the last thirty years of my life."

"So you know the landscape pretty well?"

"Of course. What would you like to know?"

Sam grinned. "Have you ever seen a pyramid?"

Chapter Twenty-One

The Skyhawk was covered in sand. It was painted light blue which poorly disguised the dirt and sand which had lightly coated her aluminum frame. Tom walked around the aircraft from wingtip to wingtip, looking for any significant faults or damages. He manually moved the articulated joints of the ailerons, rudder, and elevator. They moved freely and Tom smiled. He could see that despite only two hundred and ninety hours on her clock, she had already had some rough treatment ferrying clients into the desert. Not that it mattered, he knew that Cessna built robust aircraft to take abuse and last. There were still a number of Cessna 152s from the early 1950s still in service today – a massive testament of their reliability.

Tom clambered into the pilot seat. He pulled the latch at the side of his chair and slid it all the way to the back until his seat virtually touched the empty one behind. At six foot four, his knees bent awkwardly in the small single propped aircraft, but he was remarkably comfortable nonetheless. He carefully flicked through the Skyhawk's running sheet and spec sheet. He paused at the description of the engine. It was powered by a Continental Motors CD-135 turbo-charged 4-cylinder in-line diesel engine. He'd heard some companies were experimenting with using diesel instead of aviation fuel, but had never flown one.

Tom worked his way through the start-up check sheet, running the engine to maximum and then bringing it back to an idle. He ran the flaps through their range and then left them at zero degrees for take-off.

Outside, Sam paid the charter fee, shook Bjorn's hand and climbed into the co-pilot's seat. "What do you think?"

"About the aircraft?"

Sam nodded.

"It's good," Tom said. "She will serve our purpose handsomely no doubt. Did you know she's got a diesel engine?"

"Whose bright idea was it to put a diesel in single propped aircraft?"

"The additional torque makes it an estimated twenty-five percent more fuel efficient than her aviation fuel counterpart, bringing her range to just under a thousand miles to the tank. Besides, diesel's a lot easier to get a hold of around here than aviation fuel."

"Interesting," Sam said indifferently. He then placed a topographical map of the region in front of Tom and circled a small coastal city named, Swakopmund. "We need to fly here."

"What's there?"

"Not much. Bjorn tells me that if I want to know the truth about a rumor I'd heard about some abandoned pyramid that once existed in the Namib Desert, then I needed to speak to a man named Leo Dietrich."

"Who is he?" Tom asked.

"He's a registered Master Hunting Guide in Namibia and a drunkard, apparently," Sam said. "He offers private tours to big game hunters in search of trophy animals."

Tom nodded. "And Bjorn thinks he might have heard something in his travels?"

"It's better than that. He says Dietrich is a fifth generation hunter in the region. His family has lived there since Germany founded the city in 1892 as the main harbor of the German South West Africa. If anyone knows about an ancient pyramid that was still standing back in 1655, he would."

Chapter Twenty-Two

The little Skyhawk took off easily in the cold air. Tom reached a cruising altitude of 3000 feet and settled into a bearing due west and watched the arid and inhospitable land below go by. It took just over two hours to reach the Skeleton Coast – so aptly named because the combination of violent seas and the regular setting in of a thick fog, that it caused ships and whales to constantly become beached along its shores – where the Atlantic met the Namib Desert.

He watched as the massive sand dunes below rolled into the ocean, where they were met by the violent whitewash of the incoming waves. He banked nearly ninety degrees to his left and followed the coast south until he reached Swakopmund.

Tom landed and they caught a taxi to Dietrich's address. It was an old German colonial-style house. A dozen or more unopened newspapers lined the porch. Sam banged on the door. There was no response. They backed away from the front door to see if there was any way to see inside. A neighbor noticed them snooping round the side of the house.

"What do you two think you're doing?" She scolded. "You think it's any easy place to rob while he's away?"

"No ma'am," Sam and Tom replied in unison.

Tom looked at the woman. She was probably in her mid to late eighties and still commanded an air of German authority as she spoke. "You think he hasn't taken precautions while he's away? Well, he has. The rest of the street look after his house."

"I'm sorry," Sam said, turning his palms upwards in defense. "We're trying to find Leo Dietrich. Do you know when he'll be back?"

"You came here looking for Leo, did you?" she asked.

"Yes."

She laughed. "Then you'd better get comfortable because you'll be waiting a long time."

"Why?" Sam asked.

"Because he's gone to Ozondjahe for the hunting season."

"If we fly there now, how would we find him?" Sam asked.

She paused for a moment, as though she was picturing the place in her mind. "There's a Public House at Tsumeb where he normally stays and drinks at night. Mention his name around and someone will be able to point him out to you when he comes in from the day's hunt."

"Thank you very much, ma'am," Tom said.

"You're welcome." As an afterthought, she asked, "What are you looking to hunt, anyway?"

"A pyramid in the Namib Desert everyone keeps telling us doesn't exist."

Chapter Twenty-Three

It was another four hours before the Skyhawk landed on the narrow outcrop of blacktop that lined the road to the south of Tsumeb, before taxiing to a stop out the front of a small road house. The town was situated to the southeast of the Etosha Game Park and to the west of the Kalahari Desert. It was known as the gateway to the north of Namibia. Once a thriving mining town providing some of the rarest precious and semiprecious gemstones in the world. The town now thrived on tourism – wealthy travelers searching for big game to hunt.

They stepped out of the aircraft and into the roadhouse. A man in his late fifties with a rotund belly and a ruddy face that gave Sam the impression he'd spent an equal portion of his time serving himself hard liquor as he did his customers, glanced at Sam and Tom.

Sam greeted the man and said, "We'll need forty gallons of diesel for the Cessna – any chance you've got a line long enough to reach her?"

The man turned his gaze to outside, where the Cessna was parked thirty feet away from the single diesel bowser. He nodded and spoke as though it were entirely normal to have light aircraft asking for fuel. "I'll send a boy there to fill her up, right away."

Sam watched as a tall boy in his early teens came over with a small ladder and fuel hose. Tom opened the fuel cap and he started to fill the tank from the inlet at the top of the wing. When the young man finished putting 40 gallons into the tank, Sam thanked and paid him before walking back into the road house.

He and Tom ordered lunch and sat down at the edge of the road house – steak and chips with no choice of salad or vegetables. The steak came from wild springbok and had that distinct taste of game meat about it, but it was good. The beer was some sort of local brew that was drinkable, but he wouldn't go out of his way to have it again.

The owner came over shortly and asked, "What brings you out this way?"

"I'm looking for someone," Sam answered. "Perhaps you might know where I could find him. He comes out here for the hunting season to offer private tours for people searching for trophy game."

The man shrugged. "We're right next to a game park. I see a lot of people passing through offering hunters from all over the world their wildest dreams. Who are you looking for?"

"Leo Dietrich."

The publican laughed. "I'm sorry to say it, but you won't find him for the rest of the season."

"Why's that?" Sam asked. "I thought he comes out here for the entire season?"

"He does. Or normally does, anyway. But this year's different. He hasn't been taking anyone game hunting this year."

"Why?"

"Dietrich left here yesterday." The man poured himself another beer straight from the tap. "Do you want another one?"

Sam and Tom both declined.

The publican went on. "He said he was working for some rich man as a guide into the Kalahari Desert. He didn't say what they were looking for though. It wasn't game. That much I can tell you, because little exists in the Kalahari Desert."

"Do you know who his client was?" Sam asked, hopeful.

"Not a clue. I didn't ask and it wasn't like him to tell me things like that." The publican shook his head. "I'll tell you one thing though… his client was a strange man. Not very talkative. Not interested in a drink. And he had the most strikingly intense eyes I've ever seen. They were a deep red, possibly even purple – and his skin was white like an albino. Sorry I couldn't be more help to you."

Sam said, "Don't worry about it. Say, do you have time for one more question?"

The publican downed the rest of his glass of beer. "Sure."

"It might sound crazy, but in all your time out here, have you ever heard anyone mention a pyramid – like the ones built by the Egyptians – being found in the Namib or Kalahari Desert?"

"I've never heard of a pyramid around here. You'd need to head much further north to find any sign of Egyptian engineering…" the guy laughed. "It's funny you asked though."

"Why?"

"We primarily cater to tourists who want to see the Skeleton Coast or hunt big game and stuff like that, you know…"

"And?"

"Just last week, we had a French man here. Another strange man. He had no interest in the hunting or visiting the game park, or even seeing the Skeleton Coast – instead he'd made the journey entirely to do some local cave diving. Do you want to know what he told me he found?"

"What?"

"Drawings of a pyramid. He took a photo of them, actually. He said maybe I should put them on the website and start offering tours. Maybe get some unlucky tourist's fancy."

"Do you still have the photos?"

The man walked out the back of the bar for a few minutes and returned with a couple printed photographs. He handed them to Sam and Tom to look at. The quality was poor and the lighting was terrible. But then again, he said they were taken by a diver in a cave.

Sam stared at the photographs. Two of them were of a single pyramid surrounded by sand, as though the desert was about to swallow it whole. The third photograph depicted some sort of dark shape. The pyramid looked Egyptian, but there was something strange about it – something creepy or sinister about the way it surrounded the people in the drawing, almost like a snake stalking its prey, who were little more than stick figures. It weaved and crept through their legs as though it were alive.

He turned over the fourth picture. It depicted a three-mast ship covered with sand. He handed the picture back to the Publican. "Any idea what ship this is?"

The man shrugged. "It could be any of the four thousand or more unfortunate vessels that have found themselves caught between the Atlantic and the giant sand dunes of the Namib Desert."

Sam glanced at the pyramid. It could have been any ancient pyramid built by the Egyptians. He turned his focus back to the image of the strange smoke creature. "Any idea what this is?"

The manager looked at it. "Looks like smoke to me. Why?"

"I don't know. It seems strange this would be here. Whoever drew these images placed a lot of emphases on the smoke. I thought maybe it meant something particular to the region?"

"Like what?"

"Something religiously symbolic, perhaps?" Sam suggested. "A local fear or aversion to fire?"

The manager shrugged. "It could have. The original inhabitants of the region were often superstitious. They believed a whole range of things about different spiritual things. Maybe whoever drew this one believed the smoke was related to their ancestors or something. Who knows? I sure as hell don't."

Sam flicked over the back of the photo. In simple handwriting, written in pencil, were the words – *Found painted on a rock at the bottom of the lake. Depth 410 feet.* At the bottom of the photo was the date of discovery, which was five days ago.

"You said that Dietrich took a private hunter out on tour into the Kalahari Desert, didn't you?"

"Sure. But he wasn't a hunter, that's for sure. He was looking for something, but I can tell you now he wasn't looking for game. Why do you ask?"

"I wonder if there was any way Dietrich's client knew about these photographs?"

"It's possible, I put them up on our website just for fun three days ago – but I doubt it. If he was interested in the photographs he didn't ask about them, or anything about a pyramid if that's what you're thinking."

"No. That's all right. It was just a thought. You don't think there's an ancient pyramid buried out there in the Kalahari Desert, do you?"

Now the man laughed properly. "No. That I can tell you confidently would be impossible. I mean, think about it, for all the journeys that have taken place throughout that harsh and unreasonable environment, no one has ever mentioned finding a pyramid."

"I suppose you're right." Sam handed the photographs back to the publican. "I don't suppose you know the cave in which these photos were taken?"

"Of course I do. The same place they all come here to dive!"

"A lot of people come to the Namibian desert to dive?" Sam asked, surprised.

"Yeah, it's not our largest tourism drawing card, but it's up there. We even have a few SCUBA diving schools in town that focus on advanced cave diving courses."

"You don't say?" Sam nodded. "And what exactly do they all come here to dive?"

The publican grinned. "That would be the Dragon's Breath Cave."

Chapter Twenty-Four – Dragon's Breath Cave

The Kalahari Desert is one of the driest places on the planet. The wettest areas received a measly average of 20 inches of rain a year, while the driest enjoyed less than 4 inches. But Africa's Kalahari Desert used to be a much wetter place. Around 10,000 years ago, Lake Makgadikgadi covered most of the region before it went dry, leaving behind the massive sand dunes we see today. The region's unique dryness belies that beneath the Kalahari is home to Dragon's Breath Cave, the largest underground non-subglacial lake in the world.

One would expect that such a lake would have been possible through distant rainfalls and ancient rivers that seeped through the sands. But such speculation was wrong. Geologists believe the entire region once housed a prehistoric inland sea. As the sea dried up all life that populated the region died off, eventually forming a bed of dolomite. Throughout the millions of years since, the water would eventually seep through the dolomite, which in turn would act as a roof for the underground cave. The surface water would eventually dissipate due to the change in temperature over the aeons, leaving the underground waters undisturbed for millions of years.

Sam hired equipment and a guide from the local technical and cave diving school to help him and Tom locate the old cave drawings. The guide drove the old Land Rover Defender – one of three in the large dive party who were heading out today – south via the C42 highway into the Otjozondjupa Region, before turning east onto the private property of the Hariseb farm. After 45 minutes the small convoy pulled off the blacktop and onto the dirt road of the Hariseb farm.

The Defender entered a shallow valley and followed the narrow pock-marked trail made of a mixture of loose soil and sand that ran through the middle of a shallow valley. Sharp rocks edged the trail and small scrub lined the valley wall. The Defender fought its way through the rough terrain until a sheer wall of jagged rocks made navigation by vehicle impossible.

Their guide, Malcom, pulled up the Defender to a stop. "We're here, gentlemen."

Sam stepped out of the Defender. His feet dug into the soil, which was a burnt red and ran all the way out to the horizon. The empty sky was a rich cerulean blue. The crisp air was starting to warm up. He glanced at the landscape. Jagged rocks lined the valley wall, along with small scrub and a series of sharp uninviting cacti. There was no sign of any caves, let alone the entrance to the world's largest known subterranean lake.

He looked at the guide who was opening the back door of the four-wheel drive. "How far is the entrance from here?"

"Not far." The guide pointed to the west. "About a five minute walk toward that ridge."

"Great," Sam said.

"Before you get too excited," Malcom said, smiling as though he was taking pleasure in relating the next piece of information, "just remember, the dive party will need to move nearly half a ton of equipment by hand to the entrance."

Sam and Tom nodded in unison. "Nice day for it."

It took the remainder of the day to move the small mountain of equipment that would need to be carried by hand into the cave before any diving could take place. A large array of diving tanks went first, including separate tanks of helium and oxygen. An air compressor followed next. They established a surface to lake phone line to maintain communications. They moved three large inflatable rafts that would serve as the dive platform on the surface of the lake followed by two inflatable boats. Guides checked over existing rigging of ropes and wire caving ladders in preparation for tomorrow's expedition into the strange world.

By eight a.m. the next day Sam stared at the entrance. Barely more than a black hole in the middle of a few jagged gray rocks of dolomite, it would have been innocuous enough that he would have easily walked past it without giving it a second thought. But he would have been wrong. It was called the Dragon's Breath Cave because the hot, humid air that intermittently arose from it gave the impression that it was being exhaled by a dragon. But today, Sam saw no such humid air being exhaled. All he saw was a small hole, just large enough for a fully grown man to squeeze through. But he knew that appearances could be deceptive.

Sam entered the mouth of the cave.

He wore a pair of climbing overalls, harness, and helmet with light. He descended a wire caving ladder approximately twenty feet into the first passage. It was a narrow hallway, where a rocky slope ran in a gradual downward slope for approximately sixteen feet. Bats lined the ceiling above. Sam slowly made his way downward until he was forced to stop at a narrow collection of rocks that obstructed his passage, known in spelunking as a choke. He scrambled over the aptly termed choke by placing most of his weight on his hands and chest as he slid over the lip of the boulder, through the confined space that squeezed him with the stone above. He pulled himself through to the other side, where a fixed ladder descended another twenty feet onto a small ledge.

Sam studied the narrow crevasse into complete darkness below. It was small enough that he wondered how Tom would squeeze through. Their guide had spoken about the choke during their pre-caving and diving briefing. Malcom had identified the spot on the map and assured Tom that he would fit, but it would be a narrow squeeze. Now that Sam stared at the place, he wasn't quite as confident. The only positive fact was that they would descend feet first, so if it became narrow for Tom, he could always climb out again.

He attached his figure eight descender to a fixed rope and descended vertically thirty-eight feet onto another ledge with a large pocket in the back, affectionately called *The Closet* by the guides who used it as a final gear staging area. The narrow passage and pocket were already crammed with climbing gear.

A guide from one of the other dive teams prepared an additional set of climbing equipment up on the ledge. The guide glanced at Sam as he descended. "How are you travelling, Mr. Reilly?"

"Good. Much further?"

The guide pointed along the edge. "Not much. You're about half-way there. Malcom is down on the raft, getting your dive equipment set up."

Sam nodded. "Thanks. See you down there."

He disconnected from the first rope and attached himself to a new rope. With his descender firmly in place, he made the forty-eight foot abseil down a steep slope onto a bridge between two walls. Without changing ropes, Sam kicked off the final ledge, and abseiled into the free space one hundred and twenty-five feet onto the inflatable rafts on the water.

Four massive floodlights lit up the cavern that protected the nearly two hectares of subterranean lake, while a single submarine light glowed from fifty feet below the water's surface. Sam glanced around the ancient world. Stalactites lined the roof like some sort of a fairy grotto, while stalagmites and fallen stalactites littered the beach to the east. The shallow water near the beach was a bright cobalt blue, while the deeper water toward the west of the lake was a rich ultramarine.

Chapter Twenty-Five

Sam watched as Tom abseiled down the final drop of the hole in the ceiling. He had apparently made it through the choke. The inflatable raft shook under his 260 pounds of muscle. He smiled through a state of hardened concentration as he landed. It was good to see him more like his usual self. They still had no idea where Billie had been taken prisoner, but at least now they were able to focus on something that might lead to her.

Sam said, "You made it."

"Of course I made it." Tom's face softened into a smile. "Did you really think I'd get stuck in the narrow slot?"

"I did have some doubts," Sam admitted.

Sam and Tom quickly changed into their dry suits. Lying on the raft next to them in a series of makeshift holding containers, were twelve steel dive tanks. Most were filled with Trimix, a unique combination of oxygen, helium and nitrogen designed to allow a diver to reach extraordinary depths. Two were white with black on top – 100 percent oxygen – if something went wrong and either of them suffered from any sort of Acute Decompression Sickness they would be too far from any hyperbaric chamber. Instead they would have to take the 100 percent oxygen and then perform in-water recompression in the lake.

The problem with SCUBA diving at great depths was that the additional pressure the further down you went turned otherwise harmless gasses lethal. Below a hundred feet, the increased partial pressure of nitrogen in the blood leads to a syndrome called nitrogen narcosis, where the person experiences symptoms similar to drunkenness and eventually loss of consciousness. Below two hundred feet, oxygen toxicity occurs, leading to seizures and death. The solution was Trimix, a unique combination of oxygen, helium and nitrogen. The current world record was held by a diver who reached a depth below 1000 feet using Trimix.

Malcom glanced at the number of tanks. Sam and Tom would each wear two on their back and one in front of them. The remaining tanks would be positioned at prearranged decompression stops. Even so, the risk was enormous. "You still want to dive to the bottom?"

Sam attached his first regulator. "We don't have a choice. If there are drawings of a hidden pyramid down there, we need to see them."

"You realize it might just be a hoax?"

Sam nodded. "Even so, we need to find out for ourselves."

"It's a long way down." Malcom leaned over the edge of the raft to look into the ultramarine blue of the unmapped lake that emphasized its extreme depth. "Apart from the person who left that photograph at the Tsumeb road house, no one's ever reached the bottom of this lake. They did do a deep dive here last week, but there's no way to prove whether or not they reached the bottom, or even if its 410 feet."

Tom slipped into his buoyancy control device. "We'll let you know when we reach it."

Malcom grinned at his temerity. "There's something you haven't thought about if you think that photo of hand drawings of a pyramid in the desert is at the bottom of this lake."

"What's that?" Sam asked.

Malcom smiled sympathetically, as though what he was about to reveal would crush their dreams. "How did they get there?"

Sam paused. "That's a good question. The drawings, if they were true, depicted a ship from 1655. How often does this lake change its depth?"

"Since its discovery," Malcom said, "the water level hasn't changed a foot."

Chapter Twenty-Six

Sam lowered the additional dive tanks to the staged decompression stops. He and Tom completed a final check on each other's SCUBA equipment and stepped into lake. He sank to roughly five feet and checked his dive computer and equipment. Everything was working fine.

"How are you looking, Tom?"

"Good. Let's go find that picture."

Sam swallowed to allow his ears to equalize as he descended. He and Tom dropped quickly, maintaining visual contact with each other throughout the process. The light from above served them adequately until they reached sixty feet. Sam switched on his dive flashlight and pointed it below. A large golden cave catfish glanced at them from blind eyes and swam past.

"I wonder if it tastes any good?" Tom asked.

"Don't even think about it. That fish is unique to this cave only, and its numbers are estimated at less than a hundred and fifty."

"Sure. But do you think it tastes any good?"

Sam ignored him. Instead he concentrated on his depth gauge. With no rain or other runoff affecting the lake, the visibility was unbelievably good, making it difficult to judge their descent. The lake started shallow at the beach on the eastern end of the cavern and headed deeper to the west. The tunnel narrowed the further west it went; the subsequent result being that while the lake's surface measured at nearly two hectares, the bottom was no more than fifty feet at its widest point. It took Sam and Tom just under ten minutes to reach the cave's bottom.

"I guess the bottom's not so mythical after all," Tom said.

Sam glanced at his depth gauge. It read 405 feet. "It looks like whoever took that photo either was a really good guesser, or they actually were the first to ever reach the lake's floor."

"Yeah, and if that's true, then hopefully they were telling the truth about the pyramid, too."

"Let's go find out."

They swam to the closest wall of dolomite. The bottom of the inland abyss wasn't quite round. Instead it was more like an uneven oval. Sam shined his flashlight against the wall. There was relatively little silt built up on the wall. If there were any hand drawings on it, they would have seen them. He scratched his hands along the wall, removing the little silt, until it he was confident he would identify the same part of the wall when he reached it again.

Sam then started moving in a clockwise direction, constantly keeping his flashlight pointed at the wall along the way. Directly behind him, Tom made a second sweep of the same spot. They moved quickly. The deeper you go, the greater the pressure exerted on all gasses, which means the Trimix becomes compressed. At a depth of 410 feet, they were diving at twelve atmospheres, which meant they were using their gas twelve times faster than they would if they were on the surface and their bottom time wouldn't be very long at all.

It took less than five minutes to make a complete circuit of the bottom of the lake and return to the initial spot where Sam had made his mark.

Tom looked at him. "Where's the damned hand drawings?"

Sam shook his head. "I have no idea."

"Did we miss something?"

"Like what?"

"Maybe it goes deep at center."

"I don't think so," Sam said. "But we may as well have a look before we start our ascent."

They swam toward the middle of the oval-shaped bottom of the lake. The lake definitely didn't descend any further. Sam was about to suggest they start making their long ascent to the surface, when he spotted the boulder. It was probably originally at least eight or more feet tall, but a lot of it had sunk into the surrounding floor of the lake.

"I just had an idea," Sam said. "What if that boulder was once well above the lake inside the main cave in 1655?"

"Of course!" Tom kicked his fins and swam toward the boulder. "They documented their loss on the stone. Sometime since then, the dolomite weakened and the rock fell into the lake, hiding with it any evidence of a pyramid in the region."

Sam shined his light on the boulder. There was nothing. He swam to the opposite side and there in front of him was a hand drawn picture of a pyramid. Next to it, was a ship with three masts fighting a losing battle with a terrible storm. Wisps of dark smoke ran through the legs of the stick figures who stared up at the pyramid. In between the two pictures was a note written in modern English with some sort of red ink. Sam stared at the message.

Don't let the Third Temple rise!

"What the hell does that mean?" Tom asked.

"I have no idea. It looks like whoever took that first picture was sending us a message."

"Or someone else."

"The question is, who?" Sam took several digital photos of the pictures on the rock.

"Famine?"

"Maybe. But I don't see why someone would be trying to leave him a message. Besides, he didn't look fit enough to make it here." Sam put his camera away. "One thing's for certain, there was a pyramid in Namibia at some time and I'm pretty confident that's the *Emerald Star* being sunk off the Namibian coast."

"Not sunk," Tom said. "Judging by this image, it was swallowed by the sand."

Chapter Twenty-Seven

It took more than four hours to reach the surface by the time they had completed the necessary decompression stops along the way. Sam thought about the *Emerald Star* for a moment. The discovery was irrefutable evidence the ship had been lost along the shallow waters of the Namibian Coast. If that was true, it was also likely the second part of the note found in the hidden chamber below Derinkuyu was as well – inside the ship was the key to the Third Temple, and their only chance of finding Billie. He also equally knew that it would likely be impossible to find her after all these years.

At Malcom's insistence, they completed a mandatory three hour sit time on the raft before making their way to the surface. It then took nearly an hour to make the slow climb to the surface. One of the guides had a hot dinner waiting for them.

Tom studied the photos taken on the digital camera. His eyes leveled at the ship and then glanced at Sam. "You're certain that's the *Emerald Star*?"

"Yes."

"So why don't we head to the Skeleton Coast and go find her?"

Sam shook his head. He knew the constantly changing coastline would make it impossible to locate. "We're better off trying to locate the pyramid instead, now that we know it was here."

"Why? We already know the *Emerald Star* was carrying the key to the Third Temple?"

"Because it's been lost for just over three hundred and sixty years."

Tom shrugged indifferently. "And you think, that's too long?"

"It is along the Namibian coast."

"Why?" Tom asked. "With the introduction of ground penetrating LIDAR, we can survey the area by air. It can't take too long. We've found ships buried in harder to find places."

"It won't work."

"Why not?"

"Because at last estimate, the Namibian government predicted approximately four thousand shipwrecks were buried beneath the sands of the Skeleton Coast. But the National Oceanic and Atmospheric Administration predict that number might actually be much higher."

"We've overcome worse odds before. Besides, we have nothing to go on with the pyramid – if that is even the same pyramid where Billie has been taken."

Sam said, "The problem is the Namibian and Angolan coast isn't static. With its massive sand dunes dropping directly into the cool waters of the Atlantic, the Skeleton Coast has no set lines. It's constantly changing shape and location. The prevailing southwest wind is cooled down by the cold Benguela Current to the extent that no cloud formation can take place, but instead a thick fog bank develops and penetrates miles deep into the Namib Desert. Every so often – maybe once every few decades – a powerful storm causes the winds to change direction. When this happens, a powerful eastern wind races across the desert and dumps millions of tons of sand into the Atlantic, moving the beach hundreds of feet further westward."

"The sands are reclaiming land from the sea?" Tom thought about it for a moment. "The image of the *Emerald Star* that we found inside the Dragon's Breath Cave shows the ship being swallowed by a sea of sand. There must have been a massive storm coming from the east."

"Yes."

"Then could we calculate backwards?"

"You mean, work out the known movement over a decade and then work backwards until we have the shape of the coast in 1655?"

Tom nodded. "Why not. It might work?"

Sam shook his head. "Unfortunately, while the eastern winds like to move the sand further west, the powerful and destructive force of the Atlantic Ocean often tried to reclaim its coast. The subsequent tug a war means there is no way of predicting where the coast was when the *Emerald Star* sank."

"What we need, is a survey of the coast."

Sam nodded. "Yes. But where are we going to find one taken on the year of the great storm?"

Tom paused. "There must be historical archives from the Portuguese expeditions into Southwest Africa? Surely they must have some sort of survey of the coast?"

"I'm sure they do, but how accurate could they be?"

Tom paused and then nodded in understanding. "John Harrison wouldn't have completed building his first Sea Clock until 1730 – which means that any reference to the Skeleton Coast prior to that would have been based on a known latitude and visual guess work, without any reference to longitude."

"Exactly, which means we're back to square one. Looking for the lost pyramid of the Kalahari Desert."

"Yeah, without any leads," Tom said. His voice was hard and despondent as he spoke. "We could try ground penetrating LIDAR swathes from the air... but the Kalahari Desert's a big place. We might just end up spending the rest of our lives searching before we found any evidence of the pyramid."

Sam's cell phone rang. He answered it, spoke briefly, and then hung up. A small glint of a smile creased his lips. "Change of plans. Forget the Kalahari for the moment. That was Elise on the phone. I need you to go to Istanbul instead."

Tom nodded. "Sure. What's in Istanbul?"

"Elise thinks she's tracked down Peter Smyth and he might have an idea where the *Mary Rose* sank in the Black Sea in 1653. The *Mary Rose* was the first expedition to the Third Temple, so theoretically, if we find her, we might find a link to where she was going."

"Great. When do we leave?"

"Not we. Just you. I've told Elise to recall the rest of the *Maria Helena* crew from their vacation and send them to the Black Sea to meet you."

"Okay, you're not coming, too?"

"No. I have somewhere else to be."

"Really?" Tom asked. "Where are you going?"

"Paris. I have to attend an auction."

"An auction? What are you looking to buy?"

Sam's jaw fixed into a hardened grin. "Finally, some answers."

Chapter Twenty-Eight –
Derinkuyu

Dmitri Vernon pulled up at the house in a rented black sedan. Out the front were several police officers making notes and talking animatedly on their cell-phones. It was late in the evening, and they all looked like they'd been there all day. A local news crew was filming from thirty feet away, just behind the cordoned off police lines. He took a deep breath and stepped out of the car. They were already making a circus out of his damned show.

He wore a tailor-fitted black suit with no brand name. He was six foot-two, but his perfectly proportioned physique gave him the appearance of a more modest stature. He wore dark impenetrable aviator sunglasses and the surly expression of a man accustomed to displeasure. He took little interest and no pleasure in his work today. It would be yet another false alarm. Not that it mattered. The timing was definitely getting closer. He had waited long enough and soon he would find what he was after. He ignored the local law enforcement officers, ducked under the police containment line, and entered the house.

A detective quickly approached. "Excuse me! Who are you and what are you doing here?"

Dmitri acknowledged the man. "Are you in charge here?"

"Yes. My name is Harun Ismet and this is my scene. Who are you?"

"My name's Dmitri." He handed his credentials to the detective. They gave his name as *Dmitri Vernon*. Below on the identification card were the words, *Interpol, Special Agent*. Under country of origin, were the letters, *U.S.A.*

The detective scrutinized the ID and then handed it back to him. "You're an American?"

"Yes. But I'm based at Interpol's headquarters in Lyon, France."

"Are you taking over my case?" the detective asked.

Dmitri shook his head and feigned a gracious smile. "No. I'm just here to have a look at something."

Contrary to popular perception, the international policing organization does not have its own prisons or carry out arrests. Instead it acts behind the scenes, collating masses of intelligence and coordinating police efforts internationally. Dmitri liked to think this added to its mystique. His work generally went unnoticed, eclipsed by the national police forces that make the arrests and headlines, while Interpol rarely receives more than a line or two in news reports. The organization is a ghostly presence, informing operations on the ground, but never getting its hands dirty.

A wry smile came over the detective's face. "What interest does Interpol have with this case?"

"Probably very little. But the MO triggered something on our database for a previous crime, so they sent me to have a look."

"You could have called. We could have faxed you our report."

"No. I needed to see the scene with my own eyes."

Ismet nodded. "Follow me through to the back of the house. He's on the bottom level."

Dmitri followed without speaking. The house, like many of the other ones in the region, had been dug into the side of the hill, where porous volcanic stone had been easy to tunnel.

"How did you get here so fast?" Ismet asked, as he climbed down the ladder. "We only got called to the property three hours ago."

Dmitri turned to climb backwards down the narrow ladder. "I just happened to be in the area."

"Really? I wasn't aware of any operations with Interpol currently being run in my jurisdiction?"

Dmitri forced himself to smile. "No. I was here entirely on vacation when they called and asked if I could check it out."

Ismet stared at him. He wore his opinion in his open face – the man didn't believe a word that Dmitri had said – clearly Dmitri was here for a purpose. Unable to find a reason to challenge him, Ismet ignored the statement. "All right. He's on the other side of this door, but it's not a very nice sight. Of course, you'd already know that."

"Do you know who he is? Or technically, who he was?"

"His name's Kahraman Sadik."

He didn't recognize the name. "Is he known to you?"

"Does he have any priors?" Ismet asked. "No. He's good citizen. At least on record anyway."

"What did he do?"

"He worked as a tour guide in the ancient city below for nearly twenty-five years."

Dmitri nodded and opened the door. The light switch had been left on and it shined directly on the deceased man's face. Dmitri took in the entire scene in a glance. The deceased was short. He had been stripped bare and his hands and feet had been nailed onto the wood of a small cross at the center of the room. His stomach appeared unnaturally large. A recent surgical incision was noted just above his naval which had been neatly sewn up. Next to the body was an antique set of brass weighing scales. Although the nails appeared painful, he had no doubt they weren't the cause of the man's death.

He glanced at the detective. "Do you have a cause of death?"

"No. Only the wounds you can see clearly and none of them is lethal." Ismet chuckled. It was the sort of thing only a seasoned detective could find amusing. "Of course, we don't know what was done to his insides before being stitched up."

Dmitri nodded and studied the deceased more carefully. A few minutes later he stopped at the man's mouth. There was something inside. He removed a pair of blue nitrile gloves from his pocked and placed them on his hands. "Do you know what that is?"

"No idea. I wasn't informed there was anything."

Dmitri carefully opened the man's mouth. "Do you mind if I have a look. See if it might answer some questions?"

"Sure," Ismet said, appearing happy to have someone else perform the task.

Dmitri studied the item more closely. It was leathery and had been stuffed deep inside the man's mouth to form a thick seal over his windpipe and esophagus. He slowly pulled at it until it came out. It was made of vellum, the old animal skin paper used for parchment writing.

A moment later – about the time it took him to take a single breath – the deceased man's mouth started to open on its own like some sort of evil incarnation of the dead coming back to life, as hundreds of tiny red locusts filled the room.

Dmitri ignored the insects as they scattered throughout the living room, but their symbolism was hardly refutable. Instead, he focused on the words written on the vellum scroll.

A quart of wheat for a day's wages, and three quarts of barley for a day's wages, and do not damage the oil and the wine.

Ismet glanced over his shoulder and said, "What the hell does that mean?"

Dmitri removed his aviator glasses, revealing deep purple eyes that fixed on the detective's rapt expression of horror. He swallowed hard. "It means there's a famine coming."

Chapter Twenty-Nine –

Dardanelles Strait, Turkey

At 9:30 a.m. the day was already shaping up to be pristine. There were no clouds and no wind at all. The tide was slack and the normally fast flowing entrance to the Dardanelles appeared calm with the dark blue of aquamarine. The *Maria Helena* motored up the Aegean Sea, through the Dardanelles – the narrow and natural strait that separates Europe and Asia Minor in what was once known in Classical Antiquity as Hellespont, or the Sea of Helle – and into the Sea of Marmara. Once there, the ship motored slowly to the other end where the city of Istanbul lay nestled on the edge of the Bosphorus Strait and entrance to the Black Sea. It was dark before the *Maria Helena* finally came to rest at her anchor, off the coast of Istanbul.

Tom Bower stared at the seemingly millions of lights which illuminated the shores of Istanbul. His eyes followed the ancient castles which spread out along the foreshore of the Bosphorus Strait, up to the ancient walls of Constantinople, erected in the 5th Century by the Emperor Theodosius II to protect the city from invasion, and standing strong even today. Massive domed buildings glowed golden in the lights. He was taken in by the city's rich architecture which came from a melting pot of Byzantine, Genoese, Ottoman, Roman, Greek and modern Turkish sources.

There was no doubt why the city was known worldwide as one of the greatest cultural and ethnic melting pots. Haggia Sophia, once the largest masonry dome in the world, and the Topkapı Palace – once the main headquarters of the Ottoman Sultans – stood proudly near the Bosphorus Strait, while the Sultan Ahmed Mosque, known as the Blue Mosque, rose grandly over the skyline.

Matthew, the skipper of the *Maria Helena* approached and interrupted his momentary thoughts. "Are you ready?"

"Yes," Tom said.

"Good. We've been given approval to cross the Bosphorus Strait at first light tomorrow morning. Make certain you're back here by then, will you?"

"Of course," Tom said.

Genevieve took Tom to the shore on a small Zodiac inflatable tender. Neither spoke during the short trip. She motored the Zodiac gently up to the shore. Tom shuffled his position so that he could climb out.

Genevieve stopped him with a firm and affectionate grip on his left hand. "Tom. Whatever happens, you know I want to get Billie back as much as you do?"

Tom nodded and smiled. There was more than a little relief in his heart, too. He'd been surreptitiously dating Genevieve for nearly six months now, but Billie had once been the woman he was going to marry. He'd been uncertain how Genevieve would take the news that Billie might be back in their lives soon.

He squeezed her hand affectionately and kissed her lips. "Thank you."

A moment later he climbed up onto the foreshore and began walking toward the Blue Mosque. The Sultan Ahmed Mosque had five main domes, six minarets, and eight secondary domes. From what he'd read before arriving, Tom knew the design was the culmination of over two centuries of Ottoman mosque development. It incorporated some Byzantine Christian elements of the neighboring Hagia Sophia with traditional Islamic architecture and was considered to be the last great mosque of the classical period. Its architect aimed for overwhelming size, majesty, and splendor.

At its lower levels and at every pier, the interior of the mosque was lined with more than 20,000 handmade Iznik style ceramic tiles in more than fifty different tulip designs. The tiles at lower levels are traditional in design, while at gallery level their design becomes flamboyant with representations of flowers, fruit and cypresses. The tiles were made under the supervision of the Iznik master. The price to be paid for each tile was fixed by the sultan's decree, while tile prices in general increased over time. As a result, the quality of the tiles used in the building decreased gradually.

The upper levels of the interior were dominated by blue paint. More than 200 stained glass windows with intricate designs admit natural light, today assisted by chandeliers. On the chandeliers, ostrich eggs are found that were meant to avoid cobwebs inside the mosque by repelling spiders. The decorations included verses from the Qur'an, many of them made by Seyyid Kasim Gubari, regarded as the greatest calligrapher of his time. The floors are covered with carpets, which are donated by the faithful and are regularly replaced as they wear out. The many vast translucent windows confer a spacious impression. The casements at floor level are decorated with opus sectile – stone mosaic scenes. Each exedra – curved seating nooks for the faithful – had five windows, some of which are blind. Each semi-dome has fourteen windows and the central dome twenty-eight. The colored glass for the windows was a gift of the Signoria of Venice to the sultan.

Tom removed his shoes and entered the building from the hippodrome in the west side. The Blue Mosque was open to the public twenty-four hours a day and constantly filled with tourists and people in worship, making it an easy place to meet Peter Smyth who had spent the last two years trying to blend in and disappear from those who hunted him. Tom stopped and waited at the southern end of the mosque, where three of the blue traditional tiles had been recently repaired, showing a slightly lighter color. He studied the motifs on the tiles which included cypress trees, tulips, roses, and fruits designed to evoke visions of a bountiful paradise. Of the three recently repaired, the tulips were of a different shade of red.

A man next to him spoke quietly. "They were unable to match the tulip's color with repair."

"They should have used purple," Tom said, repeating the phrase Elise had told him to say.

The man glanced furtively around the room, before quietly completing the secret words. "No. I think they should have used yellow."

Tom smiled. "Peter Smyth?"

"Not here."

"Where?"

"Just follow me."

Tom followed the man out of the mosque, leaving a small donation. The man in front of him was sweating profusely. Despite the warmth of the summer's night, he wore a thick jacket with its hood pulled partially over his face and his head turned downward. Peter's gait was awkward and furtive, looking over his shoulder as though someone was watching him, ready to take him at any minute.

It was more than twenty minutes before Peter turned a final corner, and entered a small stone building. It looked like not much more than a dilapidated hovel. Tom followed him inside. The place looked barely livable. It was dark, the only window covered with a black sheet.

Tom asked, "You've been hiding here?"

Peter Smyth placed his finger to his lips to shush him and mouthed the words – *They're listening to us.*

Tom stared at him silently. *Had he just followed an insane man into his depraved irrational world?* A moment later – the time it takes a person to take a single breath – Peter removed a stone tile from the floor below him. It was so narrow that Tom was surprised to watch the man slip down into it.

Peter then motioned for Tom to follow. Tom shuffled his way through the tiny opening into a room large enough that he could no longer feel the walls in the darkness. Peter replaced the stone tile above and the place became devoid of any light.

Tom felt like he'd just descended into an old tunnel used by the Viet Cong. He switched on a small key light, and stared at his new environment. The place opened to a large, almost modern looking living room. There were multiple computer monitors set up. On the other side of the room were a number of large oil paintings and charcoal drawings. His eyes rested on the last of them, where a large barquentine with three masts was sinking in violent seas, only it wasn't surrounded by water, it was surrounded by sand and at the very bottom of the painting was the date 22nd of December 1655. He opened his mouth to speak, but instead took a deep breath and smiled.

Peter grinned at his reaction. "Yes. That's the *Emerald Star.*"

Chapter Thirty

Tom glanced around the room. It was something between a high tech computer lab one would expect to find in the CIA and an ancient history museum. There were high speed internet cables attached to hard drives stacked on glass cabinets, with the constant flicker of green lights showing the constant movement of data. In direct contrast were the old oil paintings and charcoal drawings, which had obviously been studied intensely by their owner.

Tom looked at Peter. "What is this place?"

Peter said solemnly, "This is my sanctuary."

"From what?"

"The people who have been searching for the key to the Third Temple – and they will gladly kill me to further their aims."

Tom considered what he'd said. "What makes you so certain others are searching for the temple? Maybe no one knows about it?"

Peter shot back, "You are, aren't you?"

"Sure, but I'm not willing to kill for it. You look terrified. What do you know that I don't?"

"My great ancestor, a man by the name of Hammersmith, referred to a man with intensely purple eyes that had paid him and the rest of the crew from the *Emerald Star* to retrieve an artifact that was hidden in plain sight within a pyramid along the African west coast."

Tom nodded. Elise had briefed him on Peter's claim. "Go on."

"In the journal, Hammersmith noted there would be four men, competing for access to the key to the Third Temple. Their names were Conquest, War, Famine and Death."

Tom felt the slightest pang of fear rise in his throat like bile as he recalled what the man who attacked them inside the tunnel of Derinkuyu had said – *My name is Famine and my time is now.* "So they're four nutcases competing to find the key to the Third Temple?"

Peter nodded. "And right now, I think Death's winning."

"Winning what?" Tom would have laughed at how ridiculously implausible the entire story was, if it wasn't for his recent memories of Famine and his heavily armed group of devout followers. "This is some sort of Biblical competition?"

"No. It's not about religion."

"Really?" Tom was surprised. "Then why all the references to the Four Horsemen of the Apocalypse?"

"I don't know. I've been studying the New Testament of the Bible where the Four Horsemen of the Apocalypse are described in the Book of Revelation by St. John of Patmos, one of the original Apostles. The chapter tells of a book or scroll in God's right hand that is sealed with seven seals. The Lamb of God opens the first four of the seven seals, which summons four beings that ride out on white, red, black, and pale horses. The Christian apocalyptic vision is that the Four Horsemen are to set a Divine Apocalypse upon the world as harbingers of the Last Judgment, so that only the good shall rise… or the chosen few."

Tom said, "You think the Four Horsemen are trying to bring forth the Apocalypse so the Third Temple can rise?"

"Maybe." Peter paused as though he was having difficulty trying to decide how to explain his theory. "What if they're not trying to bring about the new order, what if we're looking at this all wrong?"

"Sure," Tom said. "But what way should we be looking at it?"

"Consider this… what if the Four Horsemen weren't sent to set a Divine Apocalypse – instead, they were merely messengers, sent here to protect those who could be saved, from an imminent disaster. Some sort of disaster first discovered during the first few centuries A.D. when Christianity was taking off in the western world, but wouldn't occur for nearly two thousand years."

"They would need a way of continuing the message throughout many generations, without revealing the secret to the masses."

"A covenant of some kind?"

"You think the Four Horsemen are part of an ancient covenant?"

"Yes and when the time comes they will reveal the Third Temple and the chosen few will take shelter."

"There's an imminent disaster awaiting that will affect the entire world?"

Peter nodded. "And that's why they need to find the Third Temple – to seek shelter."

Tom asked, "But what disaster affects the entire planet?"

"I can think of any number of catastrophic events. A massive meteorite, an enormous volcanic eruption, and giant tsunami, or a deadly virus that's evolving faster than we can create treatments. Our existence has always been globally precarious."

Tom looked at Peter's rapid breathing and the fine tremors of his hands. "You've given this some serious thought, haven't you?"

"It's occupied most of my mind over the past two years," Peter admitted.

Tom changed the direction of the topic. "All right. I know at least one of the Four Horsemen is still around – or maybe just a guy who fancies himself as one of them.

I was attacked by him in the subterranean city of Derinkuyu in Turkey. He said his name was Famine and that his time was now. Do you know of any others?"

"I was contacted by two of the Four Horsemen separately. One named Famine and the other Death. They both told me I would die if I didn't tell them where the *Emerald Star* sank."

"Did you ever meet either of them?"

"No. I learned what I could about both of them. I had no idea how much danger I was in at the time – but I know now."

"What changed?"

"I was out of town for two weeks and a friend of mine was squatting at my apartment. I told him I wasn't allowed to sublet the place out to anyone and that if the landlord came by for any reason, to simply tell him his name was Peter Smyth."

"Okay. So what happened?" Tom asked, not quite sure how this related to the Four Horsemen.

"Someone with deep purple eyes came by while I was gone. He asked my friend what his name was. Of course he gave my name, thinking the man was my landlord. The man then forced his entry into my apartment and repeatedly questioned my friend about the *Emerald Star.*"

"Which your friend knew nothing about?"

"Exactly."

"What happened in the end?"

"When it became obvious that my friend didn't know anything about the *Emerald Star* or an artifact called the Death Mask, the stranger with the purple eyes killed him with his bare hands."

"How did you find all this out?" Tom asked.

"I have a digital security system. It records the inside of my apartment constantly. I'm able to remotely access its logs from my smartphone. When I started to receive messages from my neighbors asking if I was okay, I logged onto my security account and watched the footage."

"What did you do?"

"The only thing I could. I withdrew my entire savings in cash, keeping the bulk of my life-savings stored in untraceable Bit Coins. Then I got on a train in London and traveled through to Paris, Munich, Vienna, Budapest, Bucharest and finally Istanbul – where I've been hiding ever since."

"Why Istanbul?"

"My great ancestor made a note about *Emerald Star* being the second expedition to steal the Death Mask. The first attempt failed in 1653 when the *Mary Rose*, carrying a stone map of the desert was sunk in a storm in the Black Sea. I have a map he drew of the two expeditions."

Peter handed it to him and Tom scanned the map, drawn on well-aged vellum. It formed a primitive outline of the African continent, Mediterranean Sea through to the Black Sea. An asterisk was observed in the middle of the Black Sea approximately forty miles out from Istanbul, if the drawings were to a correct scale. Next to this, was the name, *Mary Rose*, 1653 – First failed expedition. Tom studied it for a few minutes, making sure he read each word correctly.

Tom smiled. "You came here to find it, didn't you?"

"Yes."

"And what did you find?"

"It took nearly a year but I found the wreck. It's located about thirty miles north of Istanbul and was supposed to be carrying a stone map chartered the position of the ancient pyramid of the Namibian Desert."

"Did you find it?"

"No," Peter said. "I found the shipwreck, but it may as well have remained lost for all the good that it does me. The ship that was moving the stone across the Black Sea struggled with the weight of the stone in a storm, and floundered."

"Why didn't you recover the stone?"

"I headed over there. Hired a boat and some dive equipment. You see I couldn't go in with a big professional group of divers, because the treasure hunters would then all get involved."

Tom nodded. "Go on."

"In the end, the Mary Rose was too deep to reach."

"How deep does she rest?"

"Nearly three thousand feet. Impossible to reach using anything but commercial dive equipment."

"If I could reach it, would you be willing to give me the precise location?"

"Sure. Why, do you have some experience deep sea diving?"

"A little." Tom grinned. "There's a chance I might just have a way to reach it."

Chapter Thirty-One – Paris, France

It was a warm night in Paris and the Eiffel Tower glowed golden as local Parisians and tourists walked the airy and restaurant lined streets of one of the most romantic cities on earth. Few of those out tonight realized that, at the time of construction, Gustave Eiffel had built a secret apartment for himself at the very highest level of the tower at a height of 1,063 feet. Fewer still knew that tonight a very private arm of the Christies Auction House had managed to secure the apartment for just three hours in order to receive bids for one of the most startling auctions in their history.

Sam Reilly sat in the very narrow apartment, which was barely large enough to fit the four bidders and a single auctioneer. The item in question was being handled by a very private section of Christies Auction House, which specialized in extremely rare and esoteric artifacts. He doubted the validity of the claim, and had it not been for the reputation of Christies he wouldn't have been interested, but as it was, the item being sold tonight might just buy him the answers he'd been looking for in his search for Dr. Billie Swan.

Bidding was on an invitation-only basis. He glanced around the room. With the exception of the auctioneer, he recognized a man called John Wallace who worked for the Swiss Guard at the Vatican, but two other men he didn't recognize at all. They both wore dark suits and looked like professional antiquity buyers – people who purchased items on other people's behalf – and they were talking to each other animatedly. The auction was held in the strictest privacy and none of the bidder's names would be revealed. Not that it mattered to Sam. He didn't care less who was involved, so long as his bid won.

The auction was set as a first-price sealed-bid auction, known as blind auction. In this type of auction, all bidders simultaneously submit their sealed bids, so that no bidder knows the bid of any other participant. The highest bidder pays the price they submitted. In theory it was the most powerful way to drive up the price, particularly with something this valuable and important, where the bidders were willing to invest heavily to secure the item. In an open auction the winning bidder would theoretically still be willing to pay more than what he or she paid, whereas in this case, everyone will have placed their utmost highest price on the bid.

The auctioneer waited until he received radio confirmation that no one else was on the Eiffel Tower. Privacy was of the utmost concern in this matter for two reasons. First the bidders all intended to remain anonymous, so that no-one else would attempt to follow them to the location when it was time to collect the item. And secondly, the item on sale tonight was entirely illegal – so the auction house needed to distance itself from the transaction.

Having received the confirmation, the auctioneer began to describe the item including scientific data to support the claim's validity.

The man coughed. "My name is Raymond Howser. I'm here on behalf of the current owner of the item. As you are all aware the item on sale tonight is the location of what appears to be an ancient temple. Inside which are some very detailed drawings of people, most notably a very good depiction of the crucifixion of Jesus Christ."

Raymond coughed. "What makes this discovery even more valuable is that inside the mostly frozen cavern lies the remains of a wooly mammoth, an animal known to become extinct in the region more than ten thousand years ago. Radiocarbon dating shows that it 9130–8800 BCE."

There was a slight stir from the four bidders. They had all heard of the discovery, of course, or they wouldn't even be there, but hearing someone from the highly esteemed and reputable auction house of Christies confirm its authenticity was nevertheless a thrilling confirmation of the auction's value.

Raymond continued. "As you are all aware the location of the cavern is not private land and as such we don't have the ability to sell the actual ancient temple ourselves. Instead, what is on offer today is the location of the cavern, which we can guarantee that currently no one other than the offeror and the employees of Christies know." He paused slightly to allow the bidders to consider what was actually being sold. "As a representative of Christies, I would be remiss if I did not remind each of you that an archeological treasure trove such as this would need to be reported to the local government, and after doing so, it would be almost certain that you would lose possession of any item or image discovered inside. Do I make myself clear?"

There was a quiet sound of acknowledgement throughout the small group of men in the apartment at the top of the Eiffel Tower, as each tacitly agreed to ignore this advice.

"Good, then on your chairs you will find an envelope. Inside I would like you to write your final offer for the said item." Raymond looked around at the four men. "You may or may not know the other buyers in this room, but I assure you this is an extremely exclusive group or purchasers. Each of you has been granted the opportunity to bid on this item because Christies believes you have a particular interest in what is on hand, and the substantial financial resources at your disposal to purchase it. The winner tonight, I assure you, will have paid a very high price."

Raymond glanced around the room. Once confident everyone had written their price and resealed the envelope, he retrieved the four offers. "As you can appreciate because of the unique and legally intangible status of the item, I will not be revealing the concluding winner. Instead I will contact him within the next twenty-four hours to complete the final transaction. Then, the man who discovered the ancient temple will take you to it."

Sam stood up and glanced out the window. The Parisian city was lit up with a golden glow with the black ribbon of the Seine River splitting it in two. To the east, he spotted the Cathedral of Notre Dame standing proudly. His eyes drifted to the north where the Basilica of Sacre-Coeur rose magnificently above Montmartre. It was no wonder Gustave Eiffel had no end of offers to rent the apartment, the views were amazing.

Raymond interrupted his thoughts. "I'm afraid it's important that you all leave now so that a decision can be made and the Eiffel Tower can return to the people of France. Once again, I thank you all for making the trip after such short notice."

Sam walked down the narrow spiral staircase onto the third level of the Eiffel Tower and what was considered the top by tourists. An elevator, along with its security guard, was waiting for the four bidders. Sam stepped in without saying a word to the other bidders and the elevator descended in silence. The elevator dropped quickly, a far cry from the original Edoux elevator that ran off steam until being replaced by electricity in 1912. The elevator stopped at level two and the bidders were ushered to the waiting elevator on the north pillar to descend finally to the ground.

Sam stepped out of the elevator. The two men he didn't know immediately walked in separate directions. He looked at John Wallis, trying to judge if the man would be willing to talk to him now, or if he'd been frightened by the auction. He held out his hand, "It's good to see you, John."

"Ah, Mr. Reilly." John Wallis took his hand and shook it firmly with a warm smile as though he were welcoming an old friend. "It's good to see you. I am, however, surprised to see you involved here."

"It's an interesting story," Sam said. "Do you think there's any truth to it?"

"I'm not sure. I know my boss certainly hopes not."

Sam laughed. "No. I can't imagine His Holiness would be very happy to hear that Jesus Christ was a rip off of a guy who lived around ten thousand years earlier. What's the Catholic Church going to do if your bid wins, bury the discovery?"

"Far from it!" Wallis said. "His Holiness would like it examined. We've offered a large sum for its location and we intend to get something out of it."

Sam smiled. "Probably too much."

"Nothing is too much if this is what it takes to disprove a dangerous lie. And if the cavern is real and the paintings are true, then it will be much too important for the Church to leave to treasure hunters." Wallis looked at Sam. "No disrespect to the work you do."

"None taken."

"His Holiness appreciates the work that you do."

"I find that doubtful. The only times I've been to church is weddings and funerals."

"That's why he wants you to come along."

Sam said, "My goodness. You were the winning bid?"

"Yes."

"But I thought it wasn't going to be announced for twenty-four hours?"

Wallis smirked. "You didn't think we'd wait twenty-four hours to get started on something as important as this, did you?"

"No, of course not."

"So, are you ready to go to the Charles de Gaulle airport?"

"You're serious. Why does he want me to dispute the very bases of his entire religion?"

"What better person to examine the data than an atheist?"

"Are you asking for my help?"

"We're offering you a chance to join an expedition. And I hope you'll accept."

Chapter Thirty-Two – Mount Ararat

It took five days for Sam, Wallis and Mioli to reach the summit of Mount Ararat. During that time, John Wallis spent much of his time in silent contemplation, while Sam got to know Gianpietro Mioli quite well. Despite the constant time they spent together on the journey to the top of the sacred mountain, Sam hadn't yet decided what to make of the man.

At twenty-five, Mioli was definitely intelligent and driven. That much was fact. Having completed a major in archeology, he was currently pursuing a doctorial study at Italy's University of Bologna into prehistoric human origins. The University of Bologna is a European equivalent to an Ivy League school.

What Sam didn't understand was Mioli's appearance of altruism. The kid appeared to genuinely want to help the world, through his research. He often spoke about how much we can learn from our ancestors if the world was going to survive. He spoke of the corruption of greed and the tyranny of a generation who bought into the ideal of the worship of money – and yet, when he made one of the greatest archeological discoveries he straight away auctioned it off to a private bidder.

Mioli withdrew his GPS and began studying his location. He waited until there were nine satellites overhead, giving his GPS an accurate reading down to a single foot. For what he was after, Sam knew Mioli would need every inch of that accuracy. Sam waited as Mioli studied his GPS. He stopped trying to work out the man and instead looked down from the snow-capped peak of the mountain to a very old monastery on the plains of Armenia, named Khor Virap.

In an instant, his mind was taken back to 2005 and the day he first met Billie Swan. She was investigating a place called the Temple of Illumination. A place Grigory Lusavorich visited in 286 A.D. What he had found there, led Tiradates III, his king, to have him locked in Khor Virap. Billie had never told him what Grigory the Illuminator found in that temple, but she did tell him that, whatever it was, brought Christianity to the region and gave him hope of a new world.

Sam's mind returned to the present, as he heard Mioli shout, "It's over here."

"I'm coming over," Sam scanned the plateau. It was covered with thick snow.

Mioli started hammering deep climbing anchors into the ice.

Wallis dropped his backpack on the ground. "This is where we need to dig?"

"No." Mioli fed a piece of climbing rope through the eye of the anchor. "This is where we'll all tether ourselves while we dig. Last time I was here I made the mistake of disconnecting from the tether and I fell through the crevasse. I won't make that mistake again."

Sam and Wallis clipped into the anchor and then followed Mioli to a place twenty feet further along the plateau. The sun was above them, but there was enough wind to make it icy cold. Mioli started to dig in the hardened snow. It didn't take long. Within a few minutes he'd broken the hard surface and was able to dig through the soft snow below. It was obvious the snow had only recently been turned – most likely when Mioli first discovered the cavern below.

Fifteen minutes later, a wire climbing ladder was fixed to the entrance and Sam abseiled down into the large cavern thirty feet below. The walls were jet black and glassy. Like Mioli had told them, the place was positioned inside a large lava tube.

Sam disconnected his descender from the rope. "All right, I'm off the rope, come on down."

He watched as Mioli abseiled next, followed by Wallis a couple minutes later. Sam stared at the walls. The pictures were larger than he'd expected, and definitely much more detailed than any other cave-paintings he'd seen in Neolithic caves. The images depicted a man riding a wooly mammoth and another one with a man fighting off a sabertooth tiger. The depictions of their common life events certainly matched the suspected timeframe of ten to twelve thousand years ago, but paintings of an era alone did nothing to prove the validity of Mioli's claims.

Next to him, Wallis made a silent prayer to the image above of Jesus Christ on the Crucifix. Sam turned to Mioli. "What about the other thing?"

"There's a lot of strange images in here, which one are you referring to?"

"The frozen beast."

Mioli smiled. "You want to see it?"

Sam nodded. "Without it we have little but your speculation to go on."

"Right this way."

Sam was about to ask Wallis if he wanted to come have a look at it too, but decided not to interrupt the pious man's silent prayers. He followed Mioli along the lava tube until it reached a solid wall of ice. It appeared an ancient glacier had forced its way into the tunnel many years ago. Inside the ice, about five feet deep, a large wooly mammoth stared back at him.

Chapter Thirty-Three

Sam set up his drill and took two separate core samples from the wooly mammoth. He placed them in vacuumed sealed containers and then placed a liquid sealant into the holes created by the drill. If it turned out not to be a hoax, someone would one day want to come back and study the find. It wouldn't be him, and it wouldn't be for a long time, but that didn't mean Sam wanted to damage the discovery by exposing it to the hostile effects of air.

He secured the two samples and turned to Mioli. "You said there were other drawings?"

"There are more drawings, but I want to show you something else first." Mioli smiled, like a magician about to perform his greatest act, saved until last. "Mr. Wallis, you're going to want to see this, too."

Wallis sauntered over to meet them, shining his flashlight along the walls as he went. "I'll follow you."

Sam followed Mioli deeper into the tunnel. The tunnel changed direction where the ice glacier had once penetrated the lava tube, as though it had been pushed further to the left, before turning on itself and descending much deeper into the mountain.

Mioli walked with the brisk stride of a young man, full of impatience. There were more paintings along some of the walls that Sam would have liked to look at, but Mioli was determined they should go where he suggested first.

After a few minutes Sam felt his ears equalize under the change of pressure. He started to wonder how deep they'd come. He glanced behind, where he saw Wallis's flashlight keeping up from behind. He began to become concerned after following the ancient tunnel for thirty or more minutes.

He increased his pace and caught up with Mioli. "How much further?"

"Not far. Trust me. You're going to want to see this."

"Why?"

Mioli smiled. "Because I think the rest of the cave drawings at the entrance were merely a sign. A hint of the future or the past. Maybe even a message from the past to the future. But the whole purpose of this place is located at the end of this tunnel."

Sam nodded in silence. He was happy to go along with it for the time being.

The tunnel rounded another bend and dipped steeply so that Sam had to grip the edge of the tube to stop him from sliding down into the darkened abyss. About forty feet down the tunnel leveled out and the lava tube came to an ending of solid obsidian. At the middle of the jet-black wall a small alcove glared at him.

"Well," Mioli asked, "What do you think?"

Sam stared at the alcove. It took a split second to recognize the image, because the glossy appearance of the obsidian made it difficult to determine the shape. Now that he'd recognized it, the image was obvious – it was shaped like a human skull. The resting place for a human skull.

"A little macabre, if you ask me."

"But it's piqued your interest, hasn't it?"

"You mean, why someone all those years ago would have gone to the trouble of creating such a spectacle all the way down here?"

"Yes. I mean, it's obvious isn't it – the strange alcove must serve a purpose."

Sam nodded, knowing Mioli was right. Such effort must have meant there was indeed a significant purpose to it all, but what that was, he had no idea. He flashed his light over it again. There was space for four small pendants to fit, a small recess, carved meticulously into the ancient lava rock. Sam ran his hand over the alcove and the four individual recesses in front. They were arranged at the ends of a shallow carving in the shape of a crucifix, but there was something else where the two crossed. It was hard to make out exactly what the shape was. It could have been an animal or a person. Whatever it was, it would have taken a master craftsman a lifetime to achieve the degree of precision for such masonry. He ran his fingers along the tiny grooves. Not masonry, this quality of work was in the field of lapidary –jewelry worked into the natural glass.

Behind him, Sam heard Wallis in a cross between a controlled fall and a slide down the steep section of the tunnel. He was breathing heavily as though the climb had finally shaken his usual resolve, but he reached Sam without stopping. His eyes were fixed in a steely gaze, as though he'd seen or recognized something that had affected him to his very spiritual core.

Sam glanced at Wallis. "What do you make of this?"

"I have no idea." Wallis shook his head as though the question was entirely irrelevant. "But I'd sure like to know what that man's doing here."

Fear is unique. It's like wildfire. Dormant while its confined, but spreads quickly as soon as it breaks free and catches. Right now, Sam felt that fear spread through him in an instant. His muscles tightened, and his chest pounded as his eyes followed the beam of Wallis's flashlight.

There at the end of the obsidian vault, in a yellow jacket was the body of a man lying on his back. His chest was covered in dried blood, evidence of multiple gun shots taken long ago. His eyes stared vacantly upward, as though permanently fixed with hatred and regret.

Chapter Thirty-Four

Sam's eyes darted to the deceased man and back to Mioli. Gianpietro breathed out gently. He looked guilty as hell, but not surprised. To Sam, it looked more like he'd been waiting for this, and now it was just another part of the parcel he'd sold to the Catholic Church. Wallis looked no less concerned now that he realized the man was dead.

Talking to Mioli, Sam asked, "Was he here last time you were down here?"

"Who?" Mioli replied. Wallis and Reilly looked at him as if he were insane. Both had their flashlights trained upon the dead body. Then, Mioli, glancing at the body, casually said, "Oh the stiff? Yeah, he was here last time."

Sam knelt down to search the man. "And you didn't think to mention it when the find went to auction?"

"I didn't think it was relevant."

"Not relevant?" Wallis spoke with a quiet reserve that somehow had the ability to afflict more fear in a person than had he been yelling. "You sold a discovery in which you knew someone was murdered!"

Mioli shrugged. "I didn't realize he was murdered."

"Not murdered?" Sam repeated the word. "There are one, two, three, four, five shots through his chest. What did you think happened to him – he slipped and fell to his death?"

Mioli pointed upward. There upon the ceiling was a perfectly round opening that potentially led hundreds of feet above them. "Yeah, I just assumed he fell from somewhere up there."

Sam looked at the ceiling. He could almost see how Mioli assumed the man had fallen to his death and dismissed it as one of hundreds of tragic climbing accidents where the body is never discovered. That's assuming that Mioli was like most people and didn't go to the trouble of inspecting the body closely enough to notice the bullet wounds. Still, one would think he might have mentioned the presence of a dead man at his great discovery.

The opening was dark, so wherever it went no longer saw daylight. His mind returned to 2005, when he first met Billie Swan. *She had been searching an ancient temple – what did she call it? The Temple of Illumination.* She said that one of her fellow archeologists had turned on her, trying to kill her, and she had been forced to shoot him. She never said why the man had turned on her.

"Don't worry about it," Sam said. He stopped searching the body and forgot about Mioli's folly in an instant. He removed a golden chain from around the dead man's neck. It was long enough that the pendant at the end of it would hang below his nipple line. At the end of the chain was a golden crucifix. At its center, where the two parts of the cross joined, a pendant made from a solid piece of red garnet was expertly crafted into the shape of a horse and rider. In the rider's right hand was a broadsword.

Sam took the pendant and placed it over the first of the four indentations in front of the skull shaped alcove. It was close, but didn't quite fit. Sam swore. He was certain that he'd found a purpose for everything.

"Try the next one," Mioli suggested.

"Okay." Sam placed it in the second obsidian indentation. The small alcove swallowed the stone. Sucking it in as though the garnet belonged there, imbedded in the obsidian. It was an identical match. "It fits!"

"That's great, but where are the rest of the pieces – and what are they supposed to do?"

"May I see that?" Wallis asked.

"Sure," Sam said. He reached for the stone pendant, but withdrew his hand the instant he touched it. He shook his hand, nursing the pain.

Wallis looked at Sam. "What happened?"

"It burned me!"

"Ah, guys…" Mioli said, staring at the pendant, "It's now glowing."

Sam and Wallis turned to stare at the red garnet pendant, which now glowed brightly like the sun. Sam placed his right hand in his leather abseiling glove and carefully pulled the stone free of the small recess. It didn't come willingly, as though the obsidian was trying to hang onto it. He threw it onto the cold ground.

All three of them watched it until the red glow faded.

Wallis stepped forward and tentatively picked it up. He studied the carving for a moment and then handed it back to him. "I suggest you store this somewhere for safekeeping."

Sam took it, not quite sure he wanted the damned stone. "You have any idea what it means?"

Wallis spoke with warm, even voice. "When the Lamb opened the second seal, I heard the second living creature say, 'Come and see!' Then another horse came out, a fiery red one. Its rider was given power to take peace from the earth and to make men slay each other. To him was given a large sword."

Sam nodded. "Okay. Well, I'm going to head back to the surface to see how Tom's progressing, because this hasn't led me to anything."

"Sam, I think Wallis is talking about the Book of *Revelation*."

"Really?"

"Afraid so," Wallis confirmed.

"What about it?"

Wallis placed his hand on Sam's shoulder and said, "Tell me, how much do you know about the Four Horsemen?"

Chapter Thirty-Five

Sam placed the heavy gold chain around his neck and tucked the pendant into his jacket. There was no way to know for certain how it worked, but it was obvious that the pendant formed one of four keys used to activate something – but what he had no idea.

He took another photo of the strange alcove and then glanced at Wallis. "All right. I've seen enough down here. Let's go. I want to take some samples of the paintings to radiocarbon date."

"You can carbon date the paint?" Mioli asked.

"Not all of it," Sam said. "The red ochre comes from iron oxide in the earth and the whites come from lime. Neither of those will tell us when the drawing was completed. But the dark paints are most likely derived from charcoal – and we can get a reading date off that easily enough. We don't need much of a sample."

Wallis gestured with the flashlight at the dead body and the skull-shaped alcove. "What about those?"

Sam nodded. "The dead guy looks to me like he fell from a climbing accident. As for the strange alcove and its Four Horsemen recesses… well, you can fill me in with anything I don't already know about the Biblical reference as we walk."

"Okay." Wallis concentrated on climbing the steep section of the lava tube and then began to tell what he knew about the Four Horsemen. "There were Seven Seals in the Book of *Revelation* that secured the book or scroll that St. John of Patmos saw in his *Revelation* of Jesus Christ. The opening of the seals of the apocalyptic document occurs in *Revelation* and marks the Second Coming. In John's vision, the only one worthy to open the scroll is referred to as both the *Lion of Judah* and the *Lamb having Seven Horns and Seven Eyes*."

"Go on," Sam said, although this much he'd heard before.

"As you know, the seven seals were said to contain secret information known only to God until the Lamb or Lion was found worthy to open the scroll."

"And the first four seals opened released the Four Horsemen, Conquest, War, Famine and Death?" Sam asked.

"Yes," Wallis confirmed. "As you know, each had their own purpose. The Four Horsemen of the Apocalypse are described by John of Patmos in his Book of *Revelation*, the last book of the New Testament. The chapter tells of a book or scroll, in God's right hand that is sealed with seven seals". The Lamb of God, or Lion of Judah – most commonly thought to be Jesus Christ – opens the first four of the seven seals, which summons forth four beings that ride out on white, red, black, and pale horses. Although some interpretations differ, in most accounts, the four riders are seen as symbolizing Conquest, War, Famine, and Death, respectively. The Christian apocalyptic vision is that the Four Horsemen are to set a divine apocalypse upon the world as harbingers of the Last Judgment."

"So do you think the four keys lead to an apocalypse?" Sam asked.

"I have no idea what to think. The point is quite moot at this stage given we only have one of the four keys so far and no idea where the skull is."

They continued walking in silence as Sam wondered how everything was connected. His mind returned to the strange man inside Derinkuyu who claimed to be Famine – and the fateful words the man had said – *My name is Famine, and my time is coming*. He also thought about Billie Swan. She had told him that Gregory the Illuminator had climbed Mount Ararat to make an offering to God at the end of the third century. What he found up there had caused King Tiradates III to lock him up in the dungeon of Khor Virap.

He paused and looked at Wallis. "When was the story of the Four Horsemen first noted?"

"In Revelation."

"No. Not where – during what time period?"

"Oh, I believe it was during the end of the third century." Wallis thought about it for a moment. "Or, possibly the early fourth."

Sam felt his heart race as he saw the connection. "Do you know anything about Gregory the Illuminator and Khor Virap?"

"I read that he was locked in a dungeon for a number of years for preaching Christianity while his Pagan king ruled. Years later, his king became sick and only Gregory could heal him. Afterwards, the king converted, and Christianity took its first foothold in the region. Funny you should mention that now, though."

"Why?"

"Because I do believe that one of the theories of the Four Horsemen started in Armenia around that time. One reading ties the Four Horsemen to the history of the Roman Empire subsequent to the era in which the Book of *Revelation* was written. That is, they are a symbolic prophecy of the subsequent history of the empire, and a lead up to the fall of Rome."

"Interesting. I wonder if those Four Horsemen here were based on the Biblical reference."

"They must be. What else could they be based upon? Wallis asked.

"Well. If this cave is as old as it looks, there's always the possibility it's the other way round."

Wallis stopped walking. "You think *Revelation* was based on a much older story – some sort of warning about the coming future?"

Sam nodded and stopped directly in front of a cave painting. It depicted four people staring up at the image of Jesus Christ above. Their bodies were covered in robes, but their faces were easy to see and well defined. He studied their faces. There were two men and two women. He didn't recognize the first three, but the sight of the fourth one took the breath right out of him.

Her face was quite beautiful. She had a high jaw line and strong features. They were almost over the top, as though the original artist wanted to glorify her, as he or she would their God. Only she wasn't portrayed as a God. *If anything, she looked…* Sam thought about it for a moment… *like a royal messenger.* He was quite certain he'd never seen this woman before, and yet, at the same time, a hundred percent confident that he had seen someone very much like her.

The more he thought about it the more certain he became. He'd never met the woman in the painting, but certainly a close descendant. He'd never been more certain of anything in his life, and at the same time knew that it was entirely impossible. He took a couple steps back and took a couple photos of the painting with his phone.

His eyes drifted down toward the bottom of the painting. A dark wisp of smoke meandered through the legs of the four at the foot of the cross, and into their mouths. *Or was it coming out of their mouths and then sliding through their legs?* The smoke, like a blurry haze, had no definite form or shape. Yet there was definitely something serpentine about the way it wrapped itself around the four people. Without a doubt, he was certain the smoke creature was the same one he'd seen in the Dragon's Breath Cave in Namibia.

"If your theory's correct, do you think we're looking at the original Four Horsemen?" Wallis stared up at the painting and corrected himself. "Or two horsemen and two horsewomen?"

"I have no idea what to think, yet. But you might be right. This could be the first visual depiction of the Four Horsemen."

Sam stepped forward and carefully scratched a few small pieces of the dark creature, painted with charcoal, into a few collection canisters. "Wallis, have you ever seen this smoke creature before?"

"No. But it's full of imagery and hidden meaning, isn't it?" Wallis stared at the painting. "The serpentine smoke isn't an uncommon metaphor for evil. Perhaps the artist was trying to represent the evil tidings of the four horse... people?"

"Maybe." Sam stepped back and took one last look at the woman at the end of the picture. "Anything else you think I ought to see, Mioli?"

"No. I think you've seen the lot of it."

"Good. I'll take one more sample from the painting of Jesus Christ on the ceiling, and then I want to get back to a lab to see some sort of scientific facts."

Thirty minutes later they had climbed the wire ladder and reached the surface of the crevasse. Mioli covered the surface with a small wooden board carried specifically for this purpose, and then quickly filled the rest of the opening with snow until it was once again completely buried from view.

Sam took off his gloves and withdrew his cell phone. It was an Iridium Satellite Phone. He scrolled down until he found the name he was after and pressed the call button.

"Tom, how did it go with Peter Smyth?"

"Good. He knows where the *Mary Rose* sank. She's on the bottom of nearly three thousand feet of water in the Black Sea. What's more, he knows she was carrying a map to the pyramid in the Kalahari Desert – what we believe might be the Third Temple. I took the *Sea Witch II* down to have a look this morning. Found the wreck all right, but I'll need to send an ROV in to find the stone inside her hull. I have a dive planned for tomorrow. How did you do with the lost tomb of Jesus Christ? Do you think it's legit?"

"We never called it that, but yes we found some things. Can you hang on for a moment?" Sam didn't wait for a reply. Instead he started to text the image he'd taken of the Four Horsemen. "Listen, I'm going to send you a picture. I want to know what you're first thought is when you see it."

"Okay," Tom said. A few moments later he said, "Got it."

"What do you think?" Sam found himself holding his breath as he waited for Tom's answer.

"I think you took a photo of Elise's sister or even her mom. Why? Where did you get this?"

"What would you say if I told you I took it inside the ancient temple?"

"No way!" Tom said. "What the hell does that mean? Elise's great ancestors built the temple, or do you think we're being led into one gigantic hoax?"

"I don't think it is a hoax. Then again, if it is, it sure is a good one." Sam shook his head.

"Are you going to show Elise? She's going to want to know."

"Of course I will. She has a right to know, but not yet. Not until I know a bit more about the scientific facts. I've taken a number of samples and I'll run the radiocarbon dating myself on board the *Maria Helena*, but right now, I think this is heavily connected to whoever has Billie and the Third Temple."

"What makes you so sure?"

"Forget the woman in the picture for a moment. There's something about the image that I think you should see. Look at the bottom, what do you see?"

Tom swore loudly. "It's the same creepy smoke thing we found in the Dragon's Breath Cave!"

"Exactly, and it's looking up and staring at the image of Jesus Christ."

"No. I think you've got it all wrong," Tom said. "I don't think that's what the image is meant to represent at all."

"You don't?"

"No," Tom said. "I think Jesus Christ is staring down at the Black Smoke in fear."

Sam studied the photo again. Tom was right, the image of Jesus Christ was pleading with the Black Smoke below. "I think you're right. Jesus appears worried about the Black Smoke, but what the hell was it?"

Chapter Thirty-Six – Maici River, Amazon Jungle, Brazil

The Maici River is a tributary of the Dos Marmelos River in the Humaita National Forest, in northwest Brazil, one of the most isolated and remote jungles on the planet. To this day, few Europeans have ever penetrated far enough into the Amazon Jungle to reach it. Those who have, struggled to survive. But for the Pirahã tribe, who have lived in total isolation from those outside the Amazon, it was home.

Dr. Billie Swan sat on the edge of a large boulder as she stared at a few of the strange tribal people whose land she'd shared for the past two years in complete wonderment. They were catching fish from the edge of the Maici River. The children and the adults all smiled constantly while they worked. Their eyes were wide, as though they were taking in the day in a way that made her question whose civilization was the most advanced – those from western society, or these primitive people? As an archeologist she'd traveled to many remote and distant regions of the planet. For a time, she thought she'd seen it all, but then she met the people of the Pirahã tribe.

She was one of five people alive who'd spent enough time with the Pirahã tribe to learn their language. After nearly two years, she felt no closer to realizing her grandfather's dream of uniting the remaining Master Builders. She watched the unique people working by the river. They would be considered primitive by western standards, yet out here in the deadly jungle, they were supremely gifted in all the ways necessary to ensure their continued survival. They knew the benefit of various important plants and where they were located, they intrinsically understood the behavior of local animals and how to catch them or avoid them, and they had the uncanny ability to walk into the jungle naked, with no tools or weapons, and walk out again with a basket of fruit, nuts, and small game.

Their culture was concerned solely with matters that fall within direct personal experience, and thus there is no history beyond living memory. Pirahã have a simple kinship system that includes their immediate family. Daniel Everett, an anthropologist who spent more than thirty years living and working with them, noted the strongest of Pirahã values is no coercion. You simply don't tell other people what to do. There appears to be no social hierarchy and the Pirahã have no formal leaders. Their social system can thus be labeled as primitive communism, in common with many other hunter-gatherer cultures in the world, although rare in the Amazon because of a history of agriculture before Western contact.

The adult man whistled a melodic tune, and his son ran to the edge of the river and began dropping stones into the water. He made a different sound, and the boy stopped. A moment later, the man threw a spear at a group of fish that were swimming away from the falling stones. The spear connected with a fish. The man withdrew the spear and examined his catch. He smiled. It was a medium sized fish. No other sounds were made and all five of the family came over and quickly ate the fish raw.

Billie smiled. Their language was unique and totally unrelated to any other extant tongue. Based on just eight consonants and three vowels, the Pirahã had one of the simplest sound systems known. Yet it possessed such a complex array of tones, stresses, and syllable lengths that its speakers can dispense with their vowels and consonants altogether and sing, hum, or whistle conversations. They had no name for numbers or colors, although they occasionally joined two words to make the description of a color, such as blood-stone or bone-powder. They used morphological markers that encode aspectual notions, such as whether events were witnessed, whether the speaker was certain of its occurrence, whether it was desired, whether it was proximal or distal, and so on. Yet, none of the markers encode features such as person, number, tense or gender.

One of the other splendid features of their language which particularly separated it from all other spoken languages in any civilization currently living or not, was the fact that it was entirely devoid of any type of grammatical recursion – an attribute that every other language in the world shared. Grammatical recursion basically means that a story may have a subordinate idea or ideas inside. For example, in English, one might say a simple sentence such as, *Michael has an earthy spear.* Adding recursion to that sentence might lead the speaker to include the following, *Michael, whom you know very well, has a brown spear.* The recursion can continue almost indefinitely. For example one could say, *Michael, whom you know very well, has an earthlike spear and it's lying there beneath the tree.* But of the three sentences, only the very first could be understood or communicated by the Pirahã.

Billie watched as one of the children, now full from the fish, patiently hand carved an airplane he'd seen in the sky, out of a piece of wood over the course of a number of hours. The same child, as with the rest of the tribe, was incapable and uninterested in drawing even simple shapes or pictures in the sand. Yet he was masterful at modelling complex shapes or designs. Once he finished making his airplane, he played with it for a few minutes before discarding it and walking away. She watched the boy disappear into the forest.

A moment later she stood up and strode down to the river to quench her thirst. She reveled in this time, with these strange people, because she knew the beast would return soon – and all of them, herself included, would once again be cast under its strange spell.

It would be coming for her – for all of them – very soon. The thought terrified her, while at the same time enthralling her and sending her heart into a flutter. It was nothing more than a cheap gimmick designed to enslave the primitive Pirahã tribe. There was nothing mysterious about the creature they called the Black Smoke. The thick smoke which engulfed the jungle like a blanket. It was immediately followed by an incredibly distinct and strange sound, which could be heard for miles – and, like the Sirens of Homer's Odyssey, it drew all souls who heard it to follow.

She thought about the creature for a moment. The smoke could easily be explained by someone burning damp leaves. The voices were those of mortals and not Gods. The persuasiveness of those voices was enhanced by some chemical being burned. The smoke of any number of hallucinogenic, neurotoxic, or psychotropic plants had the power to enslave.

The one thing she couldn't understand was the collective power the monster achieved with the primitive tribe, herself included. It was as though they were all hypnotized. She'd never been reduced to submission by anything or anyone before in her life. No one since the first grade right through to her most recent employer, Sam Reilly, had found a way to make her obedient.

But the Black Smoke rendered her powerless.

The thought of losing control again terrified her, but there was something else there, too. When she considered fleeing now, there was definitely a good chance she'd survive, but she couldn't force herself to take the risk. It wasn't because she was afraid of dying. Better to die than become something's slave for an eternity. So why didn't she want to run? *Was it because she liked the idea of being subservient to the creature again?* Even if she wanted to escape, she didn't even know how far she'd have to go to escape its net. She was frightened by what it would do when it found her, but most of all she didn't want to disappoint the creature. She laughed at herself at the thought. The creature – she was thinking of it as a living breathing thing now – was just smoke.

And there she had it. Something about the smoke was comforting. It was addictive, and she needed the generalized warmth, comfort, pleasure and satisfaction it provided. She recalled the euphoria at being able to perform a series of ancient masonry skills, which she'd never been taught. This, she realized, was how the Master Builders had achieved the construction of the pyramids. Not like a heroin addict needed the drug to feel okay, but more like she wanted to please it. She wanted to prove that she could build the most spectacular temple in the world. That she had been honored to be chosen to be part of this great process.

She could not run from it any more than a child could run from its mother. When the depth of her situation had become complete, she realized why the U.S. Military was so concerned about the Master Builders. Why they had spent so much money funding Sam Reilly's research in secret. They knew about the mind controlling drugs the Master Builders had developed – they had the power to control the human race, turning everyone into puppets.

That was the final thought, which made her decision for her. No matter what she wanted, Billie needed to escape. She needed to get back to civilization. Someone needed to know of the most terrifying threat to the human race. She filled her bottles with water, and packed her backpack with the last of her food. Her pleasure and her joy were irrelevant given the situation. She needed to escape. She needed to get word to Sam Reilly, before it was too late.

Billie took her first step into the jungle and away from the Pirahã tribe, and then she stopped, because the jungle darkened with a thick cloak of smoke. Through the forest, she heard the strange and eerie whistling of four hundred Pirahã. It was somewhere between the high pitch scream of a child and the piercing trill of an exotic bird. A voice in her head told her it was time to resume the work.

The Black Smoke had returned.

Chapter Thirty-Seven

The helicopter rested its skids on the deck of the *Maria Helena*. Sam opened the door and stepped out while Genevieve was still in the process of shutting down the engine. It was another warm day, late in the summer. A cold breeze suggested a change was coming. The sky above was clear but dark clouds were on the horizon suggesting the change would be violent when it arrived. Hurried by the weather, he entered the ship's main structure.

Spotting Matthew first, he asked, "How was your vacation skipper?"

"Good," Matthew said. "What I got to take of it. You recalled me a week early."

Sam shrugged. "Hey, no one said I was easy to work for. But the pay's all right and you get to go to some amazing places."

"The pay's modest and the places you take us to usually nearly get us killed."

"Hey, you're still here." Sam was always surprised by how conservative his skipper was. Their job was dangerous, but so far he hadn't lost a single one of the crew. "Have you seen Tom?"

"Down below. He's looking at launching the *Sea Witch II* within the hour."

Sam glanced at the dark storm clouds on the horizon. "Will they have time?"

Matthew handed him the synoptic charts from the communications room. "The weather report says he's got twenty-four hours."

"All right, that'll have to do."

Sam walked down the steel stairs into the dive-room. He spotted Tom and Veyron going over the dive plan next to *Sea Witch II*. The submarine was a bright yellow Triton 36 000/3. Cables were already secured to its lifting hooks, ready to maneuver the sub into the water for launch. It often reminded Sam of a futuristic hovercraft. It had twin yellow hulls and a large borosilicate glass dome in the middle that housed up to three divers. Two pilot seats were located at the front of the bubble, and one passenger crammed behind to form the shape of a V. The dome provided 270 degree visualization. The unique glass had been slowly built over nearly eight months, using boron instead of soda-lime, which gave it the unusual property of compressing upon itself the deeper it went. At the back of the dome, a square box stood out like a small doghouse. Inside a very expensive ROV– Remote Operated Vehicle or basically an underwater drone – was attached to an umbilical tether like a leash.

"Hello, gentlemen," he greeted both men.

"Welcome back," Veyron said. It was an acknowledgement of his presence and then Veyron immediately returned to his calculations for the dive.

"Sam!" Tom smiled, genuinely pleased to see him. He turned to a man who strolled over from the opposite side of the submarine. "This is Peter Smyth. He was the first to locate the *Mary Rose* and is keen to stay with us while we complete our search for the map to what we think is the Third Temple."

Sam shook Peter's hand. "Good to have you on board."

Tom said, "Peter and I were about to take the *Sea Witch II* down to the *Mary Rose* and then run the ROV out to see if the stone tablet is in her lower decks. There are some interesting things I'd like you to see. Did you want to join us?"

"To dive to 3000 feet and search an old shipwreck?" Sam asked.

"Yeah."

"Absolutely." Sam looked at Veyron who was eager to launch the submarine. "Elise is shore side in Istanbul. She has my samples from the ancient lava tube I looked at and she's carbon dating them at the Marmara University. If she gets an answer for me before I return, have Genevieve take the chopper and bring her in. I want those answers as soon as possible."

Chapter Thirty-Eight

Tom piloted the *Sea Witch II* in a direct line to the bottom. On the way down, Sam filled him in with what he'd found in the lava tube and Peter brought Sam up to date with everything he'd learned about the *Emerald Star* and the pyramid inside the Kalahari Desert. The entire journey took thirty minutes. He checked the depth gauge at 2800 feet and reduced his descent until 2950 feet. Once there, he leveled the submarine and hovered motionless.

He turned to Sam. "All right, you ready to look at this thing?"

Sam nodded. His eyes were wide and his jaw set firm, with a slight glint of a smile that betrayed his wonderment. Some things, Tom realized, one never got bored with.

Tom flicked on the powerful floodlights, which hung out from above the dome like a pair of giant bug-eyes. The *Mary Rose* lit up in front of them.

Sam gasped. "I'd heard about the salinity, but had no idea how much it would preserve the wreck."

"Told you needed to see some things in person," Tom said.

In front of them the *Mary Rose* stood upright in the silty seabed. The individual planks of wood that made up her hull were undamaged. All four masts of the Spanish galleon were entirely intact and a series of ropes showed how the great vessel was rigged. The intricate wood carvings of the helm flickered in the light, as though a restless ghost was commanding her through the dark. The wood was so well-preserved that chisel and tool marks were still visible on individual planks. Rigging materials, coils of rope, tills, rudders, and even carved wooden decorative elements survived. It was conceivable the ship might have been sunk a year or two ago, but in 1653? The concept was absurd, and yet that made it no less true.

If there was any doubt left in their minds about the age of the ship, it was shattered when the brass bell located amid ship, hanging from the main mast, bore the name, *Mary Rose*.

Sam said, "I heard the high levels of salinity preserved some of these ships, but I had no idea."

Peter spoke, with the confidence of a man who'd been studying the Black Sea and her depths for the past two years. "During the last Ice Age the Black Sea was really the Black Lake. As the planet warmed and sea levels rose, saltwater from the Mediterranean began spilling over a rock formation in the Bosphorus Strait. This meant the Black Sea was now fed by saltwater as well as freshwater rivers, resulting in two distinct layers of water – an oxygenated upper level with less salt and a lower level with plenty of saltwater and no oxygen."

Sam said, "That's amazing. In most seawater, wood and rope are among the first things to decay. But here they look entirely untouched. All right, time to get the ROV out, and find our stone map."

Tom set *Sea Witch II* to hover automatically, locking in a depth alarm – something that would alert him the instant their depth substantially increased or decreased – and then turned his focus to the computer monitor that displayed the image seen from the front of the ROV. There were two monitors. The first one showed the primary view, while the second one was split into five barely visible views – above, below, left, right and behind. Any of them could change the primary view so that the larger image was the one they viewed.

Sam switched the machine on, and the sound of its multiple propellers spinning suddenly whirred. The ROV was stored facing outward, in the same way you would park a car in a garage so that the exit was easier than the entry. The view on the primary screen was set to the frontal camera so it even looked as though you were peering through the windshield of a car.

Tom watched as Sam expertly navigated the ROV toward the shipwreck. His right hand made minor adjustments to the joystick like a kid playing a computer game. That was Sam though – a kid through and through, playing a game. The only difference was his toy was worth nearly two million dollars, and the stakes were life and death.

The ROV hovered over the top deck. Sam said, "I don't believe this. There isn't even a way inside. The damned hatches are still intact!"

Tom scanned the deck. "There! The aft castle has an entrance hatch."

"I see it." Sam whirred the ROV toward the hatch.

Peter asked, "The question is, can you open it?"

Sam grinned at the challenge. "I can open it."

Sam changed the primary view to the left side. He hit a buoyancy maintenance button – similar to the one Tom had used to keep the *Sea Witch II* in an exact position – and then turned to a new joystick. Sam maneuvered the single robotic claw until it reached the hatch. A moment later the claw gripped the handle and pulled.

The entire hatch came free from its rotten hinges. Tom said, "That'll work."

Sam returned the primary monitor to the dashboard view and entered the aft castle. He then turned to Peter. "I don't suppose you have any idea where this stone tablet was stored?"

"I don't know for certain, but in Hammersmith's journal he wrote that the stone map was seen as a gift from the gods. It was a map that was supposedly going to take them to great treasures. Where would you keep a treasure map secure from the greedy crew of a seventeenth century pirate ship?"

"The captain's quarters!" Tom and Sam said in unison.

The *Mary Rose* had two decks that ran the length of the ship's hull, plus an additional level in the aft and fore castle. Traditionally, the aft castle housed the captain's quarters, but there was no telling that her original Spanish builder conformed to the normality of her time.

Tom watched as Sam maneuvered the ROV into the aft castle. Despite the surprising preservation of the outside hull and rigging, the inside of what might have once been the captain's quarters had been reduced to a mass of silt. There was no sign of the stone tablet or any other definable structure.

Sam took the ROV down into the main deck, which ran the length of the ship. The ROV was equipped with a low amplitude sonar transducer in its belly – which basically meant that she could receive a graphical display of any structure below and in her immediate vicinity. The ROV took two sweeps of the first deck, without any sign of a stone structure. It then whirred through another opening amid ship that led to the second deck. Sam took another sweep of the sonar through this level, but the only stones it located were the broken ones in the bilge used for ballast.

"I don't believe it!" Tom said. "We've overcome so much to find this, and the damned thing was never here to begin with."

"All right," Sam said, heavily. "I'll take her back in and we'll return to the surface. That storm's coming, we might have to postpone another dive for a few days."

The ROV turned and slowly retraced its path back to the open deck. It whirred loudly as it approached *Sea Witch II*. Tom glanced at the third monitor, where the sonar image provided a simple view of the terrain below. He went to switch the transducer off and then something stopped him.

"Wait!" he yelled.

"What is it?" Sam asked.

Tom pointed at the monitor. "Does that look like something to you?"

Sam and Peter both studied the screen. It looked very much like the head of a tomb stone, only much smaller.

He watched as Sam descended the ROV until it was hovering just above the stone. The primary view was switched to the camera pointing straight down. The stone had been chiseled to form a very specific shape, but there was nothing written on it.

Peter asked, "Can you turn it over?"

Sam nodded.

Tom found himself unintentionally holding his breath. A moment later the ROV's grappler tipped the stone over. There beneath them was a perfect delineation of the west coast of Africa and a whole bunch of numbers he couldn't read.

Chapter Thirty- Nine

Sam stepped out of the submarine and onto the *Maria Helena*. He immediately set up a cleaning trough to wash the stone. He used a low pressure water jet to remove the silt until the image was clearly visible. The African coastline was unmistakable. This had to be the ancient map that Hammersmith had written about – the one they'd lost when the *Mary Rose* sank in 1653.

Veyron climbed down from the control box of the small crane. "Sam, you wanted to know about Elise as soon as you reached the surface?"

"Yes."

"She called an hour ago. Said she needed to see you right away. Genevieve's gone to pick her up right now."

"That's great," Sam said.

He felt it, too. An hour ago he suspected he'd reached a complete dead end on his search for the Third Temple and for Billie. He couldn't find the stone, and he was still waiting for Elise to tell him the truth about the painting in the hidden cavern inside Mount Ararat.

Within minutes he, Tom and Peter were staring at a perfectly restored stone tablet. He wondered what the original mason who chiseled the markings would think about it being read all these years later. The stone had one recognizable image and two sets of numbers. The numbers were in base eleven and he could decipher them easily enough, but he'd never seen the word after the numbers – although he could guess its purpose.

There were two numbers. Most likely two points of reference and where they intercept is the precise location. The unfamiliar word, *Carrib*, most likely represented a measured distance, such as a mile or a kilometer – only it didn't. The purpose of the word was obvious. He stared at the numbers. Converted into base ten they read, 318 and 325.

But 318 and 325 what?

Sam breathed out, purposefully slow. He ran his fingers over his forehead and through his brown wavy hair. "It appears the Master Builders worked out a similar means of defining precise locations long before GPS."

Peter said, "That even looks like a latitude and longitude reference."

Sam swore. It was a sudden and loud show of frustration, and it was unlike him. "It may as well be the location of a secret treasure hidden on another planet for all the good it's going to do us."

"Why?" Peter asked.

Sam shook his head. They had come so far to find the map, and yet it was entirely useless to them. "Because by the looks of things, the Master Builders were using a completely different numerical reference point. This map shows us clearly where the Third Temple was located. It's at the point where reference number 318 *Carrib* and 325 *Carrib* intercept – but I don't have any clue what a *Carrib* is."

"But that doesn't make sense," Peter said.

"I know it doesn't. I just told you it doesn't."

"No, not that."

Sam asked, "What then?"

"Hammersmith wasn't a Master Builder, so how did he know how to follow the map?"

Sam paused, as he thought about it for a moment. "I have no idea. Maybe there's an easy conversion."

Tom sighed. "Or there was a Master Builder on board."

Sam nodded. It was the most likely possibility. "All right, I'll give it to Elise when she gets. If there's any way of extracting the code, she'll work it out."

A few moments later, the *Maria Helena* reverberated under the downward whoop, whoop of the Sea King landing. Sam looked at Tom and Peter. "Speak of the Devil."

Sam jogged up the steps, taking two at a time. He stepped out onto the deck and opened the helicopter's front passenger door. It was empty. He looked up at Genevieve. "Where is she?"

"She wouldn't wait for the blades to stop turning. She's gone inside. She said she had to see you straight away."

Sam nodded. "Okay. Thanks for getting her."

Genevieve smiled. She knew how much he appreciated her, but it was rare for him to voice it. Every one of his crew worked hard and put a hundred percent into the job twenty-four hours a day. It's what he expected from them and more often than not, what he needed. Genevieve said, "Go find her."

He found Elise coming back down the stairs from the bridge.

She spoke before he could speak. "I've got the results from each of the samples."

"And?"

"You're not going to believe what they show."

Chapter Forty – Vatican City

Sam sat down on an old leather armchair opposite John Wallis who sat behind the heavy oak desk of his office. A wooden placard read, *Swiss Guard. Minister for the Future.* Eight weeks ago, Sam had sat in the very same chair, when he'd first been introduced to the man. Since that day, he had no revelation as to what Wallis's official title meant. Sam had found him because, among other things, Wallis documented the history of the Master Builders, going by a Latin name which meant, *Witness to the Master Builders.* It was a very old title, and it stretched back to the days of the Great Plague, when Nostradamus had accurately predicted a young monk in training would one day become the Pope. Wallis had been instructed to continue to perform the task of *Witness,* even though he had never met one of the great descendants.

His eyes swept the office. It was scattered with unique memorabilia from history. An early edition of the Holy Bible, strange Mayan weapons given or taken during the spread of Catholicism to the New World, an incomplete world map showing the ignorance of the 16th century Conquistadors, photos of the various Heads of State from around the world – on closer inspection, Sam saw that Wallis was in the background of every one of them – it was obvious, the man provided specialized services to the Holy See above and beyond Pontifical Security.

Wallis stared at him in silence. His hardened face perched in a permanent question, as if to say, *I'm ready, let's hear the truth.* Sam quickly gave it to him; handing out the facts as they had been given to him. Even he hadn't worked out why someone would do such a thing, or how it could have been achieved. None of it mattered. The fact was, he was happy to have been invited by the Church to find the truth, but now that it was out, it wouldn't serve him or Tom any benefit in achieving their goal of finding Billie.

"A hoax?" His eyes narrowed. "I was there with my own eyes. There was a damned wooly mammoth there frozen in solid ice!"

Sam smiled, politely. It was all he could do. "Well that part was true."

"I don't understand. You'd better start from the beginning."

"The wooly mammoth was dated as roughly 12,000 years old."

"So, the strange temple is at least that old?"

"No. You have to remember the extinct creature was forced into the cavern by a slow moving glacier sometime in the past two thousand years. Only part of it had dropped into the lava tube, while the rest of it continued further into the mountain. The only remaining ice was what you saw a few days ago."

"Okay, what about the paintings?"

"They were done around 300 A.D. give or take 50 years. But I'm willing to bet money that it was in April 286 A.D."

Wallis sat up in his chair, as though his rigid muscles could coax his mind into some sort of understanding. "You think it was Gregory the Illuminator?"

"I do."

"You think he found the frozen wooly mammoth, a monster he knew died out long ago, and decided to impart some sort of crazy lie, so that future generations might... what... believe in Christianity?"

Sam answered like a child in trouble, who knew that none would be adequate. "No."

"That Christianity was fake, because Jesus Christ was based upon another person who died ten thousand years earlier – I don't understand – for what purpose could Gregory the Illuminator have possibly performed such a horrible hoax?" Wallis paused, as though his mind was still trying to make some sort of sense of the news. "Even if he went to the tremendous lengths required to achieve it, what about the Four Horsemen? What part do they play in all this?"

Sam closed his eyes, waited for a moment and the spoke. "I've been thinking about the Four Horsemen and about Gregory."

"And?"

"This isn't some sort of juvenile hoax made up to get attention. This wasn't for fun. It had to serve a purpose, and I think I might just know what it was."

"Go on."

"The entire elaborate deception was all designed to make us focus on one particular thing – the time period. He wanted us to examine a very specific time. He wanted us to look at what happened roughly twelve thousand years ago."

"Why?"

Sam swallowed. "I think he was trying to give us some sort of warning. What if he was trying to warn us that the disaster that caused the period of mass-extinction of twelve thousand years ago, was hurling toward us again?"

Wallis spoke the words with a quiet solemnity. "The extinction of the human race."

Sam nodded in silence. He'd had the same concern. Eight weeks ago he'd discovered that the final vision Nostradamus had seen was the extinction of the human race, and somehow – Sam Reilly was the only person on earth who might have the power to change the outcome.

It was Wallis who broke the silence first. "What about the Four Horsemen?"

Sam said, "I've been thinking about that, too. What if the Four Horsemen were set up to act as a final defense against the imminent disaster? Like an ancient covenant to come into effect when the time was right."

"But how would they know when that was?" His face was etched with doubt and cynicism.

Sam nodded. It was a hard stretch to believe. "What if Nostradamus wasn't the first?"

"You mean, what if someone else knew the future?"

"Sure. What if that person knew a precise date for a cataclysmic event, and how to stop it, but no way to be certain that the Four Horsemen would achieve their goal?" Sam took a breath and then continued. "People die, stories change over seventeen hundred years. The remaining Four Horsemen may not exist."

"So?"

"So, maybe that person saw that we'd have an unusually warm summer this year. He or she saw the snow, which capped the upper third of Mount Ararat, begin to thin. It would lead someone to fall into the cavern. Maybe they knew the shifting glacier would bring the frozen wooly mammoth from twelve thousand years ago into the lava tube and our plain sight. That the twist about the age of Jesus Christ was so compelling that no matter who found the cavern, the message would reach the Vatican – where you would contact me to become involved.

"It's a whole lot of what ifs for me to believe." Wallis took a deep breath and then slowly breathed out. "Even if I did believe you, the fact remains, what are we supposed to do about it?"

Sam smiled, and withdrew the pendant out from beneath his shirt. It was made of solid red garnet and its rider carried a longsword. "We need to gather the Four Horsemen."

Chapter Forty-One

Sam stared at Wallis as he took in all that he'd been told. Wallis's face was hard and impassive. It was impossible to know what to make of it. The concept was impossible, yet the man had seen the impossible before.

"Do you have any idea where they are?" Wallis asked.

"No. I've been following a lead about a recent movement by the Master Builders in the hope of finding a temple where our friend, Dr. Billie Swan, is being held prisoner. It's led us to search for something called the Third Temple – a pyramid we believe is in the Kalahari Desert."

"I wasn't aware there were any pyramids that far south."

Sam smiled impatiently. "Yes, well we haven't been able to find one either. That said, while we were searching for it, we were attacked by a strange man. Do you know what he told us his name was?"

"No."

"He said his name was Famine and his time was now."

"Okay, so we find the Third Temple and we might find the rest of the Four Horsemen."

"The only problem is all of our leads have run dry."

"If there's anything I could do to help I would, but right now, I think we're both out of options." Wallis stood up to shake his hand. It was a courtesy and at the same time a dismissal. "What will you do?"

"I don't know. I'll head back to the *Maria Helena* to follow up on some other leads."

Sam turned to face the door and then stopped. His eyes caught sight of the old world map hanging up on the wall. He'd spotted it before, but hadn't taken any particular interest. It was only now that his eyes fixed on the date of production – *January 1655.*

"Do you know when this map was surveyed?"

Wallis seemed surprised by the question. "Not a clue. The date's on there somewhere. 16 something."

"Then it's not a fake?"

"Absolutely not. Why would I have a fake map hanging on my wall?"

"Why would you have a map you know nothing about?"

"Touché." Wallis smiled patiently. "It's not a fake. It was taken during a period when the Catholic Church was sending missions to all corners of the globe to promote God's will. Of course, God – in his almighty wisdom – chose to repeatedly sink a number of our ships in the process. That's why his Holliness ordered a complete survey of the African coastline and that of South and North America. Why would you think it was a fake?"

Sam apologized. "It just appears drawn incorrectly."

"How should I know?" Wallis grunted. "I'm not a cartographer."

"But you're certain it's not a forgery?"

"No. Why are you so concerned with it?"

"Because I've extensively studied maps of the region, dating as far back as 1655…"

"And?"

"This part here." Sam pointed to a large bay along the west coast of Africa.

"Yes?"

"In my maps, the coastline starts all the way out here."

John Wallis shrugged indifferently. "Is that a big difference?"

"It's nearly ten miles."

"So? Lands change. Particularly sandy ones, it would appear. Why are you so interested?"

"Because the last visitors to the Third Temple became shipwrecked there. Since then the sandy coast has shifted inward and outward a hundred or more times, like the turning of the tide. But if we know what the coast looked like during the same year the ship sank while at anchor, then I think Tom and I might just have a chance of finding her."

Chapter Forty-Two – Istanbul

Dmitri waited just inside the dilapidated hovel Peter Smyth called home. He still wore a dark custom made suit, but had removed his sunglasses. He didn't carry a handgun. Contrary to what popular culture and movies would have you believe, Interpol agents never did. And even if he had, Dmitri wouldn't need it today. His hands were strong and his reflexes inhumanly fast. If Peter needed more persuasion, Dmitri was confident he knew how to provide it using his hands alone.

He had been keeping track of Peter for the past three years. After finding information about the Third Temple, the man had become a problem for Dmitri. *But all problems have solutions.* He thought about ending this problem three years ago. In retrospect, he probably should have, but there was always the concern that maybe, just maybe, the man might lead him to what he was after – access to the Third Temple.

So instead of killing him, Dmitri kept digital eyes on him. The man, frightened they were after him, had naturally gone to ground and removed all evidence of his life. In the past three years there were no records of any banking transactions, passport hits, credit, rental applications, cell phone use, or social media. As far as modern society was concerned, the man was already dead. Hell, if Dmitri had to kill him now, no one would ask questions – you can't be punished for killing a ghost.

But Peter hadn't died and Dmitri never stopped watching him, or the progress that he made. The most recent of which, had genuinely surprised him. He could have guessed roughly where the *Mary Rose* had sunk, but given her location, he'd never bothered. It would be too difficult for him to reach a depth of 3000 feet and if he hired a team of professional divers to do so it could cost far more than he could afford, and bring dangerous attention to himself – from the others.

He watched as the tile that hid the entrance moved. He waited until the tile had slid all the way to the side. When he was confident the tile couldn't be shifted back into place and latched from below, Dmitri stepped out of the shadow.

"Hello, Peter – it's been a while."

Peter stepped off the ladder below, trying to drop to the ground. He was quick, but Dmitri was faster. He gripped Peter's wrist and pulled him up into the above ground section of the hovel. Peter twisted and wrestled to free himself.

Dmitri looked at him, amused by the man's efforts. His fingers were like a vice, and would simple dig deeper into his arm the more he struggled. Peter whimpered under the pressure. When he caught his breath, he redoubled his effort to escape.

Dmitri shook his head. "I can do this up here – where THE OTHERS may be listening. Or we can do it downstairs and speak where they can't listen."

Peter looked at him, his eyes wide with terror. "Okay."

"I'm going to let go so you can climb down all by yourself. If you try to do anything at all not to my liking, I won't simply catch you again. I will extract what I'm after and then I'm going to give THE OTHERS the tracking code."

Peter glanced at the small tattoo on his wrist, where Dmitri had imbedded a GPS tracking chip three years ago. For an instant, Dmitri wondered how many times the man had considered lopping off his own wrist, simply to get away from it. Peter looked up and nodded in acquiescence.

"Are you certain?" Dmitri's voice was firm.

"Yes."

Dmitri let go, and Peter hurriedly climbed down the stairs. His eyes glanced at the couch and then back to Dmitri. One glance and Peter stood perfectly still.

"What do you want?" Peter asked.

"You found the map, didn't you?"

Peter nodded.

"Do you have it or do they?"

"I have it," Peter said. "It's over there, resting against the wall."

Dmitri stepped toward the stone tablet. At a glance, he knew it was authentic. The timing couldn't have been better. "Well done, Peter. It appears it was worth my while keeping you alive these past three years."

Peter was holding his breath.

"You look like you disagree?"

"No, not at all."

"Then what is it?"

Peter said, "It's just – the map won't do you any good."

"Why not?" Dmitri asked.

"Because the map makes reference to a type of measurement never seen anywhere else before."

"So the stone's useless. It provides a grid reference based on measurements that don't exist. Even GPS doesn't serve a purpose if you don't know what those numbers mean, right?"

"Right."

Dmitri smiled. It was creepy and inhuman. Almost serpentine. "But I remember how to read it."

Chapter Forty-Three – Skeleton Coast, Namibia

The Sea King's massive rotary blade lifted the huge helicopter and her passengers skyward, as Sam Reilly took off from the *Maria Helena,* which had taken anchorage roughly three miles out from Terrace Bay, along the fatal coastline. Next to him, Tom studied the copy of the survey map from 1655, which Sam had been given by the Vatican. The map identified a large section between Terrace Bay and Cape Cross, where the sandy coastline had shifted nearly ten miles further out to sea. If the *Emerald Star* had indeed been sunk while anchored during the sandstorm, it would most likely be somewhere along the long forgotten coastline.

He flew in an easterly direction out to Terrace Bay and then banked south to follow an invisible line from the past, as depicted by the map in John Wallis's office.

Tom said, "All right, we're right above the line."

"Good." Sam manoeuvred the helicopter into a straight and level flight path approximately twenty feet above the first sand dune. "All right, switching it on."

Tom flicked a few switches and the ground penetrating radar started to work its magic. Ground penetrating radar was designed to use radar pulses to create images of the sandy subsurface. The non-destructive method used electromagnetic radiation in the microwave band, known as UHF and VHF frequencies of the radio spectrum, in order to detect reflected signals from subsurface structures. The plan was to run a grid search along the invisible line of the forgotten coast, as depicted by the map in John Wallis's office from the same year the *Emerald Star* was sunk at anchor.

To Sam, the device felt close to cheating in the world of treasure hunting. Using technology people could have only dreamt about twenty years ago, the state of the art equipment was relatively simple to use. It ran a continuous swath. It was then decoded by an on board computer, which then spat out the image of any solid shapes within the subsurface. Tom studied the monitor, but in reality he didn't have to. The computer would identify any objects, and provide a list at the end of their search, meaning there was little active input during the process.

Tom turned to Sam. "Still no word from Peter Smyth?"

"No."

"It seems unlikely that the man would disappear right when we were about to discover the truth?"

"I know. I don't like it. Anything could have happened since we left him in Istanbul. He might have got cold feet and decided to go to ground again – or THEY caught up with him?"

"What do you want to do about it?"

"There's not much we can do about it. I've left Elise running a continuous online search for his image anywhere near Istanbul. If he's gone to ground, we might still get lucky."

The computer pinged loudly – they had received their first positive response from the ground penetrating radar. Sam glanced at the monitor. It looked like a ship, but a very small one. If it was along the current coastline, he would have suspected it to be a small motorboat, but given its location, it was more likely to be a skiff. He made a circular search around the object, so that the radar could plot a more precise size and shape of the object.

A few minutes later Sam returned to straight and level, following the imaginary line from the past. He studied the hostile but fascinating coast with a mix of awe and respect. It was no surprise that such a land could be unforgiving. The coast was predominantly soft sand, with the occasional rocky outcrop. To the south were large gravel plains, while this far north, around Terrace Bay, the landscape was dominated by some of the largest sand dunes in the world.

His mind returned to a recent account of the region he'd read, in which the Bushmen of the Namibian interior called the region, *The Land God Made in Anger*, while Portuguese sailors once referred to it as, *The Gates of Hell*.

On the coast, the upwelling of the cold Benguela current gave rise to a dense ocean fog for nearly two thirds of the year. There is a constant, heavy surf on the beaches. Here the cold and unpredictable Benguela Current of the Atlantic Ocean clashes with the dune and desert landscape of north-western Namibia. Numerous ships have stranded at the Skeleton Coast thanks to the thick fog, the rough sea, unpredictable currents and stormy winds. The sailors who were able to make it to the land did not stand a chance of survival at this inhospitable coast and died of thirst.

Strangely, it was the same Benguela effect that allowed the region to teem with life. Although less than ten inches of rain fell annually throughout Namibia, the dense ocean fog extended nearly a hundred miles inland. Large wild animals adapted to the arid climate and survived surprisingly well, including desert-adapted elephants, rhinos, desert lions, brown hyenas, jackals, giraffes, seals, oryx, kudus and zebras. The riverbeds further inland were home to baboons, giraffes, lions, black rhinoceros and springbok. The animals get most of their water from wells dug by the baboons or elephants.

By the time they reached Cape Cross, they'd found a total of five ships in the sand's subsurface. Two were much too small to be the *Emerald Star*, but the other three were in the vague vicinity of the size and shape expected of the seventeenth century Barquentine.

Sam banked to the right and made a beeline for the *Maria Helena*.

Chapter Forty-Four

The *Orson Scott Card* was an eighty-foot dredging vessel. Her futuristic design looked to Sam like a cross between a tank with its massive twin rubber tracks and a conventional battleship. It had a large hydraulic snout, and a massive claw attached to an arm off the rotating bridge, the entire ship looked like it was straight out of science fiction. He guessed her owner was inspired by the ship's strange impression to pay tribute to the classic science fiction writer of the same name.

Its shallow draft and tank tracks gave her an amphibious capability. Under power from the tank tracks, the vessel drove due east, slowly climbing the monstrous sand dunes of the Skeleton Coast before dipping down their backside. It had cost a small fortune to hire the vessel and her operator for an entire month. The first day was spent just moving the damned ship to the first location.

Sam and Tom rode up high in the main bridge with Max Heinemann, the owner and operator of the dredger – a solid man of roughly sixty, sporting a thick, white beard that to Sam looked very becoming a sea captain. The reddening of his cheeks, and rotund belly suggested he liked his drink perhaps a little too much. He seemed knowledgeable and competent at his job. More importantly still, he was available for hire.

As the heavy tracks dug deep into the upcoming sand dune, Sam asked, "Have you had such an unusual request before?"

"Unusual?" Max changed into a deep low gear, and the vessel slowed to a crawl up the dune. "It's not even the first time I've been asked to dig up an old ship long since buried in the sand.

"Really?"

"Yes. There's been many a book written about lost treasure being inside shipwrecks buried in these sands. Did you know the desert is slowly moving west, reclaiming the land?"

Sam nodded, he knew exactly how far the dunes moved. "Has anyone ever found any real treasure?"

"Course they have. Not that it makes any sense to me."

"Why not?"

Max gave him that sort of smile that said he was going to let him in on a secret. "Think about it. You spent a small fortune hiring the dredger. You might not find anything of real value to show after a week out here. Even if you do, it won't cover much of my fees, unless you really do strike it rich. So the entire thing seems to me like a giant waste of time and money – not that I mind of course – it's your money and I'm glad to receive your business."

Sam and Tom laughed.

Sam said, "Thanks for your honesty. We're not really looking for treasure, so it's okay."

Max met his eye, with the hardened stare. "Really? What do you hope to find inside an old shipwreck?"

"Just history. I have a friend whose great ancestor lost his life on this ship. We're hoping to find it for him."

"A noble cause. I wish you luck."

Sam asked, "Just out of interest, if someone was to search for something beneath the sands of the Kalahari Desert, could you move the *Orson Scott Card* there?"

Max shook his head. "If you were to give me months, I might be able to get a permit to travel with her along the highways at night time, but it would be expensive. Probably cheaper to have a mining dredge or digger built on sight. Or even bring in a bulldozer or two. What are you really looking for out here, Mr. Reilly?"

Sam smiled. "Ancient history."

Chapter Forty-Five

The first dig took a total of two days to reach and then a further day to excavate enough sand to determine the ship was the *Alicia May*, a French merchant ship. It took the fourth day to reach the next structure. On the fifth day they discovered the ship was actually the remains of a small whaling cabin, discarded at the end of the whaling era which the coast was named after.

Sam studied the map. Tom had circled three main structures in the sand's subsurface with the ground penetrating radar. He'd made the decision earlier to search the larger structures and skip the smaller vessels altogether. There was only one vessel left to search. If that came up with nothing, he would have to rethink how he was going to progress with the search. There was a lot of sand and just as many shipwrecks.

In truth, he'd been quite lucky to discover the first two weren't the *Emerald Star* early. If he hadn't found the nameplate of the *Alicia May*, he might have been digging for a week and still not know if it was the correct ship or not.

On the tenth day they reached the final shipwreck. Sam marked out the location, which would hopefully correlate with a section amidships, where he hoped the main opening might still be accessible. Max started up the large dredging machine.

The Orson Scott Card used a fourteen inch pipe connected to a large centrifugal pump to suction the sand. Its 550 horsepower engine spun two impellers at a rate of 600 RPM. In water, it moved approximately 8,000 gallons of water and sand per minute. In the dry sand, Max was forced to reduce the RPM to 300, which shifted approximately three tons of sand an hour. It ran at a pressure of seven BAR, two below its maximum output, for six hours – before the sand gave way to untarnished wood.

"Stop!" Sam shouted. "We've reached something."

The loud grind of the pump came to a halt, leaving a slight residual ringing in Sam's ear. Behind him, Max pulled back on the automated suction arm so that it was out of the way. "Okay, Sam, she's all yours. Go have a look at what you found."

Sam nodded. He climbed down into the large opening in the sand. "Hey Tom, can you please bring a shovel down here – we might need to manually shift some of this sand."

"Here," Tom passed one to him.

Sam ran the back of the shovel along the thick wood of what appeared to be the remains of an old mast. He felt the blade chip away at wood and sand. A moment later, the sound changed. It was something different, something distinctly metallic.

He used his hands to quickly dig away the rest of the sand. Breathing hard, he pulled at the sand and with each movement he began to see a new piece of the puzzle. The item was brass. It made him work harder. In two minutes he removed enough sand that he was able to dig his fingers in underneath. Sam pulled hard. Whatever it was he'd found held under the suction of sand compressed by hundreds of years. But then it started to move. Sam pulled harder and in a moment the entire thing broke free and Sam fell backward.

He scraped the remaining sand free of the brass item. It was the ship's bell. There was a small engraving at the top of the bell. Sam felt his heart lurch into a gallop. He held his breath as he blew the remaining sand that filled the tiny gap of the engraving and then stared at the Bell.

His lips then curled into a winning smile, because the name on the centuries-old engraving was still clearly visible – *Emerald Star*.

Chapter Forty-Six

Sam switched his flashlight on and climbed down. The wooden ladder creaked under his weight, but the wood was otherwise very well preserved. At ten feet down, he reached the main entrance cabin. It was shaped like a small semi-circle with an empty weapons rack at the end. The skeletal remains of a man lay on the ground in front of him. Through the hollowed ribcage, a steel-tipped spear still pointed to the stars.

He turned his flashlight away. It was obvious how the man had died and he had no morbid desire to study him further. To a certain extent, he figured the guy who had landed on the spear received a far kinder death than those who had survived long enough to become entombed by the sand.

Tom carefully tested his weight on the ladder above. "Do you think it will hold my weight?"

"Yeah, should do. Just watch the spear at the bottom."

Sam felt the structural beams that supported the deck above. They'd held the weight of many tons of sand for a little over three and a half centuries. He ran his hand over the first four he found. They were made out of some sort of red hardwood. A dendrologist might have told him the wood had come from *Lebanon Cedar* – the most prolific hardwood used in ship building throughout the Mediterranean until the eighteenth century, when overcutting reduced it to extinction – and that the arid environment had allowed it to maintain its strength after all these years. Without the specialist knowledge, Sam felt a healthy fear for the stability of the old vessel.

He took another step. The floor creaked and he turned to Tom. "On second thoughts, you might want to wait here. There's no way of telling how safe the wood is after all these years. No reason to put both our lives in danger."

Tom nodded. "I'm here if you need me."

Sam continued deeper into the main cargo hold. He was surprised to see the ship, which had been so well preserved inside, didn't seem to have any other skeletons. He dropped down to the lower level that housed the now dry bilge. He flashed his light around the deck, but it was empty of what he was after.

Sam retraced his steps to the main deck and then headed aft. At the very back he found a step up into the aft castle and Captain's quarters. He climbed the stairs and entered the room. Sam flicked his light across the room. His eyes fixed on what he saw in front of him and he inhaled sharply.

A large navigation, come dining table, took up the vast majority of the captain's private quarters. It was an aft cabin from the glory days of shipbuilding, when the privileged class ruled the world. It was big enough to have entertained eight or more persons at one time. The table had been intricately carved out of mahogany, and in the middle of it, still sitting at the table were the skeletal remains of one man. Facing directly at the human skull was a very different one – a golden skull.

The two skulls were facing each other, their eyes locked for eternity.

Sam fixed the light on the empty skull. The void where the eyes once stared out, somehow betrayed the man's profound loss. Next to him was an empty bottle. Nothing remained to suggest what was inside, but Sam figured if it was him, he'd want some pretty hard liquor. In a moment, Sam realized the significance of the find. It meant that this man was the only one alive when the ship had become buried beneath the sand.

By the looks of things, the poor wretch had the time to wander the ship in isolation before starvation or dehydration eventually took his life. Sam almost forgot what he was searching for as he wondered who the skeleton once belonged to. His eyes swept the room. There was something else he hadn't noticed immediately.

A leather bound book graced the table next to the golden skull. He hoped he would find the answers he needed inside that journal, but now was not the time to read it. Instead he studied the golden skull. He'd heard Peter Smyth refer to it as the *Death Mask* or the *Key to the Third Temple.*

Sam picked up the heavy skull.

It was hollow inside, but even so, he felt the weight in his arms and was thankful he hadn't needed to carry it across a desert. He turned the skull to face him. Its ivory teeth grinned hideously, as though it was begging to tell one hell of a story about its past.

What do you know?

As Sam turned the skull he felt something move inside. It wasn't quite as fluid as liquid, but more likely fine like a powder. He stared into the hollowed eyes. *Or was something inside?* Sam shined his light into the dark space. The entire area behind the eyes and nose appeared hollow. It was only on the second look, that he spotted it. Not that he knew it was anything at all. He inserted his finger deep inside the left eye socket and felt it move.

But what was it?

He pressed upward with his index finger and felt it move all the way upward. He grinned as he withdrew his finger and shined the flashlight back inside. It had been a clever latch and it had caused an intricately carved piece of obsidian to swivel outward, allowing access to whatever was stored inside.

His eyes narrowed as he tried to interpret what had been stored inside. There was a sweet scent to it like a mixture of hard liquor and chloroform. Sam instinctively took a step back and held his breath as he examined the black powder. It was so fine and delicate he worried that one whiff and the entire contents would be inhaled. The powder shifted in an almost liquid-like state as he tilted the skull.

Sam made a mental note to have the powder tested in a lab. He then used his index finger to reach inside and pull the latch downward. The piece of obsidian returned to its resting space, and the black powder was once again secured.

He turned the skull over and stared at it from below, where solid gold had been flattened to make space for a unique image, delicately etched inside. It depicted two mountain peaks, leading together with a small lake or possibly snow in the middle. He'd recognized the snow-capped mountain of Mount Ararat and in an instant realized the skull was a map.

But not the map he wanted.

He already knew where the key to the Third Temple was supposed to be taken. What he needed was to locate the pyramid in the Kalahari Desert and find Billie Swan. Sam considered his next move, wondering whether the man's journal might shed some light on things, when he saw it.

His heart raced and he felt the goosebumps prickle over his skin as his eyes fixed directly in front of the skeleton, where the mahogany table had been scarred by the deep etchings of a knife. Sam stared at them for a moment, carefully reading the words that struck him like lightning – *Don't let the man with purple eyes have the Death Mask.*

Chapter Forty-Seven

Sam spent the next three days reading and then rereading the journal of Harper Smith on board the *Maria Helena,* while the preparations were made. The *Death Mask* was secured inside the ship's armory, where a state of the art security system would scare off the most seasoned bank robber. He sent a sample of the black powder off to a biochemist to study and left Elise in charge of making sense of whatever the scientist discovered.

On the fourth day, the final resources arrived and Sam and Tom set off east into the Namib Desert on camel back. Sam had located Smith's Kamal and having read the old explorer's journal, now knew that the early navigation device allowed him to accurately follow a specific latitude defined by the marking of an additional knot into its line. Per his journal the men had traveled for three days by camel to the east, starting out at the *Emerald Star*, before they located the ancient pyramid.

The camels were loaded with a similar weight as those used by the crew of the *Emerald Star*. The plan was they would travel east using Kamal, and keeping pace with the original expedition as recorded in Smith's journal. This would get them within a basic vicinity of the pyramid. It wouldn't get them to the exact place, because the sand dunes would have changed during that time, but it was a start.

Once they reached that area, then they would contact the *Maria Helena* and Genevieve would bring in the Sea King and the ground penetrating radar. It would then be a time consuming process of expanding the search in ever evolving larger circles. Sam realized it might take months to locate, or he might get lucky. Either way, the camel trip was only the start.

At the end of the second day, Sam received a call on his satellite phone.

It was Elise, and as per usual, she got straight to the point. "Sam I got a hit on Peter Smyth."

Sam asked, "Where?"

"The Daily Sabah, an Istanbul based newspaper, ran a report on a body that washed up on the shore of the Bosphorus Strait."

"They killed him, didn't they?"

"I'm sorry, Sam. It would appear so."

Sam thought about the consequences. There was nothing he could do to save the man now, but there were still consequences to consider. What had his murderers found out? How much could Peter have told them? Were they on their way to the Skeleton Coast already?

He paused as he considered this possibility. If Peter talked before he was murdered, it would mean that THEY would come to the Skeleton Coast. The entrance to the Emerald Star had been intentionally buried again, but there was a possibility if they got to Peter they were smart. If so, they would start asking the right questions to locals in the area, who would be quick to talk about two strangers who spent a fortune hiring a dredging ship to remove sand covering an old ship nearly ten miles inland. It was an amazing story, and one they'd quickly find.

So what if they dug up the Emerald Star?

The Death Mask was no longer there, and Smith's journal was in his hand, so there was no evidence of where the pyramid might be. Sam thought about that for a moment. Were they safe? He knew the answer was no. It wouldn't take long for their pursuers to make the connection that the pyramid would have to be east of the *Emerald Star*. It then wouldn't take much for aerial surveillance to locate two men on camels.

Sam instinctively touched the pouch on the right hand side of his camel, thankful that he and Tom brought Heckler and Koch MP5 Assault Rifles. If they had visitors, they were prepared to meet them this time.

Over the course of three and a half days, Sam and Tom followed the same route that Harper Smith had taken three and a half centuries earlier. When they stopped after spending the exact same amount of time on camel as their predecessors, it turned out to be a little under two hundred miles from the *Emerald Star* – making the pyramid just inside the Kalahari Desert.

Both men stared down at the rows of sand dunes that continued all the way to the horizon.

"Well, we made it – as much as I hate travelling by camel!" Sam stared into the distance. "The pyramid must be somewhere in this vicinity. Of course, it might take us months to locate it from the air."

Tom looked over the crest of the dune, squinted and then shook his head. "I don't think we need to worry about that."

"Why?"

Tom swallowed. "Because it appears someone beat us to it."

Chapter Forty-Eight – The Buried Pyramid of the Kalahari

The opening looked more like the entrance to a mine shaft than a pyramid buried in sand. Three old railway sleepers formed the framework for the adit. It ran at a gradual decline right into the base of the next sand dune. Inside the makeshift timber set, used to support the roof inside, mingled with a series of posts, jacks and roof bolts used to prop up the sandy ceiling. They had been placed haphazardly, giving Sam the impression of an old gold mine built during the American gold rush era.

Sam glanced around at a series of recent vehicle tracks leading toward the entrance. There were two distinctly different tracks. One looked wide as though it belonged to a large vehicle, like a truck or four wheel drive, while the other was narrow but deep, and ran all the way inside the mine shaft. The smaller of the two looked like it possibly had been caused by a small digging machine, possibly a backhoe or frontend loader.

Tom dismounted his camel and removed his Heckler and Koch assault rifle from its pouch. He set it to full auto and approached the entrance to the shaft. He glanced back and said, "You might want to call Genevieve and tell her to bring in some reinforcements."

Sam grinned and followed suit, removing his own weapon and setting it to full auto. It felt like a final shoot out scene from an old western movie, where the final standoff occurs inside an old ghost mine. Only in this case, the mine wasn't a mine at all, it was a tunnel to an ancient pyramid and the good guys were carrying assault rifles.

He made the call to Genevieve, who said that she and Veyron would come with the Sea King armed to the teeth to secure the area.

Sam stopped at the entrance and listened. There were no sounds coming out from the mine and nothing outside it, either. He scanned the horizons in each direction. There was nothing but sand. No sand clouds or wisps of upturned sand spewing toward the sky, indicating a truck might be approaching.

"Genevieve says she can be here within an hour." He turned to Tom as he filled a small bucket with water for the two beasts to drink. "What do you reckon?"

Tom attached a light to his weapon's scope. "I think it's time we find some answers."

Sam nodded. "That's what I thought you'd say."

Chapter Forty-Nine

The tunnel extended a quarter of a mile before it reached the horizontal entrance to a pyramid. Sam found himself unintentionally holding his breath, listening for any signs of other persons inside. He heard none. He and Tom switched their flashlights off and waited another few minutes. The faint glow of the outside world was barely visible looking backward, and no light surfaced from inside.

Sam exhaled. "All right, let's go."

Tom stepped inside first. Thirty feet inside the angle of the tunnel changed from horizontal to a steep decline. Another four hundred feet inside and the tunnel separated into directions. The original tunnel continued to descend at the same angle, while the second tunnel ran at the exact same angle, only at an incline instead.

Sam said, "It's the same anatomy as the Pyramid of Giza."

"So which way do you want to go?" Tom asked.

"Up. Down probably leads to a storage chamber. We need to reach the king's Chamber if we're to find the location we saw from the looking glass."

They continued climbing for another four hundred feet. Again the tunnel split into two. With the main tunnel following the same incline, while the second one ran horizontally deeper toward the pyramid's core.

Sam shined his flashlight into the horizontal tunnel. "The queen's chamber. Let's keep heading upward."

They continued to climb the stairs. The ceiling above opened to about thirty feet. If the anatomy of the architecture matched the Pyramid of Giza as the sunken pyramid on Infinity Island had, it indicated they were now traveling through the grand gallery. At the top of the incline, the tunnel leveled out horizontally and they stepped into the king's chamber.

The room was rectangular with a ceiling just short of twenty feet. At the center of the room where Sam would have expected the sarcophagus to go, a single limestone pedestal stood. Sam recognized the recess built into the top of it as being the perfect match for the base of the Death Mask.

He shined his flashlight around the rest of the room. Two pictograms lined the east and west walls. The first was a series of numbers, most likely indicating an intersecting point on a map. The problem was, the distance was referred to as the *carrib* – that same ancient word they'd found on the stone tablet on board the shipwreck of the *Mary Rose* on the seabed of the Black Sea. There was an image next to it, which left no doubt in his mind of the location the map was referring to. The drawing depicted the two volcanic peaks of Mount Ararat.

The second consisted of three sets of Roman Numerals, which appeared highly at odds with their Egyptian environment. The size of each numeral changed dramatically from number to number so that the three sets formed the shape of a small pyramid. Sam took a photo and read the numbers out loud. They appeared vaguely familiar to him, but he couldn't recall where he'd seen them before.

They certainly didn't sound like any location he'd been to, and they were too long to refer to any sort of period of time. It irked him that he couldn't recall where he'd seen the numbers.

Tom swore and then looked at him. "It's the wrong place, isn't it?"

"Yes."

"Any of this mean anything to you?"

"Not a thing, but my guess is it will."

Sam finished taking photos of the chamber. When he was done, he said, "All right. We're not going to learn anything more from here, let's hitch a ride back to the *Maria Helena* and see what Elise can find out about either of these images."

"And if she can't?" Tom asked. "Then what?"

"Then we'll have to take the Death Mask to its resting place on top of Mount Ararat."

Sam gripped his Heckler and Koch assault rifle and started to walk down the descending passage. He made it two hundred feet and stopped. Because up ahead, he spotted the flicker of someone else's flashlight.

Chapter Fifty

Dmitri switched off his flashlight.

In the narrow ascending passage sound traveled quickly. He heard the distinct click of a weapon being switched into a firing position and the labored breaths of two men approaching in the dark, having just extinguished their flashlights in an instant. He turned and started to slowly feel his way down the passageway.

After thirty or forty feet, his hand dipped into the horizontal passage that led to the queen's chamber. He heard the sound of heavy footsteps, as though someone large was now running toward him. Only an insane person would try to run in the dark to greet a hidden enemy. The thought almost made him laugh out loud.

Dmitri was quick and time had hardened him against fear. But somewhere in the back of his mind, a voice said he had to get out of there. He had no gripe with the two men who were approaching, but he was less confident they would share the sentiment. He wondered if he could outrun the strangers in the dark to the surface of the mine.

The steps grew louder and he knew there was no way to reach the surface before them, and even if he could, there was no telling that once on the surface he could escape before being shot by the two men. No, he was better off hiding.

He stepped into the horizontal passage and started to move quickly and silently toward the queen's chamber. When he reached it, he found there was nowhere for him to hide. No sarcophagus. No limestone pedestal. It was a rectangular chamber, only just smaller than the king's above, and it offered him nothing in the form of concealment.

He listened hard. For several minutes there were no sounds at all. Had the ruse worked? Had they continued running to the surface? Even if they did, how long did he have before they worked out he was still inside and decided to backtrack?

Dmitri was about to take the chance and make his way to the king's chamber, to find what he'd come here to get. He needed to reach the temple on Mount Ararat before the others did and the king's chamber was the last place he knew which had an ancient map.

He stepped into the horizontal passage and quickly shifted back inside the queen's chamber – because he heard the sound of footsteps approaching once more. Dmitri shot his back against the stone wall of the queen's chamber. He stayed about a foot away from where the horizontal passage entered, and there he waited.

A bright light flashed toward the tunnel.

He heard a confident voice shout, "Come on out. There's two of us and we're both carrying assault rifles, so you're trapped."

Dmitri waited. He breathed silently with the practiced equanimity developed over a very long lifetime and he listened to every step of his attackers.

"We're going to shoot you if you don't come out…" the same voice boomed.

Dmitri slowly inhaled and then held his breath.

The queen's chamber was completely silent. He heard the gentle cadence of his unsettled heart increase its pace slightly. It pounded in the back of his ears.

About three feet away, he heard someone take another step. It was so quiet, the sound was almost imperceptible.

He started counting.

Dmitri had only reached two, when the shadow of a man as big as a small house, stepped into the chamber. It was a fifty-fifty chance the man would look to his left or right. They were bad odds, but they were the ones he was dealt.

His attacker glanced to the left first.

It was a small win, but it was all Dmitri was going to get. He moved with inhuman speed toward his assailant. His hands gripping the monster from his shoulder and pulling him backwards, while simultaneously driving his left foot hard into the soft spot behind the giant's knee.

He heard the man grunt. It would normally bring the toughest of men to the ground in a wail of agony, but this man remained standing. Dmitri wrapped his left arm around the man's neck, locking his elbow, so that he could apply pressure on his windpipe. He felt the monster thrash, as though he still believed he could win from that position. Dmitri brought up a small blade to the man's throat with his right hand so the point gently pierced his skin and then applied more pressure behind his knee so that he was leaning back into him.

"Okay, that will do…" Dmitri whispered, as though he were trying to hush a child. "I think this will end much better for the three of us if you tell your friend to put his weapon down."

"My name's Sam Reilly." A light shined directly at him. "I have a Heckler and Koch assault rifle pointed straight at your head, so I suggest you let my friend go."

"Sam Reilly?" Dmitri couldn't believe what he heard. "How the hell did you find this place?"

"I found the remains of the *Emerald Star* and then from there followed the journal to this place. But of course, you would already know that, wouldn't you?"

"What do you mean, wouldn't I?" Dmitri asked. "I wouldn't have asked if I already knew."

"I mean you wouldn't be here if you didn't already know." Sam's voice was calm, but there was a coldness to it that bordered on vehement animosity.

The big guy he'd taken prisoner spoke. "I don't mean to interrupt your bickering, but you mentioned before that if my friend puts his weapon down, this would go better for all of us. Did you have a plan in mind?"

"It's quite simple really."

"Go on," the giant said. "I'm listening."

"You remove the magazine from your weapon and eject each of the bullets. Then your friend here does the same. As you already know I only have a knife, so that leaves us all without an instrument that goes bang."

"How do we know you're not carrying a gun?" Sam asked.

Dmitri made a big show of sighing, as though he was trying to explain something to a simpleton. "Because if I had, I would have used it by now, wouldn't I?"

"You'll still have a knife and we won't have anything…" Sam pointed out. "The move's stacked a little heavily in your favor."

"True. But someone's going to have to give something here. Alternatively I slit your friend's throat now, and then we see who gets the first shot off. It's probably going to be you, but either way, your friend here dies. So, what do you want to do?"

The big guy spoke again. "If we empty our magazines. Then what?"

"Then I run like hell, gambling that I might just be able to run faster than you can reload your bullets." He sighed again. "Or you could just let me leave here."

"All right." The big guy started to eject bullets from his magazine.

Dmitri counted twenty-five bullets hit the ground – a full magazine. After the last bullet fell he heard the assault rifle follow. Dmitri glanced at Sam Reilly. The man's piercing blue eyes were fixed on him with unreadable glare. "Your turn."

"Okay," Sam said.

Dmitri counted twenty-four bullets hit the floor – one short of a full magazine.

Sam never blinked. "Your turn."

"I'm afraid I'm going to need you to eject the last bullet from your magazine."

Sam opened his mouth to lie. Then, appearing to think better of it, he said, "You have really good hearing."

He waited until the last bullet was ejected and dropped on the floor. "Okay, now I want you over there, at the end of the queen's chamber."

"Sure." Sam moved over to the back of the chamber. "Now what are you going to do?"

Dmitri smiled. "I'm going to walk out of here, and you're both going to let me."

He pulled the big guy backwards and then stepped out of the way, kicking his leg in the process. The big guy turned with surprising speed, narrowly avoiding hitting the floor and then picking up his assault rifle the man launched at him, gripping the weapon like a baseball bat.

The stranger moved quickly, but he responded faster. Dmitri stepped back and withdrew his handgun from a concealed holster behind his back. He had it pointed straight at the man in an instant.

Dmitri said, "I told you to let me walk out of here!"

Both men backed away. "Okay, okay… go!"

"I suggest you count to a hundred before you come after me. If I catch you following me, I won't talk to you, I'll kill you both."

He bent down and picked up the two MP5 magazines to take with him and started running. He didn't look back. He just kept running. He was thankful for his decision to carry his handgun. He rarely did anymore. Didn't have a need. Today was different. He expected to see one of the OTHERS, but instead he found two strangers. His lungs pounded by the time he reached the surface ten minutes later.

Dmitri grinned. He was free and for the first time in decades he knew who had the Death Mask. He burst past the opening of the mine shaft and then stopped and raised his hands above his head – because a large helicopter stood on its skids facing him and out the door stood a man pointing a Browning heavy machine gun at him.

Chapter Fifty-One

Billie woke up lying next to the cool stream.

Her lips curved upward in a warm smile. It was the same as last time. The same as all of the previous times. Like waking up the day after a long night of drinking, where the events after the first drink were a mystery. Only it was completely different, too. She felt a sense of accomplishment, although of what, she couldn't quite remember, yet. Her muscles felt sore, but invigorated, as though they had been working hard and now she was somehow stronger.

The euphoria was there, too.

She'd never taken illicit drugs. Not out of righteousness or anything like that, simply because she'd never felt the need. Some people have an addictive personality, and she wasn't one of those. Billie thought about that while she lay there on the side of the river, basking in a sensation of true bliss. She could leave this anytime she wanted, couldn't she?

Maybe she did have an addictive personality, after all?

Billie stood up to find some food. She always felt incredibly hungry after the Black Smoke had taken her. She glanced at her wristwatch. *Could it really have been three days this time?* She ignored the nagging question, knowing full well she didn't want to know the answer. The durations were getting longer, as though someone knew the preparations were approaching their deadline soon.

She took a deep breath in and smiled. She would stay here until the Black Smoke had completed its task, and no longer had a use for her.

Life was good.

Billie felt into her shirt where her ivory pendant hung for comfort. She gasped and swallowed the fear that rose in her throat like bile – because her grandfather's ancient pendant was missing.

Chapter Fifty-Two

As the helicopter flew due west toward the *Maria Helena*, Sam slowly reassembled his Heckler and Koch MP5. Opposite him, now with his hands and feet bound by cable ties was the man he'd met inside the Kalahari pyramid. The man's violet eyes were fixed in a vacant stare, as though inside the mind was set in a constant disillusionment about how he lost.

Sam recalled the warning on the mahogany table inside the *Emerald Star*. The last thing a dead man ever wrote – *Don't let the man with the purple eyes have the Death Skull.*

He kept his eyes on the man throughout the entire flight, but both men remained silent. Not that they could have spoken if they'd wanted to with the engine and rotary wing drowning out any words.

When the helicopter finally landed on board the *Maria Helena*, Tom dragged the man out on to the ship's aft deck. It was open without anywhere to run or hide.

Sam made a show of loading the final bullet into the magazine and then clipped the magazine into the chamber. "Okay, let's start with your name."

The man had a curious look on his face as he studied those aboard. "Dmitri."

"Dmitri who?"

"Just Dmitri." The man glanced around the ship. "Where are you taking me?"

"To place the Death Mask into its slot on top of Mount Ararat and turn the key."

Dmitri shrugged. "I have no idea what you're talking about."

Sam said, "The key to the Third Temple."

Dmitri started to laugh. "Oh, this is rich. You have no idea what's going on here, do you?"

Tom hit him in the gut. "A good friend of mine is being held prisoner in the Third Temple, so we're not in the mood for your jokes. Tell us what you know."

Dmitri breathed gently, as though the punch had barely winded him. "I can tell you one thing for certain."

"Go on," Tom said.

"Your friend isn't being held prisoner in the Third Temple." He then smiled. It was one of those looks like I know something you don't know and you're not going to like it. "No one is, yet."

"What the hell does that mean?" Sam asked.

"It means I can't help you find your friend."

Sam thought about pushing him, but guessed Dmitri wasn't the sort of person who caved under pressure. "All right. Next question, why did you kill Peter?"

"Peter who?"

"Smyth. The man who you killed to find the pyramid in the Kalahari Desert."

"Peter's dead?" There was surprise in his eyes, but no remorse or loss.

"You killed him."

"No. It must have been one of the OTHERS."

"What others?"

"One of the Four Horsemen."

Sam considered the possibility. He'd already met Famine. That meant there were three more out there. He turned to Dmitri and asked, "What other name do you go by?"

"Ah... a good question." Dmitri smiled. "Some call me Death."

"If you didn't kill Peter, how did you find the pyramid?"

"I paid a guy earlier this year to search for the pyramid. A guy called Leo Dietrich, an expert hunter in the region, to search the Kalahari for signs of the pyramid. Once he'd finished building the tunnel in, he contacted me and I came to get what I needed."

"What did you need?"

"An address. I didn't get around to finding it, because you and your friend got in my way. But not to bother, by the sounds of things I don't need it anymore."

"Why not?"

"Because you're taking me to the temple on the top of Mount Ararat."

"What is this all about?"

"I'm sorry. It's not that I don't want to tell you, but I've made a promise not to tell anyone. Not now, not even in the end."

Sam looked up, and noticed Elise walk onto the deck.

As per normal, she omitted any pleasantries and jumped straight into business. "I've had a sample of the black soot analyzed by a leading neurologist in Boston."

"And?"

"You're not going to like what she had to say."

Chapter Fifty-Three

Sam read the report and then looked at Elise for clarity. He handed it to Tom to read, and then turned to Elise. "You want to explain this to me as though I'm not a chemical engineer or a neurologist?"

Elise smiled as though she'd been expecting just such a response. "All right. I sent the powder to a toxicologist for a report, who said it was something extraordinary he'd never seen before and consequently he sent it on to a leading neurologist to determine what sort of effect such a chemical make-up might have on the human brain."

Sam asked, "He'd never seen it at all, or hadn't seen it in combination with whatever was there?"

"Never seen it before, but you'll never guess what it's most similar to."

"Okay, I probably won't. What?"

"Lysergic acid diethylamide."

"What?" Sam asked again.

"Didn't you go to university?" Elise teased. "LSD."

"The Death Mask is filled with LSD?"

"Not exactly."

"What do you mean, then?"

"LSD was first made by Albert Hofmann in Switzerland in 1938 from ergotamine, a chemical from the fungus ergot."

"Go on."

"Ergotamine is a molecule that shares a structural similarity with neurotransmitters such as serotonin, dopamine, and epinephrine and can thus bind to several receptors acting as an agonist."

Sam said, "In English!"

Elise smiled, patiently. "It means the powder has the ability to affect everything the human brain perceives."

"So is the black powder LSD or not?"

"No. But it does come from a similar fungus new to science – something that no biochemist in the world appears to have ever seen. Aren't you happy, you discovered a new drug?"

Tom looked up from the report. "All right. So the ancient ones used to sit around tripping on this black smoke, is that it?"

"Not exactly," Elise said.

Sam asked, "What then, does the neurologist think its purpose was?"

"Okay, I'm going to have to refer back to LSD, because it's the closest chemical compound we have to the black smoke and the two share remarkable similarities." Elise waited for Sam and Tom to look like they were ready to follow her again. Having received it, in the form of a slight nod, she continued. "The effects of LSD are most noticeable in the cerebral cortex, which is responsible for, among other things, thought development, sensory perception, and communication. LSD appears to blur the lines between each form of incoming sensory information."

"Meaning?" Sam and Tom asked in unison.

Elise said, "You might see the sound, hear the color, feel the sight with your fingertips, or taste the music. LSD affects all parts of your sensory perception by turning up the intensity, like if you took an old television set, and turned up the intensity to make the colors brighter."

"Okay, it still sounds like the black powder was there to give people a trip. Are you telling me it served some other purpose?" Sam asked.

Elise swallowed. "I'm not trying to convince you of anything. I'm merely passing on what a leading neurologist believes."

"And what does she believe?" Sam asked.

"It was once hypothesized that the cerebral cortex was once able to receive a different sort of information. Something close to high frequency sound waves."

Sam asked, "For what purpose?"

Elise said, "If the cerebrum was intensified, this part of the brain might be able to transmit and receive information at a frequency that human ears can no longer perceive."

"Are you talking about a form of telepathy?"

She nodded.

"How?"

Elise said, "Through high frequency wavelengths no longer able to be recognized by the human brain."

"But evolution made it shrink?" Sam asked, without hiding his skepticism.

"It appears so."

"But why would evolution remove something that would have obviously been useful?"

"It's not telepathy in the same form as what fantasy books or science fiction would have us believe. Instead, it was more of a rudimentary means of communicating feelings or senses, such as, *danger, run, hide, and feed.* Simple feelings. The receiving person would then intrinsically feel the same. It would be like a sixth sense. They weren't sending and receiving information in the form of words."

Tom looked at Sam. "Does that sound like something familiar?"

Sam said, "Christ! Billie's being controlled by this drug!"

Chapter Fifty-Four – The Temple of Illumination

It was approaching the end of summer and a thick layer of snow, the first major snowfall, covered the entrance to the crevasse on the plateau of Mount Ararat. Sam cleared the space and abseiled down into the lava tube. With him, were Tom and Dmitri. Dmitri of course had grudgingly agreed to join the expedition… he had no other means to find the remaining Four Horsemen.

Sam had agreed – it was worth the risk – he knew the information that Dmitri had would be critical to discovering the nature of the relic and finding Billie. He maintained a strong sense of mistrust for the man, but also accepted the fact Dmitri didn't kill him or Tom when he had the chance inside the buried pyramid of the Kalahari Desert.

Twenty minutes later they reached the deepest part of the lava tube, where the recess in the wall perfectly matched the Death Mask. Below which, were four additional smaller recesses carved into the obsidian wall – one for each of the Four Horsemen.

Tom glanced at the dead body still lying at the very end of the lava tube. "Who's the stiff?"

"That's War." Sam flicked the light of his flashlight across the room, where the thick yellow jacket was about all he could make out from the distance. "He fell to his death a number of years ago."

"And you left him here?"

"You got a better idea?" Sam asked. "We're trying to find Billie and this is the last link we have, so I wasn't all too keen on letting the authorities come and investigate a murder here."

"Suits me fine." Tom had a strong moral compass and that included putting the need of his friends who were in trouble first.

Sam removed the Death Mask and stared at Dmitri. "Well Death, are you going to tell me what's going to happen when I place the mask in the alcove?"

Dmitri said, "No." His face was impassive and unreadable. His mind trapped in an event from long ago.

"All right."

Sam placed the golden skull in the alcove. He waited as nothing happened. The skull remained there, its hollowed eyes staring out vacantly at him. Sam studied the skull. Nothing had changed. He felt it, expecting the gold to have turned hot like when War's pendant was placed inside the recess. Yet this time, nothing happened.

Tom shined his flashlight across the skull. "Did you see anything?"

"Not a thing." He turned to Dmitri. "Should we be expecting something to happen?"

Dmitri remained silent and shrugged. It was obvious he either didn't know, or if he did, wasn't going to share his information.

Tom fixed his flashlight onto the ceiling above the Death Mask. "Hey, did you see those numbers before?"

"Numbers?" Sam shook his head. "No."

He glanced above. There were a series of Roman Numerals. Like the ones seen inside the king's chamber of the pyramid within the Kalahari Desert, the sizes of each number changed to ensure a visual appearance of a pyramid. There were three lines of numbers, with the top being the shortest and the bottom being the longest.

Tom said, "It looks like it's almost the same set of numbers."

Sam looked at the photo he'd taken on his phone. "Not just similar, these are the exact same numbers."

Dmitri said, "What a coincidence, hey?"

"What does it mean?" Tom asked. His voice firm as he spoke.

Dmitri shrugged again and Sam started to grin.

Tom said, "Do you know what it means?"

Sam shook his head. "Not a clue."

"Then why are you smiling?" Tom asked, without hiding his frustration.

"Because I just remembered where I saw those numbers before." Sam withdrew his handgun and pointed it at Dmitri. The Glock 31 doesn't have a safety. His finger hovered just above the trigger. "No more games. You need to tell us where these numbers lead to."

"Why do you suddenly think I know anything about the damned number?" Dmitri asked. "Besides, if I did I've already said I wouldn't tell you."

"Because when I clicked on the photo on my phone the digital recognition software noted three previous images were a close link. Do you know where I'd previously taken a photo of this number?"

Dmitri shrugged, treating the question as rhetorical.

"The most recent time was inside Harper Smith's journal, where he referred to the number that, without it, the Black Smoke would be irrelevant. In the journal, there was a second note that Death sought this number as much as the Death Mask." Sam looked at Tom, who was already in the process of tying Dmitri's wrists together with cable ties. "But it was the first photo I ever took of that image that makes it so valuable to us now."

He looked at Dmitri, but the man's eyes were fixed somewhere else.

Sam said, "The first time was in the lost city of Atlantis, where Dr. Billie Swan was rapt with a set of numbers she found on a wall of obsidian that served no apparent purpose. I questioned her about it afterward, but she shrugged it off, as simply being an interesting set of numbers. I took a photo. Three days later, Billie said she wanted to follow a new lead and disappeared for good. So now, I'll ask you again, where did those numbers take her?"

Sam's hand was fixed rock solid as he pointed the Glock at Dmitri. "Where? God damn it!"

Dmitri remained silent. His face set in a hard and impassive expression. His eyes, seemed to be watching something.

Sam's eyes darted between Dmitri and the Death Mask.

Something about the skull seemed different. The skull never changed. Of course it didn't, the ancient relic was an inanimate object, right? Only, somehow, there was something different about the eyes.

Sam focused on them. They had turned more sinister, somehow. *Were they mocking him?* He shook his head, knowing the skull hadn't changed shape at all. But still the feeling that there was something different about the eyes increased... then he realized what it was...

Was it warning him?

That was it. The skull was preparing him for something terrible and warning him against a tremendous evil. He felt his sixth sense go into overdrive. His skin was riddled with goosebumps. Adrenaline surged throughout his body.

Had Death tricked him, somehow?

Sam considered shooting the man right away. It might be the safest course of action. Instead, he heard a voice from behind tell him to put the weapon down and turn around. Sam turned slowly and put the Glock down on the floor – because the ghost at the end of the tunnel had just risen and was now pointing a shotgun directly at him.

Chapter Fifty-Five

Sam stared at the ghost.

It wore the same yellow Gore-Tex climbing jacket, lined with bullet holes. That's where the similarities with the body of the dead climber ended. The man in front of him had a slightly gaunt and ascetic face, with a patrician nose and unusually high cheekbones. Sam spotted the crucifix hanging round his neck and at its center a horse of pure obsidian.

Sam recognized the third horsemen – Famine.

"Mr. Reilly, I cannot begin to tell you how much I appreciate you rounding up each of the Four Horsemen for me." Famine smiled. "You have no idea how long I've searched for these."

"Are you forgetting someone?" Sam asked. "I see Death standing there, and you are already practically emaciated, so I'll take your word for it – you're Famine. I'm carrying War. But I don't see Conquest, do you?"

"Let's just say Conquest will join us soon," Famine said. "Now, I'll have you place War in its recess."

Sam paused for a second and Famine shot Death in his left knee cap. The bony fragments splintered into more than a dozen shards.

Death let out a deep, guttural roar. It lasted seconds and then was over; the practiced silence of a lifetime of pain and discomfort.

Famine grinned. "I've wanted to do that to you for a few centuries now."

Death remained silent.

"Okay. I'm placing the War pendant into its recess," Sam said. "But I happen to know for a fact that Billie Swan wears Conquest, so you're still one short."

Sam quickly removed the pendant from his neck and placed it in the obsidian recess.

"Good." Famine pointed the shotgun at Tom. "I'll have you take Death's pendant and place it in the recess now."

Tom glanced at Sam. He nodded. It was okay, there was nothing else they could do – yet. Tom removed the pendant and Death, his wrists still restrained with the cables, let him. Tom then placed the Death pendant into its stone recess.

Famine removed his own pendant and threw it at Tom. "While you're there. I wonder if you'd be kind enough to place this one, too."

Tom nodded and placed it.

Nothing happened. The Death Mask remained cold. The three horsemen warmed up inside their placements, like horses preparing for battle, while the last of their army failed to show.

Sam asked, "Now what?"

Famine stared at him with a glint of conceit. He then removed a second pendant. This one was made of ivory and depicted a horseman carrying a broadsword and a crown. *Conquest.* "You didn't really think I'd come all this way, and, as they say, play all my cards, if I already knew I was one pendant short of winning?"

Dmitri glanced at Sam. "How could you of all people have been so stupid to allow all Four Horsemen to gather at the temple?"

Chapter Fifty-Six

The next few seconds happened fast.

Sam was approximately seven feet from Famine and Tom closer to ten. He glanced at Tom. No words were spoken. Their eyes met each other with perfect honesty. There were few options left and none left much chance of survival. Each accepted the only outcome with magnanimity. A simple belief system and rule they each followed throughout their lives, which meant good must overcome evil at all costs – sacrifice was the ultimate litmus test of honor.

They dived at Famine.

It would take less than one of those feet for Famine to squeeze his shotgun's trigger. Both Sam and Tom were betting that in the process of dying, one of them might reach the murderous creature and kill him before taking their final, agonal breaths.

Famine met their attack with unrestrained disbelief. He jumped backward, adding more distance for them to cover, and rounded the shotgun to meet them.

Sam heard the three loud bangs of gunfire next. Adrenaline surged through his body. He subconsciously tensed his body in expectation of pain from the shotgun blast ripping through his earthly flesh and he dived the remaining three feet to close the distance between him and Famine.

The shotgun blast was the next thing he heard – the sound of his own death.

He fell on top of Famine. His hardened fingers tearing at the man's windpipe. A split-second later, Tom landed on the other side of him. The thunderous echo of weapons firing in the small tunnel, was suddenly replaced with total silence.

Death said, "It's over."

Sam shifted his position on Famine's throat. The man's entire body was still. His muscles were flaccid and blood ran down his chest and abdomen.

In an instant, Sam took it all in. Famine, distracted by Sam and Tom's advance had swung his shotgun round to stop them dead. At the same time, Death took the opportunity to dive to the ground where Sam had thrown his Glock. Then, instead of shooting Tom and Sam, Famine had to fire at Death. A split second before the shot was taken, Death fired three rounds, killing Famine instantly.

But a shotgun shot was fired…

Sam turned to Dmitri, who was still lying on the ground, where blood ran freely from the spread of shot pellets which littered his lower torso through to his feet.

Chapter Fifty-Seven

Sam and Tom rushed to Dmitri's aid. His eyes swept the man's injuries at a glance. The spherical pellets of shot spread out from his lower torso to his feet. Blood dribbled from each wound. There simply were too many to plug. If they were right next to a trauma hospital with a team of surgeons, his chance of survival was about fifty-fifty. Buried deep inside Mount Ararat, where it would take more than two hours to reach a hospital, the outcome was foregone.

"Thanks for saving our lives," Sam said. "Is there anything we can do to make you more comfortable?"

Dmitri shook his head. "Nothing will extend my life, but there's something I need."

"I'm sorry," Sam said.

"I've had a very long life," Dmitri said. "As the result of a unique genetic disorder shared by less than twenty people throughout history, I've lived much longer than anyone could imagine. Time, you see, blunts all instruments, even death."

Tom applied pressure to the top of Dmitri's abdomen where the greatest amount of blood spilled out. "Are you immortal?"

Dmitri started to laugh. It was halted a moment later, as blood came up through his mouth. "Do I look immortal? No. We can die, just like everyone else. We just age very slowly, that's all."

Sam wanted to ask him what genetic disorder the Master Builders all shared, and how long had he lived, but a single look at the man's ashen face made him realize the man wouldn't be conscious much longer. So instead, he just asked, "What do you need?"

Dmitri spoke quietly, lacking the strength to push his diaphragm any harder. "You have the Death Mask and the Four Horsemen. When the time comes, as it will soon, you must complete the prophecy."

"We might be able to get you to a hospital within the hour."

Death smiled. His ashen face, calm and accepting. "No. You and I both know I don't have that much time."

Sam asked, "What would it have done – if Famine had succeeded in joining the Four Horsemen?"

"You still don't know, do you?" Death was incredulous.

"No."

"It brings the rise of the Third Temple."

"I thought the pyramid in the Kalahari Desert was the Third Temple?"

"No. The Third Temple isn't a place. It's a new cycle of evolution."

"Come again?" Sam asked.

"The Third Temple is the name for the third group of human survivors."

"Of what?"

"The apocalypse that's coming our way."

Chapter Fifty-Eight

Sam stared at the dying man in front of him, terrified he would die before revealing the hidden secrets of the Death Mask. He placed a hand on Dmitri's shoulder and said, "Please, you need to tell me what it's meant to be."

Dmitri said, "It was an ancient covenant designed to protect the Death Mask. There were four keepers. Each living in different parts of the world to keep the keys separate until the right time for them to come together."

"The Death Mask was about to bring forth this apocalypse?"

"Yes. It was going to trigger a series of micro changes inside the volcano. The subsequent result would cause one of the largest volcanic clouds ever seen on earth. The result would trigger a new ice-age. Those who were worthy of the Third Temple would survive the destruction to rebuild a new order, while the vast population of the human race would succumb."

"But why?"

Dmitri paused, as he let out a deep, guttural cry. "Because by saving the few, it was the only way to save any."

"So you believe the Death Mask is vital to the continuation of humanity?"

Dmitri said, "It's probably the most important device ever built and the great masters who built it spent generations perfecting it for this very purpose."

Sam asked, "Then why did you stop Famine?"

"Because it's not time, yet."

"I don't understand. When is the right time?"

"Soon. Maybe before the end of this decade. I don't know."

"Why?" Sam leaned closer to hear the man's fading voice. "What's going to happen?"

Dmitri coughed some more blood. "Have you ever been to the Göbekli Tepe?"

"The ancient astronomer's temple just north of Syria on the Turkish border?"

"Yes. How familiar are you with the Pillar 43?"

"The Vulture Stone?" Sam opened his computer tablet and brought up some saved information on the ancient temple. "It was designed to show a snapshot of the sky at the time of the comet impact, which is calculated by the authors of a recent archeology paper to be around 10,950 BC."

"That's right. In addition, some recent archeologists have questioned whether the stone concealed two messages. The first being the image of the comet that struck, leading to the mini Ice Age known as the Younger Dryas. And the second, being that the ball-like object is the sun in Sagittarius at the time of the winter solstice between the years 1960 and 2040."

"Meaning?" Sam asked.

"That the Vulture Stone marked a coded message, conveyed across time by the Göbekli builders of 11,500 years ago, the age of Enclosure D where the stone was found."

Sam considered the revelation.

Could it have really been a warning to humanity telling us that during this 80-year window the comet responsible for a terrifying impact event at the commencement of the Younger Dryas event might once again threaten the world? It was a daring, bold, and a somewhat disturbing proposition that once made, would unlikely be forgotten. But was it right? Was it even appropriate to interpret the carved imagery of Göbekli Tepe's Vulture Stone in this way?

"It seems hard to believe." Sam's face was set hard. "Is this what you've heard, or are you telling me what the Vulture Stone meant?"

"It's one of the theories the current archeologists believe." Dmitri coughed some more. His eyes were heavily glossed over, like his internal light had finally succumbed. But then his eyes lit up, as though another surge of adrenaline gave him the tenacity to finally tell the truth. "I don't know what the truth is about pillar 43."

Sam persisted. "What do you know?"

"Pillar 43 was a lot less important than Pillar 44."

Sam watched as Dmitri took a pause in his speech, either due to his failing strength, or for dramatic flair. Sam glanced down at his tablet, where an image of Göbekli Tepe's enclosure D stared back at him.

His eyes met Dmitri's at the sudden revelation. "There was no Pillar 44."

Dmitri smiled. "There used to be a Pillar 44 within enclosure D. It was slightly taller than the other T-shaped stones, and depicted the burning tail of a comet. It was aptly named the Death Stone. The ancient astronomer's chart accurately identified another major comet – this one having the power to destroy the vast majority of life on earth in the future – a period in time that is rapidly approaching."

Sam looked at his eyes and knew Dmitri was speaking the truth. Dead men and those near to it, rarely find the need to lie.

"It's true, isn't it? Sam asked. "There is some foreboding disaster approaching earth."

"Yes. I'm afraid so."

"When will it hit?"

"I don't know. Somewhere between 1960 and 2040, but the method for knowing for certain has been lost for many years."

"The ancient's predicted the exact date of the collision?"

"Yes. But it's been lost forever now."

"How?"

Dmitri said, "The Death Stone mapped the comet's precise movements until it reaches earth during winter solstice."

Sam said, "If a second stone did in fact exist and there was a world-ending comet on its way, those who discovered it would have brought the knowledge to the world?"

"They did."

"How do you know?"

"Because it was my brother who found the stone. He notified a delegate of the UN. The next day, they came and removed the stone and put it on a ship. My brother called me and told me all about it, and then was killed in a car accident on his way home."

"What are you saying?"

"I'm saying – if high ranking members of the world knew that such an event was inevitable, would they tell anyone? What if they knew they had time to save some, but not everyone? What if, instead of alerting the world, they turned their efforts to building the world's largest bunker?"

Sam thought about it for a moment and shook his head. "What about the ship? Did your brother make a note of the ship that took the stone?"

"Yes. He kept a record."

"And where did the ship go?"

"I tried to follow it up, but the ship sank in transit and its entire crew and cargo was lost."

"Do you know where?"

"No. They wouldn't tell me, and if they did, I wouldn't believe them."

"You think it's still out there?"

Dmitri nodded. "Someone's studied it and knows the truth. Even as we speak, someone in high ranking government around the world knows the precise date."

Dmitri's eyes stared vacantly above. He was close to death. Sam had so many questions to ask, but instead he asked just one. "Where's Billie Swan?"

"I don't know."

"Where could they be keeping her?"

"I have no idea, but you were right about the pyramid numbers. Follow the numbers and they will lead you to her." Dmitri said. "I don't have much longer. I was born in this temple nearly four hundred years ago. I want to be alone with the shrine of my ancestors before I die."

Without anything adequate to say, Sam nodded and stood up.

Death gripped his arm. It was weak, but there was enough force to make Sam stop. Death looked at him, with his purple eyes fixed hard. "Tell Elise, there will be others like her. She will need to find them one day."

"The picture!" Sam suddenly recalled the cave painting toward the entrance. "It was of her?"

"No. Her grandmother."

"Where are the remaining Master Builders?"

"Scattered around the world – hiding."

"Why?"

Dmitri gritted his teeth. "Because someone is actively hunting them."

Chapter Fifty-Nine – Black Sea

In the mission room on the *Maria Helena,* Sam enlarged the image of the pyramid numbers on the digital projector. They were Roman Numerals and displayed three distinctly different sets of numbers. The first doubled to form the second and then the first and second combined to make the third.

Sam stared at the numbers on the wall. Tom, Genevieve, Matthew, Elise and Veyron all stared too. He turned to Elise, who was well known for her codebreaking abilities. "These numbers tell us where Billie is being held prisoner."

Elise asked, "Is that what Dmitri told you?"

"Yes. But it's more than that. I've seen those numbers before."

"Where?"

"Inside Atlantis," Sam said.

"What?"

"When we found Atlantis, there were a series of numbers on the wall. I remember Billie taking a photo of Roman numerals nearly five feet high."

Matthew asked, "So what does it represent? It's much too long to be a latitude and longitude."

"I have no idea," Sam admitted.

"Could it be a coordinate?" Tom asked. "Something other than a latitude and longitude? Something older, like the Master Builder's *carrib,* in which they identified the location of the pyramid in the Kalahari Desert?"

Sam shook his head. "Too many numbers there to match anything we saw about the *carrib.*"

"What about the height of a pyramid?" Genevieve asked.

Sam thought about it. "I don't know. What sort of measurement would achieve such a long number?"

Veyron added, "It could be a different height for each section of the pyramid."

"Or something entirely different," Sam said.

Elise smiled.

Sam recognized that smile. He'd seen her make it a few times before, just before she resolved a puzzle that had defeated the rest of them. "You have a suggestion, Elise?"

Elise grinned. "Or the frequency of a sound wave."

"What?" Sam was surprised by her answer.

"I thought you played piano, Sam?" Elise said, "Don't you know anything about sound?"

Sam ignored the disparagement. "Okay, so what sound does that represent?"

"It's high pitched. Probably much higher than most humans could even produce without significant training."

"There's three numbers here. What does that mean?"

Elise shrugged. "It's a very simple tune. Three separate wavelengths. I don't know what it does."

"Have a guess, for me," Sam said. "Is there any way we could trace this back to where Billie's being held?"

Elise paused, as though she was considering the problem. "Sound can propagate through mediums such as air, water and solids as longitudinal waves... oh, it can travel in transverse wave in solids, too. The behavior of sound is affected by three things. A complex relationship of density, temperature, and speed."

Sam nodded. It was painful stuff, but he knew something about her unique mind that required her to showcase her knowledge as she worked the problem. It didn't reveal her conceit, and she wasn't boasting about her IQ. She didn't have to. Everyone on board knew she was brilliant. It was simply how her mind worked the puzzle.

Elise continued. Her voice was sharp and animated as she spoke. "Physically, audio is a vibration. Typically, we're talking about vibrations of air between approximately 20 hertz and 20,000 Hertz. That means the air is moving back and forth at a rate of 20 to 20,000 times per second."

"Go on," Sam said.

"If you measure that vibration and convert it into an electrical signal through, say, a microphone, you'll get an electrical signal with the voltage varying in the same waveform as the sound."

Elise glanced around the room to see if any of them were still following. Sam guessed she saw a lot of vacant expression.

Elise continued. "Now we have an analogue signal. But not digital. Because we know voltage varies between minus one and positive one volts. Now we hook our volt meter to a computer and instruct the computer to read the meter 44,100 times per second. Add a second volt meter and you get stereo. This format is called stereo 44,100 Hertz – and it really is just a bunch of voltage measurements."

Sam shook his head. "Elise, that's great, but just tell us what these numbers mean!"

She typed them into the computer and pressed play. A strange, high pitched wail resonated from her laptop's speakers. It was eerie and compelling at the same time.

Sam said, "Any ideas where that sound comes from?"

"No idea. Hang on. Let me do a search for it."

"You can Google a sound?"

Elise nodded, cheerfully. "Basically, I'm searching a few other databases, but in short, I'm looking for digital matches of the wavelength of that specific sound."

The search program stopped. She clicked on the first link and pressed play. The whistle was identical to the one they'd just heard.

Sam asked, "What is that sound and where was it made?"

Elise grinned, because there was only one place in the world that made that sound. "The Pirahã tribe, along the Macai River of the Amazon Jungle."

Chapter Sixty – Macai River, Brazil

The Sea King landed in a small clearing at the edge of the Macai River. Elise watched as Sam, Genevieve and Veyron – all armed to the teeth – stepped out into the Amazon jungle. Tom cut the power to the motor, and the massive rotary blades started to slowly whine, until they stopped altogether. Elise was the last to climb out.

She carried an Israeli built, Uzi submachine gun.

The local tribal people fished along the edge of the river. They glanced at the helicopter until its rotors finally stopped turning and went silent. After which, they returned to their fishing as though nothing in their environment had changed. The Pirahã tribe chose to remain out of the world of western civilization, but they were far less primitive than expected. They had seen planes and helicopters overhead. They simply had no desire to interact with the strange machines.

Tom looked at her. "Now that you've gotten us this far, any chance you might narrow the location of Billie in the jungle?"

"Afraid not," Elise said. "If it makes you feel better, the Pirahã tribe number less than four hundred. So if she's living with them when she's not working on the new pyramid, she should be relatively easy to find."

Tom's eyes swept the thick Amazonian jungle. "It's a big jungle. There's a lot of area to cover. She could be anywhere."

Billie stepped into the clearing. "Or she could be right here."

Tom embraced her. It was an affectionate hug, more like that between brother and sister than ex-lovers. Elise glanced at Genevieve, who appeared to be taking it with a refined grain of ambivalence. The two had been secret lovers until recently, when both had forgotten to conceal their obvious affection for each other. Most people wondered what would happen to their relationship now Billie was back. Elise wasn't one of those. She knew that Tom and Billie broke up before she left on the pretense that she was more interested in finding the Master Builders than her relationship with him. The reality was, it was a bit of both – Billie couldn't settle down with anyone.

"How did you know where to find us?" Sam asked.

Billie laughed. "It's not like we get a lot of helicopters in the area."

Tom said, "Let's go before that thing comes back."

"You mean the Black Smoke?" Billie asked.

"Yeah."

"It shouldn't return for a few more days." Billie glanced toward a group of people in the distance. "You guys should stay and see this place. The people of the Pirahã tribe are amazing!"

Sam intervened. "Sounds like it, but all the same, we should leave."

"Leave?" Billie repeated the word. "I'm not leaving."

"What do you mean you're not leaving?" Tom spat the words.

"I like it here." Billie shook her head. "I can't leave yet. I haven't finished my work and the Black Smoke needs me."

"Needs you!" Tom said. "That thing isn't real. We had it chemically analyzed. It's basically LSD on steroids. They've been using it to control you."

"Yes." Billie smiled, stupidly. "I know."

"And you're okay with that?" Tom asked.

"Yes. Of course I am. You guys don't understand what it's trying to achieve. What it does for you… I've never felt more alive in my life."

"That's great." Sam gripped his Heckler and Koch MP5, scanning the rest of the jungle around them. Some of the Pirahã tribe, who'd taken little notice of them five minutes earlier, were now slowly making their way silently to greet them. "We've got to go."

"Why?" Billie asked, holding on to Sam's arm. "Please, I'd like you all to stay."

Her hand gripped his arm so tight it hurt. Sam ripped his arm free. "What's got into you? I said, we have to go."

Billie's eyes filled with confined rage. "Please, I just want you all to stay… just for a little while longer."

Black smoke seeped out of the lower ground and surrounding valleys like a rising sea, that would soon swamp them all.

Genevieve interrupted. "Listen bitch! I don't know what the drugs are telling you to do, but we've come a long way to get you out of here, and it's time to go."

Billie's head snapped to face Genevieve. Her almond eyes were wide and her mouth opened – an instant later, her lips thinned and she started to form the lower notes of a high pitched whistle.

Chapter Sixty-One

The high pitched whistle was relayed across each member of the Pirahã tribe who were now encircling them. Elise gripped her Uzi, and fired a couple short bursts into the air above the men and women who were slowly encroaching on them at a pace no faster than a slow walk. To her they appeared more like an animal patiently stalking its prey, than human's surrounding their enemy.

She shouted, "Back in the helicopter!"

Tom grabbed Billie against her will and dragged her into the helicopter. Genevieve climbed into the pilot seat and flicked on the engine, while Tom tried to stop Billie from clawing her way out.

Sam yelled, "Get us out of here, Genevieve!"

The massive rotor blades above started to turn at a painfully slow pace. It takes time to start a helicopter, and no amount of coaxing can reduce it. Genevieve checked a number of controls, waiting for the main rotor to reach its minimum take-off RPM.

Elise stared out the helicopter's windows. The thick smoke now filled the outside. It surrounded them like a sinister weapon trying to smother the life out of them. The Pirahã tribe now formed a circle around the helicopter, so close they were touching one another. Each person looked straight upon the helicopter – mesmerized by the sight but unable to advance any further.

She could make out every intricate detail of the faces. They were set hard with determination as they stared into the helicopter. Their eyes were open, but pupils were rolled back – as though they were having a seizure.

What the hell?

"Get us out of here, Genevieve!" she yelled.

But already, the thick smoke was starting to seep through the small opening in the Sea King's aluminum airframe.

"Close the vents!" Sam said, shutting the cockpit air vents.

In the rear cabin, Elise and Veyron frantically shoved blankets over the vents, where the Black Smoke still entered. Her eyes darted toward Billie, who was grinning sardonically and, like the others, her eyes were rolled back inside her head. Although she looked awake, she had no more control over her cognitive response than an epileptic having a seizure.

Elise tried to hold her breath. "We're going to be trapped here, Genevieve – if you don't get us out of here now!"

Genevieve turned around. "We're okay, now."

Every muscle in Elise's body went taut as she involuntarily recoiled – because beneath the waxy replica of Genevieve's fortitude, her eyes were fixed upward, staring at the back of her skull.

A moment later, Genevieve switched off the Sea King's engines and the rotor blades whirred into a silent idle.

"Wait!" Elise screamed, but her words went unheard, as Sam, Tom, Veyron, Genevieve and Billie all opened the doors and stepped outside to join the Black Smoke.

She followed them outside. Now all the entire Pirahã tribe was starting to enter the jungle, and her team among them. No one spoke. They simple followed, as though driven by some sort of higher power, a chemical intervention that she still didn't quite understand.

Elise fired another burst of rounds from her Uzi just above her friend's heads. It made no difference. She doubted if shooting them would have stopped their inhumane need to follow the others into the jungle.

In the back of her mind, Elise felt a strange yearning to follow them. There was no voice in her head that told her what should be done, simply that it would feel right to join the others. She watched as her friends disappeared into the jungle.

No. This isn't what I want.

She thought about it for a moment, trying to steady herself from joining the others. It was like a patient trying to stay awake after being given the anesthetic for surgery, convinced they would actually get to count back from a hundred.

It was impossible.

And yet she tried.

The jungle is wrong. It's evil. We must not follow. We want to go home...

They weren't quite thoughts, as much as feelings. She didn't shout the words out. Instead, she simply felt the strong emotions of fear, distrust, and the need to escape. The sensations became stronger. More forceful and uncomfortable. She tried to make them stop. Like a child, she wanted to crawl under her blanket and pretend she was somewhere else, a place where monsters in the dark didn't exist.

A few minutes later, she spotted Billie. She stepped out of the thick jungle and into the clearing. Behind her, Sam, Tom, Veyron and Genevieve all followed. They slowly came and stood next to her. Each one remained silent, standing there, staring at the Black Smoke as it disappeared into the jungle.

When the Black Smoke was completely gone, Billie turned to face her. "Now what?"

Elise grinned. "Now we go home."

Chapter Sixty-Two

Boston Specialist Hospital – Two Weeks Later.

Sam looked at Billie. She'd just finished getting dressed and had signed herself out of the hospital. She was back to her normal, intelligent, cynical self – filled with confidence bordering on arrogance. It was good to see her back to normal.

He said, "There's one thing I really don't get about all this."

"Really?" Billie said, "Just one?"

"Okay, one thing that's been bothering me… and you might happen to know the answer."

"Shoot."

"Why did the Master Builders focus on the biblical reference with the covenant of the Four Horsemen?"

"I've had a lot of thoughts about that. I believe they were concerned that none of them would be alive when the time came to trigger the Death Mask. You see, the Master Builders had a genetic disorder that allowed them to live extremely long lives, but they were far from being immortal. Like all people, they could die from traumatic events and their numbers were lessening. What's worse, is that the same genetic disorder that extended their lifespan was recessive – meaning in most cases, their children didn't possess the same disorder."

"Most adults outlived their children?" Sam asked.

"Yes. So most ceased to have children of their own."

Sam said, "How awful."

"So the Master Builders needed to enlist the help of ordinary people."

"But why focus on Christianity?"

"You have to understand that at the time of the early fourth century, Christianity was spreading like wildfire in the region. Armenia was the first to adopt it as its country's religion. It was the simplest means of maintaining an ongoing covenant that needed to extend well past any one person's life expectancy."

Sam nodded. "And Gregory the Illuminator?"

"At the end of the third century, when Gregory made a pilgrimage to the Gods he thought he spotted in Mount Ararat, he found the Master Builders. They told him of the Four Horsemen, and instructed him to keep the pendant of Conquest. They told him to return to his king and tell him to renounce his pagan ways. That in the years to come the king would become possessed by a demon, and that only he alone would be able to cure him."

"Go on."

"King Tiridates III was angry, but so concerned by Gregory's conviction that he ordered the man locked in the dungeon of Khor Virap. The rest is history."

Sam smiled. "The Master Builders poisoned King Tiridates III until Gregory's release?"

"There's no proof, but it's definitely a high likelihood. Either that, or Gregory did perform a miracle."

"And your grandfather. How did he become part of the Four Horsemen?"

"My grandfather followed a very old story about the day Gregory the Illuminator was thrown into Khor Virap. It said that he was wearing a pendant of a horse made of ivory, but that by the time the man was released, he no longer wore any jewelry at all."

"Your father visited Khor Virap?"

"Yes. He found a buried container inside the deep dungeon and a note from Gregory relating the story of the Four Horsemen. My grandfather spent most of his life trying to locate the hidden temple inside Mount Ararat. In the end, it's what got him killed."

Chapter Sixty-Three

Sam watched as Dr. Elaine Creswell, M.D. entered the room. She was a couple years shy of sixty, and one of the leading experts in the world on the topic of neurology. She focused specifically on unusual neural pathways. Things like secondary pathways that sometime start to grow after a stroke has caused a blockage in the usual pathway, or sometimes to circumvent information that is failing to be processed at the sight of a brain tumor. The aberrant neural pathways were uncommon, but not unheard of. She had spent a life studying them with the hope that such pathways may one day lead to a solution for patients with spinal cord injuries.

"Good morning, Dr. Creswell," Sam said.

"Morning, Mr. Reilly. I have something I want to show you." She glanced at Billie. "In private, I'm afraid."

"No problem," Billie said. "I was just leaving."

Dr. Creswell waited until Billie left the room and then closed the door. She placed a radiology report in front of Sam. "This is the report from Elise's MRI."

Sam met her eye. "What does it say?"

"Elise has an enlarged posterior cerebrum."

"She has a large brain?" Sam asked. "Hell, I could have told you that. She's several rungs above genius status on the MENSA IQ ladder."

"It doesn't quite work like that. This isn't normal, and at first it quite worried me."

"You think it's a brain tumor?"

"At first I did. I ran all the tests. There's nothing malignant or concerning about this. It appears to be her normal cerebral structure. Most likely the result of some sort of strange hereditary process."

"What do you think it means?"

"You want to know if it could have had anything to do with why everyone was affected by the Black Smoke, except Elise?"

Sam nodded. "Was it?"

Dr. Creswell said, "The posterior cerebrum is concerned with a number of cerebral functions, but communication is up there with its highest priority. The Black Smoke appeared to heighten the natural excitation of the neural responses in that region – in ordinary people – elevating it to a level where high frequency radio waves can be interpreted."

"But you're saying that aspect of Elise's brain isn't normal."

"No. In Elise's case, that region of the brain is already enlarged."

Sam asked, "What does that mean?"

Dr. Creswell shook her head. "I'm not certain, but it appears she has the ability to interpret high frequency sound waves without the chemical enhancement from the Black Smoke, and…"

Sam waited, but the Dr. appeared uncertain about giving him the next bit of information. "What?"

"And I think she was capable of transmitting high frequency radio waves, too."

"Thank you, Dr. Creswell, for your work." Sam thought about the revelation for a moment. It was a reasonable explanation. The only possible reason why Elise was unaffected by the Black Smoke – not just unaffected – she was able to convince the rest of them to return to the helicopter.

She said, "We'll need further tests, to know for sure."

A strong woman's voice interrupted the conversation. It both took charge and simultaneously dismissed Dr. Creswell. "I don't think that will be necessary."

Sam smiled and turned to face her. "Madam Secretary, I was wondering when you would show up."

The Secretary of Defense closed the door behind Dr. Creswell. She looked at Sam with concern heavy in her face. "Well?"

Sam said, "We'll need to run some more tests, but I think she might be genetically descended from the Master Builders."

"You can forget about running tests."

"Why?"

"Because I already know what they're going to say," she said.

"Really?"

"Yes." She shook her head. "I wish you'd let me know you were close to finding their hive."

"Hive?" Sam asked.

"That's what we've decided to call a group of Master Builders." She bit her lower lip. "Defense has been keen to learn all there is to know about this Black Smoke for years."

"You knew about the smoke?"

"Of course. We found drawings and signs of the strange chemical in the first temple. I don't need to tell you what such a drug could be used for during war, or worse still, if replicated by our enemies."

Sam smiled. "That's why I've always been given a long leash and an extraordinary budget. You're worried about the Black Smoke?"

She smiled. Her hardened face was stunning, yet patronizing at the same time. "We're enthusiastic about the opportunity, and terrified of the consequence of losing the race."

"What race?"

She smiled again at his naiveté. "Why the race to synthetically reproduce the chemical compound."

"Didn't the CIA already try that in the fifties with LSD? Sam asked. "How did that work out?"

She turned from his vehement gaze. "There will always be a war. For the good guys to win, we need the superior weapons. In a world where technology is changing daily, an ability to control entire groups through high frequency sound waves is a breakthrough that might just give us the edge to survive. Think of the possibilities. Our soldiers could harmonize their movement as though they were one single entity. The enemies could be manipulated to attack each other or better still, relinquish secrets."

"What about Elise?" Sam asked.

She shrugged. "What about her?"

"What do you know?"

"I think it's time to tell you something about Elise's history – before she was taken in by the orphanage."

"What?"

"I was leading a team of CIA operatives on a raid on a temple in Afghanistan, which we now call the first temple of the Master Builder. When we broke in to the temple it appeared long deserted, but it wasn't completely empty. There was a baby girl sitting underneath the middle of a large obsidian dome. She was looking up, as though she was studying it. That girl was less than one year old, and we named her Elise."

Sam swallowed hard at the revelation. "Does she know?"

"No. And I'm not certain it would be wise to tell her yet."

"Why not?"

"Because we don't know how she'll take it." The Secretary of Defense shrugged. "More importantly, we don't know whose side she'd be on."

"What are you talking about? There are no sides!"

"Maybe not yet, but there might be – when the remaining Master Builders gather?" The Secretary of Defense studied him, trying to determine his own value to her. "What else did you learn?"

"I'm not sure, yet. There might be something. Then again, it might be nothing."

"What is it?"

Sam swallowed. "Have you ever heard of the Death Stone of Göbekli Tepe?"

"No, should I have?" She answered without hesitation.

Her face remained hard, and expressionless. Sam thought he saw something else there, too – *was it the unique combination of recognition, fear and guilt?*

He smiled, obediently. "No. I was just following a lead, but I doubt it will amount to anything."

The End

Made in the USA
Middletown, DE
18 February 2023

25137103R00198